STUPID BOY
A NEW ADULT ROMANCE NOVEL

CINDY MILES

This is a work of fiction. All of the characters, organizations, and events portrayed in this novel are either products of the author's imagination or are used fictitiously.

Book design by Maureen Cutajar
www.gopublished.com

eISBN: 978-1-937776-97-8
ISBN: 978-1-942356-14-1

Other Books by Cindy Miles

The *Stupid in Love* **Series:**
Stupid Girl
Stupid Boy
Stupid Love (Coming Soon)

The *Cassabaw Island* **Series:**
Those Cassabaw Days: A Malone Brothers Novel
(Book 1, April 2015)

Other Titles:
Forevermore
(Young Adult, Scholastic books)
Spirited Away
(Adult ghost romance, NAL)
Into Thin Air
(Adult ghost romance, NAL)
Highland Knight
(Adult ghost romance, NAL)
MacGowan's Ghost
(Adult ghost romance, NAL)
Thirteen Chances
(Adult ghost romance, NAL)

Visit Cindy on her website, Facebook, Twitter, or Goodreads!
Contact her at cindymilesbooks@yahoo.com

For my mom, Dale.
My biggest fan. My best friend.
I love you.

"If adventures will not befall
a young lady in her own village,
she must seek them abroad."

- Jane Austen, Northanger Abbey

Then: Harper

"HARPER? ARE YOU IN here?"

Daddy? No, not Daddy. Can't be Daddy. Somebody else. Somebody bad. My eyes felt cold. Dry. Wide open, like I couldn't blink at all. Against my back the damp wood beneath the kitchen sink pressed into my favorite *Beauty and the Beast* tee shirt. The cabinet was dark and smelled really bad, like the old faded pink sponge Mama sometimes washed dishes with. I pulled my knees closer to my chest, held them tight with my arms, and squeezed my cold dry eyes shut. Pushed my head against the wood. Further into that smelly damp place I sank, further, further, and I shivered. *Go away! You're one of them! Go away...*

"Come on out, honey. It's okay now. No need to hide anymore. I promise."

1

The man's deep voice seeped through the cracks of the kitchen cabinet I hid inside of, and no, it wasn't gonna be okay. Never was it gonna be okay.

Footsteps, heavy, gritty, as if dragging through sand scraped across the torn kitchen floor, suddenly stopped. "Harper, my name is Detective Shanks. Me and Detective Crimshaw are here to help you."

"Harper?" This time, a woman's voice. "Come on out, sweetie. You're safe now." A pause. "The bad people are all gone. We won't let them come back." Another pause. "I bet you're hungry, aren't you? We'll take you for a hamburger. Would you like that?"

I said nothing. I hardly breathed. No, I didn't want a hamburger. My stomach felt sick. The voices sounded close, yet stuck in a tunnel somewhere, and I think I wanted them to stay that way. My eyes pinched shut, and I squeezed my knees so tightly the bones hurt my chest. *Please, just go away...*

"Jesus, Shanks," the woman called Crimshaw whispered. "She's been gone for days." Another pause. "You don't think she's really in here, do you?"

Footsteps closer to my hiding place made my breath catch like a high-pitched whistle in my throat. In the next second, the cabinet door eased open on creaky hinges. The sound made the skin on my arm grow cold. A dark head lowered and looked inside, and I closed my eyes back tight. My breath came fast now, faster and faster and I couldn't help it, and my arms began to slip from around my knees...

"Crimshaw, she's here!" Big hands that looked like rubber doll hands reached in and grabbed me under my arms and dragged me out, my legs knocking over an old plastic bottle of dish detergent. I tried to scream but the noise pushed silent out of my throat, so dry it was like a scratchy old pipe. The sound came out like a creaky whisper. I was lifted, and the man called Shanks held me tight to stop my wiggling.

"Shh, shh, Harper," his voice comforted quietly. He patted the back of my head. "Just breathe, just breathe. It's okay, honey, everything's going to be okay now. We're the police. We're here to help you and take you outta here." He patted me some more. "Shh…"

He was the police. He was gonna take me out of here. I buried my head into the man's shoulder, and he smelled good, like pine cones, and although he said everything was going to be okay, it wasn't. My breath continued, faster, faster, and then everything started growing darker and darker. My arms felt heavy, my legs just dangled.

"Dammit Crimshaw, call for an ambulance!" I heard the man say. "She's going into shock or something."

"Already called them," the woman said. "Jesus, Frank. She's been in here alone with them for days…Jesus."

Just as the smell hit my nose and then my stomach, my head felt light, felt like a balloon that was gonna float away into the air. The room got so dark I couldn't tell if my cold eyes were open or hidden hard against the man's shoulder, and I felt the air leave me. I gasped. Blackness filled my eyes. I'd smelled that awful smell before, when Mama had found a dead cat in the trashcan out back. I gagged, gasped, and began to shake.

"Poor kid. She'll never be right after this…"

Then: Kane

THE GLASS SHATTERED AGAINST the old green and gold linoleum kitchen floor. My gaze darted fast to my sister, whose eyes widened in terror. She stood there, her hand in the C shape it'd been in before the wet glass slipped out of it. Her lip quivered. We both knew what was coming. It was just some old NFL team glass he'd gotten from Burger King. It'd come with a value meal. Cheap. Stupid. So stupid. It mattered to him, though. He'd make it seem like the end of the world.

Footsteps pounded in the hallway. Heavy, familiar. Grew closer.

"Get behind me, Katy," I whispered harshly. She did, her small fingers threading through the belt loops on my jeans and holding tight. As her face pressed against the small of my back, I drew a deep breath in, steadied myself.

He burst through the kitchen and stood, staring at the broken glass on the floor. His frame filled the doorway. His face was beet red; his nose was redder. Bloodshot eyes flamed and narrowed as he fixed his angry glare on me.

"What in the goddamn hell did you do?" he thundered. Fury rolled off him like waves from a drum fire.

I drew myself up. "It was an accident. Glass slipped."

His hazy eyes moved, and he tried to focus on my sister. "Did she do it? You coverin' for her again, Kane?"

"No," I answered. "It was me."

In two steps he was there, grabbing me by the collar of my tee shirt and yanking me hard enough that the material ripped. I stumbled onto the glass and winced as a piece of it dug into my palm.

"You lyin' sack of shit," he spat. "Girl, did you do it?"

Katy sobbed behind me. "N-n-no, sir," she stuttered, then whimpered.

I hated him at that moment. More than ever. Just for making my sister scared, making her cry.

"Well, one of you has to pay for it," he said. His words slurred, and I knew he didn't mean pay for it in money. "Which one of ya's it gonna be?"

I pushed off the floor, blocking my sister from his view. "Me."

"Figured you'd say that," he replied, and he wiped his bearded jaw with his hand. "Always acting like some fucking goddamn hero, huh, Kane?" His eyes dropped to the floor, scanning the broken NFL glass. Kneeling, he picked up the bottom. It had remained intact; the sides now jagged and sharp.

My insides froze, and like all the other times, I shoved the fear to the back of my throat as I watched him rise.

"Take off your shirt, boy," he ordered. "Then turn around and grab that chair."

I glared at him, and I knew he could see the hate there. He was bigger than me, since I was only eight, and he knew it. But I did it. Did what he asked. Yanked my shirt over my head, threw it on the floor. Turned around. Grabbed the back of the chair, my knuckles turning white from my grip. Fury and fear boiled inside of me. I could feel it like a rolling pot of water under my skin.

My sister sobbed, and then my head was snatched back as he grabbed a fistful of my hair. His voice brushed my ear.

"You make one sound and you'll get an extra letter." He yanked my head. "So far you have six to look forward to. Every time you fuck up, you get another letter. You hear me, hero? You get this game now, smartass?"

I nodded, and when my eyes found my sister, I mouthed to her, *be quiet.*

My breath quickened; he'd not done this before. Fear stuffed inside my throat, my lungs and I hated that even more than the pain about to happen. Fastening my eyes on my sister's, I concentrated. Breathed.

Waited.

And just before the first swipe of that glass bottom dug into my back, I watched my sister cover her mouth with both of her hands and scream silently. I felt the first letter as he carved it into my back. Curved it around. *S.*

My head pounded, but I kept my eyes on my sister. Then I saw nothing but red.

After: Harper

WHEN THE CAR TURNED into the black iron gates and onto the long drive, my stomach started to go numb inside. Trees overhung the single lane, and it wound and wound through a pecan grove until I'd lost sight of the road behind me. The driver hadn't said a word to me, and I hadn't said one to him, either. He drove and drove and drove. I waited.

Finally, a flash of white, and then appeared the hugest house I'd ever seen. It had a double porch—one on top, one on bottom, and when the car pulled around the circle drive and stopped, I glanced up through my window. An older woman stood on that upper porch, arms folded over her chest. She wore a fancy looking black dress, one that reached the floor, and I recognized her from the funeral.

My grandmother. My mother's mother, Corinne Belle.

I'd never met her before the funeral.

With her back stiff and straight my grandmother turned and disappeared through the veranda's double doors.

My car door opened, and the driver held it for me as I climbed out. I had no suitcase; only my backpack, and he handed that to me.

"This way, miss," he said, and I followed him up a sweeping set of brick steps.

Just as my foot touched the first step, the tall doors opened and my grandmother stood there. She looked down at me then, and I looked up at her, and wordlessly she inspected me. She did that for so long I began to squirm, shift from foot to foot. Blue, icy eyes studied me hard.

"Stop fidgeting, Harper, and come this way," she finally said, and turned on her heel. Her voice wasn't friendly. It wasn't exactly hateful, either. But it was cold and as sharp as the noise her heels made across the wood floor.

I followed her through the cavernous old house, filled with old stuff and vases and smelling like lemons, up a wide staircase to the second floor, and down a long, long hallway. Not once did my grandmother turn to see if I followed; I guess she knew I would. Halfway down the hall she stopped, opened a door on the right, and turned, hands folded in front of her, waiting on me. At the opened door I stood still.

"This is your room," she said. "Go inside."

Hesitantly, I did as she asked, and her clicking heels trailed behind me. I didn't know what to do, really. Or where to go. So I walked to the bed and stopped. Laid out on the bedspread were clothes: underwear, socks with lace trim and a pair of shiny black shoes, and a dress the color of very ripe plums. Also, a large white towel and washcloth. I glanced up at my grandmother.

"Hand me your bag, child," she said, and I slid it off my shoulder and did so. With her finger and thumb, she pinched the zipper, just barely, as if it were covered in germs, and opened my backpack. There wasn't anything in it, really—just what few clothes I had, a pair of old sandals, and a picture of Mama and Daddy. It was an old picture—back...before. It was the only one I had. Corinne Belle then gave me a stern look.

"You'll discard the items you're wearing, all of them, and place them in here," she said sharply. "Then you'll wrap the towel about you and you'll follow me to the bathroom."

I hesitated; I didn't like taking my clothes off in front of her. She might be my grandmother and all, but she was a stranger to me.

"Stop pondering, child, and for God's sake stop staring at me as if you're brainless and do as I say at once. The faster you discard, the faster you can wrap that towel around you."

My face grew hot as I quickly took off all of my clothes, dropped them into my backpack, and then bound the towel around my body. My grandmother watched the entire time, and now we stood, facing one another. Again, I waited.

"I realize that what you've been through—in fact, your entire existence—isn't your fault, Harper. You're but eight years old. But the conditions of you living in this house are strict ones that must be abided by at all times." The lines around her mouth deepened. "You'll forget your past. Your mother. Your father. That squalor you lived in. Even your last name will be changed to Belle." She zipped up my backpack. "You'll forget everything in this bag and you'll not mention it again. Ever. And I'll know if you do." She leaned down from her towering height, and met my eyes with hers. "I'll know every move you make, young lady. Every one of them. This is a privilege you're receiving, to come here and live under my care. You're lucky to have anyone at all to take you in and I do hope you're grateful for it, every single day. You'll obey every rule I set and you'll not give me a minute's worry. I've already enrolled you in boarding school and you'll begin in the fall, where no one knows you and you'll not tell them anything about your previous life." Her eyes flared. "You're going to be taught proper manners and become a functioning, useful and productive being of society. You'll become a Belle. It will be as if the old you never existed at all. Is that clearly understood?"

My eyes once more felt dry, cold as I stared hard at her. My breath caught in my throat. "Yes, ma'am," I said shakily. "C-can I have my picture?"

Corinne inspected me then, from the top of my head to my bare toes, and she frowned. "Absolutely not." She turned on her heels again, and I knew to follow without question. I fought back tears as she stopped in the hallway, two doors down from my room.

"You have your own bath, Harper, and I expect you to make use of it every single day. Starting now." She looked at me. "Wash your hair twice." She stared at it. "It looks absolutely filthy. And once you're finished you'll dress and come downstairs for supper where I'll inspect you before we sit to the table. Is that clear?"

"Yes, ma'am," I said, and I tried to keep my voice steady.

With one final, stern glare, she straightened her back,

turned, and headed down the hallway toward the stairs without another word, her heels click-clicking as she went.

In the bathroom, I closed the door, turned on the water and watched the tub fill. At the same time, my eyes filled with tears, and when the tub was full I dropped the towel, climbed in, and hugged my knees.

I don't exist anymore.

I'm dead, too. Just as dead as Mama and Daddy.

Then, I cried.

After: Kane

"**Y**OU LIKE BASEBALL?"

I stared at the mattress above my bunk bed and didn't say anything. I didn't know that kid sleeping up there, and that kid didn't know me. This was my third foster home in two months. No need to make friends. Didn't need 'em. A second later, a head popped over the side from the bunk above and I studied the boy occupying the bed. He hung upside down. Wild curls flung all over, and even wilder blue eyes pierced the room lit only by a small Red Sox night-light. The kid had said his name was Brax. One of his eyes had a big purple shiner around it.

"You got a hearin' problem or something?" Brax asked, but he said it with a big smile that showed all of his teeth. "Kane, right? Well do ya? Baseball?"

"I guess," I answered.

Brax continued to stare. He was local—a Southie. I could tell that much by his mouth. Looked a little younger than me, like nine or ten, maybe.

Brax cocked one brow. "You from around here?"

I met his gaze. "Dorchester."

Brax nodded. Wiped his nose with the back of his hand. He was still hanging upside down. "You been in the system long?"

"A while." I kept my stare on Brax's.

"Well, I been in my whole fuckin' life." He swung down, landing quietly on his socked feet, and squatted beside my bed. "Been here almost two years." He shrugged his bony shoulders. "It's okay. Wicked better than the last one I stayed at." Again he cocked his head. "Wanna go to a game tomorrow?"

I rolled onto my stomach and faced away, hoping Brax would just shut up and go back to bed. "No."

"Come on," Brax coaxed. "It's more fun with a friend."

"We ain't friends," I muttered. "We ain't."

In the next second, Brax grabbed the blanket and yanked. "Don't be such a dickwad—" His words hung unfinished in the air for several seconds. All I heard was his breathing. "Jesus fuck," Brax finally said in a whisper. "Jesus."

I didn't move. Didn't look at Brax. Didn't say a word. I just laid there, and Brax set the covers in place. Over my body. I knew Brax saw. Saw my mutilated back. Saw the word there, raised and puckered and purple-red.

"Hey, I'm sorry," Brax said. His voice was even. Quiet. And he probably really meant it. "I won't tell."

13

"Doesn't matter," I said into my pillow.

"Fuck yeah, it does," Brax said. "I hope the asshole paid for it."

I didn't say a word. Just kept quiet.

"We're goin' to a game tomorrow," Brax said, then I felt a shift in the air as he swung up into the bunk above me. He was quiet for a while, and I thought he was asleep. Until he spoke again.

"The game's at two. We're playin' Kansas City. And we're goin' together," Brax said. "I know a guy at the park. He's been lettin' me in since I was seven. We can get a hot dog, might even catch a foul ball. Okay?"

I sighed into my pillow. "Okay." Anything to shut him up. It worked.

Then I closed my eyes. I knew I'd dream. I always dreamed. Only they weren't dreams, they were nightmares. *Frightmares.* Night terrors, the doctor had said. And Brax was going to hear them.

Soon, he'd know everything.

1. Now

Winston University
Texas, present day
Early November

"LADIES, AS YOU ALL know, the Kappas start every fall semester off with one of their degrading, humiliating fraternity dares. Last fall..." I sighed and stared at the aged wooden podium I stood behind, used by many Delta presidents before me. I looked up, then scanned the familiar faces of my sisters. The flames from several lit candles swayed as the air conditioning kicked on and swooshed a fake breeze through the common room. I gripped the podium with my palms. "What they did to Olivia Beaumont last year was unforgiveable. And now they've done it again. They shouldn't just get away with it."

"Poor Macie Waters," Maggie Gibson said. "How she fell for that jackass Josh Collins is beyond me. Why would she ever think he'd want to seriously be with her?"

"Macie is a smart girl. She'll get over him," I answered. "Whether she'll get over being humiliated in front of a hundred people at their ridiculous Halloween bash anytime soon is yet to be seen. It was a hard life's lesson learned for her." It'd been a Stephen King's *Carrie* sort of moment—minus the pig blood. Josh had coaxed Macie into dressing up as a slutty nurse and drinking way too much—then announced at the bash it'd all been a dare. Idiot.

"But Olivia beat them," Jane Morris said. "She and Brax won."

A murmur ran through the Deltas at the mention of Olivia and Brax. With good reason, too. They *had* won. Olivia's strength and courage had out-witted those lamebrain Kappas. And Brax? Well, he'd surprised everyone—including me. He'd proven to not only be one of the brightest guys I'd ever met, but was totally in love with Olivia. So much that he'd quit the Kappas. Since last fall's dare, Olivia had made the Dean's list. Last season Brax had accumulated more pitching records than any Silverback before him. And their romance was the talk of Winston. Like a living, breathing thing, it simply...existed. Everyone knew of Brax and *Gracie*—his endearing nickname for her. More than one time I'd wondered, *what would that be like? To have someone love me that much?* I couldn't even fathom it. The idea felt foreign. Alien. And in the end, it left me feeling hollow inside.

"Oh my God, the way he looks at her," Jane said, her voice whispery. "Like he'll suffocate, shrivel up and die if he can't touch her."

"That's true," I continued. I tucked my hair behind my ear. "Olivia is extraordinary. But still. Despite their survival, a new dare victim was chosen this year. Humiliated. All for some drunken good laugh. And I—*we*—can't let them get away with it. It's degrading. We're sophisticated, intelligent women. Not to be used as dogs."

Heads nodded and muttered their agreement.

"I thought the dares were banned," Maggie said. "Like, not allowed. At all."

The smile I gave stretched thin and tight against my teeth. "They are, as far as sexual harassment and damage to property goes," I answered. "Only, that doesn't really mean anything to the Kappas." Again, I peered out over my sisters. "I've been thinking."

"Oh," a familiar voice said. "I fancy that impish gleam in your eye, Ms. Belle."

My gaze found Murphy Polk, who was a transplant from York, England. She was as close a friend as I had. Her chestnut hair had streaks of highlight and was cut in a fashionable wavy abstract lob that brushed her collarbones, only presently she had two large braids pulled along each side and gathered in the back. She was smiling the type of smile that had meant trouble before. Modernly dressed yet with an easy Bohemian flare, Murphy was that girl who fit in with every single crowd. Everyone liked her. That smile? Like the Cheshire cat from *Alice in Wonderland.* She'd pushed me into sticky spots before, knowing I was a total rule-follower. A wicked spark now flashed in her eyes as she waited for my answer.

Murphy's grin grew. "Well, come on, then, love. Please, share." Her brows knitted into a mock frown. "And withhold not one manky detail."

I couldn't contain the grin on my own face at Murphy's heavy north York accent and favorite slang. *Manky*—meaning dirty or filthy. It reminded me of the first day we'd met, in our freshman year at Winston. Murphy had blown into our dorm room as though she'd known me forever. We hadn't instantly connected, though. Murphy...she was persistent. I couldn't help liking her. And the one thing I really loved about Murphy? She never asked questions. She simply...accepted. Unless, of course, it pertained to up-to-no-good fraternity pranks. "I think we should give the Kappas a taste of their own putrid medicine. That's what. And I have an idea how."

Several gasps filled the room, and the Deltas exchanged looks. Only Murphy kept her wide brown-eyed gaze on me. Her smile turned positively shady. "Whoa. Are you saying...you want to rule-break, Harper Belle?"

"Not exactly." I lifted my chin. "We are strong, motivated, goal-oriented women. There isn't a one of us who have less than a three point nine GPA. We're not pawns in their stupid frat dares. We tirelessly sponsor events to raise money for our house. For the shelter. And for our various clubs. The Kappas...they're a drunken joke. I'm tired of it and I for one want them to learn a lesson."

"Well, let's hear it," Murphy urged. Others joined in.

I met the expectant gazes of my sisters. "Bad. Boy. Makeover."

The sisters stared, silently and questioning at first. Then they all started talking at once, and the room sounded like a hive of bees. Murphy's gaze was still on mine, and the Cheshire Cat smile slowly stretched across her face. "Brilliant," she replied.

"So, what are the rules?" Maggie asked.

I thought about it. Straightened. Held their gazes. "Three of us will choose a subject. The absolute baddest, most ridiculously awful guy you can find. Completely reform them. Clean up their act. Teach them manners. Encourage participation in our winter events. Make them fall for you. Get them to divulge their deepest, darkest secrets." I smiled, held my head high. "Last but not least, they'll willingly attend our holiday Dash-n-Date. In a suit."

"Do they have to specifically be a Kappa? You realize how difficult that would be," Megan Conners said. "They're all jocks. Most already have girlfriends."

I thought about that. "Definitely an obstacle. If you find an available Kappa, go for it. Otherwise, target a Kappa affiliate." There were plenty of those around campus. Guys who weren't in the fraternity but who hung out with them.

Several rounds of *oh's* filled the room, and Murphy spoke up. "Definitely, Harper, you've outdone yourself this time." She grinned. "You should of course be one of the three."

I nodded. "Absolutely, I second that." I glanced around. "Who'll join me?"

Murphy's hand shot up. No one else's did. "Thanks, Murphy. Anyone else?" I gave a stern eye to the sisters. "We need one more."

I stared into the faces of the Deltas. We were known more for our brains, upbringing, and GPA rather than our beer pong prowess or how we might look in a wet T-shirt. We held ourselves on a higher level than most and took pride in everything we represented. How our sorority house had ended up directly across the street from the Kappas—total opposites—would always be a mystery to me.

Finally, a hand rose, and I nodded. "Thank you, Leslie." I gripped the podium once more, and the cool wood beneath my palms almost soothed my nerves. I didn't like games. Didn't care for pranks. Definitely didn't agree with dares, which is why I didn't dare suggest public humiliation. In my way of thinking, to emerge the victor, we must truly reform the chosen male. What better way to put the Kappas in their places?

The Kappas just needed to learn they couldn't treat women like trash. Plain and simple.

"We've got six weeks before the Dash-n-Date," I announced. "So ladies, choose your subjects and get to work."

As the sisters disassembled, their heads together discussing our latest quest, Murphy sauntered up to me. Her eyes narrowed. One brow shot up.

"You have someone in mind already?" she accused. "Don't you?"

I looked at her, surprised. "No I do not." I eyed her curiously. "What about you?"

Her smile revealed a devious plan. "A beastly specimen." She winked. "The very moment you decide, you must tell me first."

"All right," I agreed. "And you do the same."

I laid awake that night, staring up at the coarse pattern of what looked like popcorn on my ceiling. My mind scoured through the unimpressive number of guys I personally knew. None of them seemed appropriate. I thought of the Kappas. All of them seemed appropriate. But, as it had been pointed out at the chapter meeting, most had girlfriends and, despite my determination to make the Kappas pay for their stupid

Dare against Macie and Olivia, I just wasn't going to interfere with a relationship—no matter how insignificant it might be. Sighing, I turned onto my side, but my thoughts kept me wide awake. I liked it when a task had me preoccupied. It meant the past would leave me alone. At least for a little while.

I'd search tomorrow between classes. Winston was bound to have a pool of what Murphy called beastly gents. I thought about Brax. Even now, he had the look. Only I knew him pretty well and it was simply Brax's persona. It was who he was. He'd softened a bit, though, since Olivia. Didn't fight quite as often as he used to. But he definitely still had the look. I thought about it.

The bad boy appearance was incredibly difficult to overlook. They inadvertently wore it like a suit of armor. Not just the clothes they wore, because let's face it. Bad boys could wear raggedy jeans with holes in the knees or a thousand dollar Armani suit. No. It was the way they carried themselves. Confident. Fearless. Challenging. Obnoxious. A smile tugged at my mouth. Exactly like Brax Jenkins, I supposed. But there weren't any more Brax Jenkins-types wandering around Winston. He was definitely one of a kind. I sighed. This task would be a little more difficult than I'd thought. But I'd search. I'd look for those obvious qualities. And I'd reform.

My eyes fluttered, drifted, and with the plan to search for just the perfect specimen tomorrow, I fell asleep.

*   *   *

IN BETWEEN CLASSES THE next day my search began. My heels snapped against the sidewalk as I hurried across campus.

21

Determination made my jaw set; my eyes were peeled, scanning the quad, the walkways—everywhere. I would find my Dare today, no matter what. As I searched, a few caught my eye. Athletes mostly, but it seemed they always had a girl with them. Of course, though, that was a bad boy trait after all. Womanizer. I'd have to be persistent. A little aggressive, maybe. I headed to my last class.

During lecture, my mind focused on one thing. Not Rembrandt, the topic of the day. Instead? Who needed reforming? My eyes moved over the forty or so people gathered in the hall. First, not one Kappa present. And on closer inspection, not one noticeable bad boy type. They all seemed ordinary. Docile. Frustrated, I turned my attention to the notes on the overhead.

After class I set out, more determined than ever. On a mission, I sat on one of the concrete benches and scanned the sea of students milling about the quad. The late afternoon sun waned, and I glanced directly into it. Squinted. Then noticed how the light shimmered against the plum and red and ginger colored leaves of the pear trees. It'd be pretty if fall didn't lead into the holidays—

"Can you tell me how to get to the observatory?"

The soft-spoken, northern accented voice made me turn my head. A guy; tall, broad-shouldered but not bulky, with dark messy hair and soft brown eyes stared down at me. His eyes were hard to look away from. Smoky. Like expresso beans. And long, dark lashes. I'd never seen him before. And I was pretty sure I'd have remembered.

His mouth lifted in the corner into a crooked smile. Waiting. Those dark eyes watching me closely.

"Oh," I said, and stood. Smoothing my tailored blazer, I turned and pointed. "Take that pathway there. It will lead you to the Science complex," I said, and looked at him. "Look for the big dome."

He smiled fully now, with his eyes and his mouth, and it threw me off guard. "I will. Thanks."

"No problem," I answered, and watched him saunter away. He glanced over his shoulder and gave me a crooked grin, then continued to amble toward the direction I pointed him in. And I continued to stare. Leather jacket. Worn jeans. Biker boots. He didn't exactly look like an astronomy buff. But it was Wednesday, and the observatory was open to the public. I watched him for a few more moments, until a wave of students getting out of class swallowed him up.

I settled back down and examined the crowd for a while longer. Not only did I not find my Dare project, but I soon realized I kept inadvertently searching for the stranger with the smoky eyes and crooked smile. I didn't see him again, and I was surprised to find I was disappointed in that. The sun began to drop, and the air grew chilly. Fewer and fewer people walked about, the end of the day drawing them back to their dorms, or to the library, or the café, or the pubs. I watched the sky turn several shades of purple and lavender before finally getting up. Tonight was the one night of the week the Deltas had dinner together. We always met at Juno's on campus, so I hurried across the quad so I wouldn't be late. The girls were all there, waiting on me when I walked in.

Juno's was a pretty calm eatery in comparison to the rowdy sports pubs on campus. A shade of Bohemian, a shade of sophistication, the walls were painted in warm colors and decorated with pieces of local campus artwork and antique musical instruments. There was a sitting lounge with a giant sofa, four overstuffed chairs, and a small library of art and music books. I found our usual set of tables, in the corner and beneath a large canvas of a multi-colored knit scarf wrapped around the neck of a marble sculpture of an angel, and headed over. Draping my bag over the back of my chair, I sat next to Murphy. She pushed a small paper menu in front of me. Dinner at Juno's was just that. Dinner. No official business. No meeting topics. Just the sisters gathering, spending quality time with one another. Most times I'd wanted to skip out. Eating at Juno's once a week, despite having a student discount, added up. But being president of the Deltas, I didn't dare.

Murphy leaned toward my ear. "So did you discover a scrummy specimen today?"

I sighed and stared at the menu. Soon the words blurred, and the attractive stranger who'd asked for directions to the observatory popped into my head. "No," I answered quickly. "You?"

She stared hard at me for a moment. "Codswallop. I can see it in your eyes, Harper Belle. Someone caught your fancy, aye?"

I gave her a stiff grin. "Honestly. I haven't. Searched for a solid hour after class, but nothing." I sighed, wondering how Murphy's perception was so sharp. "Maybe I'm being too choosey."

"Could be," Murphy answered, then gave my shoulder a gentle shove with hers. "Don't fret, love. You'll find one." She grinned. "I've my keen eye on two, actually."

My eyes widened. "Seriously? Who?"

Murphy grinned. "Let's just say when I choose one, I'll give you the leftover."

I gave her a sideways glare. "Well, thanks."

Her grin was crooked and full of mischief. "What are you ordering? And if you say a bowl of soup I'm going to clobber you."

I shrugged. "I like soup." Plus, it was the cheapest thing on the menu. It filled me up, though.

Murphy looked at me, with that all-knowing, thoughtful gaze she sometimes had. At times I felt she knew my secrets. Knew everything about me, as if she'd hired a private detective and somehow had found out about my past. Maybe she had. If she did, she'd never once mentioned it. Her eyes softened, and she smiled. "I'll have soup, too."

I gave Murphy a hesitant smile, and she gave me one back. Unspoken acceptance. She'd never know how much I appreciated her silence.

*   *   *

THE NEXT DAY I ran into Olivia on my way to the library. She was stopped and facing away from me.

"Hey, Olivia," I said.

Olivia Beaumont turned to me. She was eating peanut butter on a spoon. Dressed in a long sleeved snap-down shirt, skinny jeans and a pair of navy All-Stars, she wore her long hair in a messy braid that hung over her shoulder. And not one smidge of make-up. I didn't know anyone else who could pull off the look like Olivia. One wouldn't think just by looking at her that she was so exceptionally brilliant. She wore her

Texas cowgirl shameless and with pride. I confessed, if only to myself, that it sparked a bit of envy in me. Never had I been allowed to be so...free with myself. Quickly, Olivia dabbed at her mouth. "Hey, Harper. How's it going?"

"Fine, thank you," I answered. I smoothed the front of my tailored suit and tucked my hair behind my ear. When Olivia glanced over her shoulder, my gaze followed. Then they widened. Brax stood, hands on hips, head down. Before him, another guy—the very same one I'd encountered yesterday. Same dark, messy hair, jeans. Boots. Leather jacket. Brax looked up and started talking with his hands. His body language seemed...angry. The attractive guy stood calm, hands shoved in his pockets.

"Who's that with Brax?" I asked cautiously, studying the two with a close eye. "It looks like they're arguing."

Olivia continued to watch the exchange. Then she sighed and looked at me. "They are. Well." She laughed lightly. "Brax is. Sort of. It's his older brother, Kane McCarthy. From Boston. They've been brothers since they were kids. Grew up in the same foster home for a while and have been joined to the hip ever since. Kane...kind of surprised Brax yesterday. He sort of just showed up at the observatory where Brax was helping me clean the scopes." She glanced at me and gave a wan smile. "A love-hate thing, I guess."

Kane McCarthy. Ever since our brief encounter the day before, my thoughts kept drifting back to him. Something about his dark stare and confident posture burrowed into my subconscious. More than once during classes, I'd thought about him. His smooth voice, his quiet stare. That easy smile. And I'd been the one to send him to the observatory. I watched

Brax throw his hands up, run them over his head, then push them onto his hips again. He took a few steps, then turned back to his brother. Meanwhile, Kane simply stood. Staring at Brax. Calm. "Why is that?" I asked.

"Well," Olivia explained. "Brax is still on probation with the baseball team from all that trouble last year. He can't afford any more. At all."

My spine stiffened. "Is that what Kane is? Trouble?"

Olivia looked at me, and her wide eyes softened. "I hope not, but it's kind of looking that way." She sighed. "This is the first time I've met Kane in person, but Brax has talked about him a lot to me. Brax loves him like crazy, but..." Olivia smiled. "They both grew up in a hard, unimaginable life on the street. Brax escaped. Kane unfortunately didn't." Her gaze moved back to the brothers. "Kane has been in trouble before. Running numbers." She looked at me. "Brax says that's what he's probably here to do. Football season, you know."

"Is he going to start school here?" I asked, alarmed. "Or just numbers?" My gaze returned to Kane and Brax.

"I honestly don't know," Olivia answered. "He'll be staying with Brax for a while, anyway. Brax will try and talk some sense into him. And you're aware of Brax's method of talking sense into someone."

My gaze moved to Olivia. "Is Kane dangerous?" I looked at him again. Still standing quiet while Brax moved around, throwing his hands in the air, shaking his head. The whole while, Kane just watched his brother.

"I'm positive Kane himself isn't dangerous," Olivia answered. "Don't get me wrong—he's been in his share of fights, so Brax tells me, and can hold his own. But I'm afraid of the numbers. That's not only illegal. It's dangerous business. And he was asking Brax about Kappa House."

The Kappa House? I continued to watch the brothers for a moment, lost in thought. Until an idea formed.

What if I could reform Kane? Although his demeanor wasn't that of a bad boy—at least, not like Brax, anyway—if he was a street-wise, number-running guy, he was bad in my book. I could steal him away from the Kappas and they'd suffer a loss. Which was pretty much the idea of the Deltas' private Dare.

Should I? Or...could I? Did I even have that kind of nerve? My eyes found Brax's brother once more.

I'd most definitely have to give it some serious thought.

2. Prospects

I WAS SURPRISED TO find I had a hard time looking away from Kane McCarthy, and was even more surprised by how the idea intrigued me. The idea of Kane as my Dare. I'd continue to search, though. Just in case a better prospect emerged. With a deep breath, I turned. "So, Olivia," I said brightly. "Have you thought any more about joining the Deltas?"

She shook her head. "Thanks, Harper. I know you guys are great but you know how I feel about that."

I nodded. "I understand. But, I had to ask. You'd be a phenomenal addition, if you ever change your mind."

"Change your mind about what?"

My eyes darted to Brax, who'd jogged up to us. He wore a Silverbacks baseball cap, bill facing the back, and a Silverbacks tee shirt. The long-sleeved button down he wore over it hung open. When I glanced over my shoulder I saw his brother leaning against the live oak tree in the quad where they'd been arguing. His arms crossed over his chest, eyes were on us. Watching. *Kane McCarthy.* I felt as though he were looking directly at me. Inside of me.

"Harper here is still trying to recruit me into their sorority," Olivia stated.

I turned and Brax's startling blue eyes and scarred face studied mine as he draped his arm over Olivia's shoulders. He pulled her close, kissed her on the temple, then grinned. "Yeah, good luck with that, sweetheart. Gracie here ain't into clubs of any sort. Unless it's the Brax club." He chuckled, and his strong Boston accent paired with a penetrating gaze as he studied me a little longer, an unsettling sort of inspection that almost had me fidgeting where I stood. I struggled not to glance away. Sometimes, he looked at me as if he knew. Knew my secrets, just like Murphy seemed to. Brax's mouth pulled up in one corner, and it was a soft, friendly sort of movement that eased his harsh features. "Nice suit."

I glanced down at my wardrobe, then back up. Corinne Belle always insisted that in order to be successful one had to dress successful, at all times. No jeans. No tee shirts. No sweatpants. Only the finest would do. My wardrobe was chosen and tailored for me each semester by Corinne.

She'd *insisted.*

And so I did just that. But I couldn't tell if it was sarcasm or a compliment. Knowing Brax it probably was a little of both, but I took it as a compliment. "Thanks, Brax."

He gave a slight nod, then looked at Olivia. "You go ahead," he said, then kissed her on the nose. "I'm going to"—

his eyes flashed quickly to me, then back to Olivia's—"get my brother out of here for a while. Come over later?"

"Of course," Olivia answered softly.

Suddenly, I felt like an intruder. I could feel the tension rolling off of Brax in waves. Was he that angry with Kane? I'd seen Brax Jenkins angry before. It wasn't a pretty sight. My eyes flicked to the slim black leather watch strapped to my wrist. "I…have to go," I said hurriedly, and smiled at Olivia. "Oh—did you sign up for the Turkey Run on Saturday?"

Olivia grinned. "We both did."

I nodded. "Super, thanks. See you guys there."

"Oh, Harper," Olivia said. I looked at her, and she smiled. "I've been meaning to ask. Do you have plans for Thanksgiving? You're welcome to come home with us. We always have a load of food."

My insides froze, and I pasted a smile as panic seized me. "Oh, thank you, Olivia, but…I'm going home." I gave a laugh that came out a lot meeker than I'd planned. And so did the lie. "It's a huge Belle ordeal. Very Norman Rockwell. You know what I mean. But thank you."

Olivia nodded, and her eyes softened. "If anything changes, the offer is there, Harper."

Brax kissed Olivia's temple and wiggled his brows. "She makes pies."

This time, my smile came easy. His love for her came off him in waves. "Thanks, Olivia. Brax."

I hurried off toward the library, and at the steps I paused and looked over my shoulder. The pair moved up the walkway, Brax's arm protectively around Olivia, his head bent close to her ear, then they stopped at the walkway leading to the Science complex and he pulled her close, pressed his mouth to hers and kissed her long. Olivia's head lifted, smiling up at Brax, and he turned and jogged away.

I couldn't imagine what Thanksgiving would be in Olivia's world. I knew she had a big family, and I envisioned it to be something similar to one of the Holiday Hallmark movies Murphy frequently watched on her laptop. I swallowed my sigh, pushing Thanksgiving and holidays and turkey and big families out of mind and turned, my gaze seeking Brax's brother.

His stare seemed dead on me. I couldn't move; couldn't look away. Finally, Brax reached him, and the pair turned and sauntered off.

Kane McCarthy. Mysteriously quiet and attractive. Street kid. Foster kid. From Boston. And he was here to run bets during football season. Not much to know about a person, and what there was to know was pretty shady and a little frightening. But by the time my last class finished for the day, he'd entered my mind at least a dozen or more times. Slightly frustrating when trying to concentrate on the notes Professor Sizemore was giving on the Ming Dynasty. That quiet, slightly accented voice and those dark smoky eyes kept interrupting my thoughts. Disruptive, to say the very least. Then there was that crooked smile—

"Hey, Harper," a familiar voice sounded behind me. I'd just escaped class and was headed to a meeting for the annual Greek bake sales when Murphy caught up to me. She eased into my pace as I hurried along. "Fancy a little curry for dinner?" she asked in her heavy English accent. "I heard of a new place that just opened in Covington." She elbowed me as I gave her a side glance. "The absolute dog's bollocks, I'm told. I'll drive."

I smiled and shook my head as we weaved through the student body of Winston. I'd learned most of her witty British slang, so I knew dog's bollocks was a good thing, despite the crude sound of it. "Your driving terrifies me."

"Ha! I'll have you know I've pinched only two violations since arriving here, Ms. Belle. My driving skill is nothing short of legendary."

I laughed. "Right, right. I can't, though." I looked at her. "I have a meeting."

"After the meeting, goose," Murphy coaxed, and we both stopped. She looked at me. "You've got to eat, Harper."

I pondered Murphy's invitation. I'd turned down her invites at least three times in the past week. Maybe it wouldn't hurt to go for just a little while.

"Harper?" She snapped her fingers in front of my eyes. "Hello in there? Curry? You know—smelly but delish?"

I smiled. "Okay, okay. After my meeting. Smelly curry."

Murphy's smile was wide and epic. "Brill! Well, chivvy along, love. Finish thy meeting, post-haste, and I'll pick you up at the house at...?"

"Six," I answered.

"See ya then!" Murphy grinned.

With a wave, I hurried to the meeting—for the bake sale— and again, I found myself having a difficult time concentrating on my tasks. Maybe it was because the information was nothing new to me; the bake sale was a standard Greek fundraiser and I'd done several already. It was to help fund the holiday Dash-n-Date, a conglomeration of the sororities. All—

well, most anyway—were taking part in it. It was a formal event and each participating sorority house would host one course in a five-course meal. And, a date would accompany them. Gown and tux. It was quite the event. Over the last three years every sorority participated.

Maybe I couldn't concentrate because for some strange reason, Kane McCarthy wouldn't leave my thoughts. Ridiculous, really. I'd only seen him once. Well, twice if you counted the interaction with Brax. Still, he wouldn't leave me...

Meanwhile, I'd keep my eyes peeled for a true blue bad boy to reform.

Murphy was waiting for me at the house when I pulled up. Black leggings, a big slouchy ivory-colored sweater and brown boots completed her casual, easy look. I smoothed my suit jacket and closed my car door.

"Chivvy along, chivvy along," she coaxed, and then jumped behind the wheel of her white Land Rover. I shook my head, crossed the lot and climbed into the passenger side. The sun had dropped behind the horizon and darkness settled over campus as we maneuvered through the tree-lined streets and out of the main gate. I surprised myself, though, as my eyes searched every group, every solitary person walking along. Looking, I suppose, for him. Kane McCarthy. And I wasn't even sure why.

Murphy filled our drive time by popping in her favorite CD mix, starting with one of her favorite British bands, The Proclaimers. It started with her number one favorite song of all time, *I'm Gonna Be (500 Miles)*. She played it every single time she got into her vehicle. Every time. To be honest, I'd come to love the song almost as much as she did. We sang along until the song ended, then she restarted it. I smiled and shook my head.

The words burrowed into my thoughts. Imagine a man who would indeed do what the lyrics stated and walk a thousand miles to fall down at the door of the one he loved? Whether it was a father walking that many miles to his child, or a man to the woman he loved. Either was beyond rational thought, to me. A dream almost. Fantasy.

Karma was a small restaurant set in a copse of trees off the highway, just inside the Covington city limits. The building looked like quite a lot of the ones in rural Texas: rugged. Once a BBQ joint, Karma, now an Indian restaurant, had retained the rugged look. Wood sided with a new sign over the entrance, painted in tall red letters: KARMA. Murphy found a parking spot near the back and stopped the Rover. She grinned. "I bloody well love that song."

I shook my head and fought a smile. "Yes. I know."

"Well, come on then," she said and leapt from the truck. "I'm famished."

I followed Murphy to the entrance and we stepped inside. Busy for a Thursday, we were finally seated near the back at a small table at the window. I glanced out as I sat, into the darkened woods behind the restaurant.

"Warning: I'm so bloody hungry I'm barking," Murphy said, studying her menu. "Oh! I'm having *vindaloo*." She winked and pointed at the menu. "It says right here that it's enjoyed by pyromaniacs. I'll be breathing fire for a fortnight. What about you?"

I scanned the menu. "Gobi saag." It'd be less than five dollars with my student card.

35

Murphy blinked. "That's it? A bit of spicy veggies?" She looked at me, her eyes soft. "One day I'm going to get you to my mum's for some pot roast and Yorkshire puddings." She grinned. "You'd eat yourself sick." She closed her eyes. "Oh God, I want that now."

I laughed softly. "It sounds wonderful. I'll take you up on that sometime."

We ordered and, as we waited for our food, Murphy leaned close. "I know I just asked you yesterday, but any prospects?"

I nodded. "Sort of."

Murphy let out a squeak. "Oh! Do tell!"

"Well," I started. I didn't want to tell her everything Olivia had told me about Kane, so I left out the details regarding the numbers. "Brax Jenkins has a brother in town. From Boston. A foster brother. I think he's here to do business with the Kappas."

Murphy's eyes widened. "What sort of business? Dodgy?"

I shrugged. "I'm not sure, but I think, yes."

Murphy stifled a squeal. "Tell me everything. Manky, and non-manky. Because this," she wiggled her brows, "is juicy. And you know how I fancy juicy."

"Yes, yes," I said with a grin. "We all know." I sighed. "I overheard Brax telling Olivia about it." My brows knitted. "Brax wasn't happy. Not at all."

"I bet not. He'd get in a tub of trouble." She eyed me, and her hazel orbs almost sparkled. "You could, too, you know."

I lifted my chin. "I won't. And neither will Brax. Or Kane for that matter."

She rubbed her chin. "Tell me how you met him."

Suddenly, it was there. The cramped, trapped feeling I got

36

when people asked too many questions. Forcing me to tell too many lies. I willed the sensation to go away. "First, he just randomly asked me for directions to the observatory. Then he saw me talking to Brax and Olivia." I shrugged. "I…noticed him watching me for a while before he and Brax walked off."

"That is uncanny, love." She lifted one chestnut brow. "Perhaps a bit stalkerish and you're most definitely off your trolley." Her eyes widened. "It's perfect. He's perfect, Harper." She grinned. "You must choose him."

I leaned forward. "I don't want to get into trouble over this, Murphy. I…can't." My grandmother's stern face flashed before me. Cowered me. Made me remember.

"Well," Murphy continued. "If he's up to no good and having shady who-knows-what sort of dealings with the Kappas, then I say take him on." She grinned. "You can do it, Harper old girl." Her Cheshire cat smile returned. "Reform the barmy beast." She leaned back and met my eye. "But I probably wouldn't let on to Olivia. You know? Being that he's Brax's brother and such. She might not be too keen on the idea."

"Right," I agreed.

And immediately, that thought sat ill with me. Olivia had been Brax's Dare; neither would like it. But I stashed it away, just like I skillfully stashed so many other things away. Out of sight. Back into a corner of my mind even I had a difficult time locating. For no one else to see.

*   *   *

IT WASN'T UNTIL THE next afternoon that I encountered Kane McCarthy again. Completely unintentional, he seemed to suddenly just be…there. In my path as I made my way to the library. He was talking to Cliff Barnes, president of the Kappas. As I passed by, Kane's gaze found mine and locked onto it, and I couldn't seem to look away. It was brief, yet much more intense than the first time. It was enough, and I was more aware of him this time. Details that had escaped me before leapt at me now. Dark eyes the color of coffee followed me, and they seemed to smolder, simmer, spear right through me as he openly stared. His skin was pale; flawless, with dark brows and thick dark lashes that were too thick and long for a man. A strong-cut chin and full lips looked as though they'd been pulled straight off a marble statue. He was the kind of gorgeous that made your eyes kaleidoscope. At least, to me. Quickly, I looked away.

*   *   *

BY THE TIME I'D finished a very poor attempt at studying for an Art test and exited the library, the tell-tale signs of pending dusk had crept onto Winston's manicured campus. The early November air felt crisp against my cheeks as it whisked through, rustling the leaves and sending several pirouetting to the ground to land in scattered colors on the grass like some strange abstract stained glass. Knowing darkness would soon swallow everything, I hurried to the campus coffee house and café that stayed open until midnight. Inside, students sat at tables studying, their laptops open, the light illuminating their faces and coffee cups by their sides. As I took my place in line I selected my usual pre-packaged turkey sandwich and a bottle of lemonade and stood, waiting to pay.

"That's all you're eating?"

I jumped at the voice behind me and turned to find Kane there. Instantly, my insides froze. He gazed down at me, his hands shoved into his pockets, those broad shoulders sort of hunching toward me, almost…cornering me; his eyes as worn and soft as the leather jacket he wore.

"Um, yes," I answered. I gave a hesitant smile. "Not very hungry, I guess." What was he doing here? Suddenly I felt closed in—a feeling I avoided at all costs.

"So what's good here?" he asked. His Boston accent was heavy and void of the letter *r*, just like Brax's, only…softer. Quiet. The kind of voice that you had to pay close attention to or else you'd miss what they were saying completely.

I couldn't believe he was talking to me. I shrugged, pretended he didn't bother me, and held up my sandwich. "Turkey?"

He said nothing as he lifted three turkey sandwiches from the cooler; his smoky gaze remained riveted to mine. Then, he bent his head close. "Kane McCarthy."

I looked at him then, taken back by how his voice washed over me and made my skin tingle. I forced myself to breathe; I wasn't used to being in this kind of situation. Guys just didn't go out of their way to talk to me. I made sure of it. But I didn't balk. I mean, after all—Kane was my potential reformation Dare. Right? Murphy's words rushed back to me. *Reform the barmy beast!* I breathed. Smiled. Pretended. "Harper Belle."

Again, his eyes softened, and as we stepped up to the cashier he gave her a nod and inclined his head toward me. Before I could say a word, the cashier had rung our orders up together, and Kane handed her a twenty.

I looked at him, embarrassed. "Oh no, really, that's okay, you don't have to—"

Kane's eyes moved over me. "Yeah," he said quietly. "I do."

3. Chosen

"THANK YOU," I SAID. I glanced around, scared to see if anyone had noticed Kane's gesture. As far as I could tell, no one had—except the casher, who'd given me a hasty look. What in the world did Kane McCarthy want with me? In my hand I clutched a five-dollar bill. Despite the sandwich and lemonade only costing three of the five dollars, the whole bill landed on the top of Kane's sandwiches. "But I don't take charity. Especially from strangers." Turning quickly, I started out of the café. I made it to the door, only to have his big hand push it open and hold it as I passed through. Silently, I did. He followed.

"We're not strangers."

I made the mistake of looking at him. I shouldn't have; should've just kept on walking. But, I didn't. His stormy eyes lit

41

on mine, holding on as if we could communicate without speaking. By just simply…looking at each other. I'd never reacted that way before. To anyone. The brown depths of his irises gleamed fathomless; held secrets, maybe. Kind of like mine did.

I cleared my throat and returned my gaze ahead of me, and continued on my way. Dusk was fading fast. "Of course we are," I said.

"We've met before," he continued in a soft, even voice. "You gave me directions to the observatory. And…" I glanced at him again, and his mouth curved. "You're friends with my brother and his girl." He inclined his head, toward the café. "I introduced myself back there," he replied. "And so did you." He ducked his head to look at me, and the corner of his mouth lifted. "Strangers no more."

I walked faster, crossing the quad to the main parking lot where I'd left my Lexus. I spared him a look. "We're friends, yes. But all the same I make it a habit never to accept handouts, even from friends." I held my eyes to his. "I don't like owing anyone. Besides. We've barely known each other ten minutes."

He gave a soft laugh. "Handouts? I was just—" He sighed. "Never mind. So why are you in such a hurry?"

"I'm late for a Greek assembly," I lied, and just like whenever I had to lie, I started feeling cagey. Ready to escape. I felt my skin prickle. I felt ready to run.

Breathe, Harper. Just breathe. Don't let them in. Don't let them see you.

He's nobody.

Another deep breath, inconspicuous, and I shook off the feeling that sometimes threatened to swamp me. That brought on confusion. Slips of memory. And what Corinne Belle called *fits of unnatural behavior.* I hadn't had an episode in, well, forever. Yet within a few moments Kane McCarthy threatened to pull one out of me. I breathed slowly. Controlled. Focused on the *now*. Tamped down what madness was brewing inside of me. I stopped at my car and, with the keys in my hand, I pressed the unlock button and opened my door. Kane was right beside me.

"It was nice meeting you," I said calmly. I'd almost forgotten my manners so I quickly flashed a well-practiced smile. "Welcome to Winston, Kane McCarthy."

As I shut the door to my Lexus, Kane stepped back and watched me silently. Crazy, but I looked at him—as if my eyeballs had a will of their own, as if they didn't care the state in which Kane almost drove me to. And it was a mistake. Not a *fit of unnatural behavior* sort of mistake, but...different. Unfamiliar. Shocking. Those coffee colored eyes bore into mine, steady and quiet and smoky and something else I couldn't identify. Didn't want to. Then, a small movement lifted his mouth in the corner, shifted his expression into what looked like amusement—or interest—and he gave a single nod of goodbye. Quickly I pulled past him and drove away.

As I drove through Winston's narrow, tree-lined streets I let my breath out. Alone, I felt safe. I felt like I didn't have to hide anything. Or lie. To anyone. Except myself.

Kane McCarthy. What had propelled him to take an interest in me? Why had he looked at me like that? And why had he made me so incredibly edgy? It was all sort of silly, really. I mean, it'd been my idea to use him as my Dare reformation. So why did I allow him to stir such a reaction in me? He wasn't supposed to be pursuing me. *I* was supposed to be pursuing *him*. It made no sense. None at all.

43

At the main gates I waited for several cars to pass, then when it was clear I pulled out, heading toward a place I frequented. My favorite place. Me and no one else. If I hurried, I'd have a few minutes before it grew too dark.

I entered the city limits of Covington and soon after veered right, down an oak-lined road. Street lamps cast a hazy glow over the pavement, and soon the entrance to Ardsley Park emerged on the left. A small man-made lake with a jogging track around its perimeter, and picnic tables along the side, families gathered here on the weekends. Not too many students since Winston had its own magnificent park. And that's exactly why I came.

I pulled in and edged along the drive until I reached my usual spot, then parked. Grabbing my turkey sandwich and lemonade, I left my car and walked to the park bench by the pond's edge.

After I wiped off the early evening dew from the wooden seat with one of the napkins I'd taken from the café, I sat, meticulously opened the wrapper on my sandwich and quietly ate. Small birds chirped and tweeted in the tree boughs above my head, and the sun had completely dropped from sight, leaving in its wake a hazy, almost blurry sort of maddening gray. A mysterious blanket that draped over everything, just before the night's blackness settled in. I watched a couple jogging along the path beneath the lamplight, and as they ran they bumped shoulders. Raced each other. Played around.

Isn't that what normal people did? Horsed around? Played? Loved?

Kane found my thoughts again, but no sooner did his somber brown eyes and gentle voice come to mind did my grandmother shove them aside. I squeezed my eyes tightly shut, trying to make her go away, back to a place where she couldn't hurt me. But she still got in there. Inside of me. Just like she always did.

"What are you doing in here?"

I knelt on the ground by the trashcan behind the kitchen entrance. I'd found my backpack in there, where she'd thrown it away. I was digging through it, and my hand held tightly onto the only photograph I owned of my mother and father.

"Answer me!"

I jumped, my hand squeezing the picture into a fold. "No-nothing," I stammered.

"Pull your hand from that bag right now."

My body began to shake as I slowly lifted my hand from my backpack. I looked up, pleading with Corinne Belle. "Please. Can't I just keep it? I'll hide it in my—"

With a firm grip Corinne yanked me up by my thin arm and shook me. "You'll not keep it. Did you already forget what I told you not an hour ago?" She leaned closer to me, and I could see every line and wrinkle in her pale, powdered face. "You don't exist anymore. Neither do they!" She snatched the photograph from my hand. "Come now."

She didn't turn me loose; instead, she pulled me, back through the kitchen, past the pantry and out into the hall. At the hearth, a massive fire roared. Corinne Belle shoved the picture back into my hand.

"Take one last look, child," she said. "Then throw it into the fire."

Tears filled my eyes as I looked at her face; cruel, mean, old. Filled with hate.

"Do it now!" she thundered.

Slowly, my eyes left her, and through tears I peered at the photograph. It wasn't a good one; a piece of the corner had been ripped off, and my parents were blurry. But I could still see them. They were young, before...the trouble began. Before me...

"Throw it in!" Corinne Belle screeched. "Now!"

I gave the picture one last look, hoping I could keep the memory of my mother's face, my father's smile, in my head. Then I let the flames take the photo from my hands. In a hiss, the old paper turned to black ash.

Corinne squeezed my shoulders and spun me around to face her. With a bony hand, she grabbed my chin, forcing my gaze to hers. "You are no longer Harper Lewis. Harper Lewis is dead. Your parents are dead. That life is dead." She shook me. "Do you hear me?"

My eyes widened, and I nodded.

"Don't you ever defy me, girl. Ever! Eyes are always on you. Do you understand? If not mine, someone else's. And there will be serious consequences if you defy me. Do you know what that means?"

I wasn't sure, so I shook my head.

Corinne Belle's face tightened. "You'll pay dearly for any mistakes you make. Your grandfather insisted we not beat your mother and look where that landed her. In the grave!" Her mouth turned flat, like a straight line across her face. "The Bible says, Spare the rod, spoil the child. I promise you, Harper. You'll not end up like your parents. Pathetic, useless drug addicts. Sneaking around my back, having sex at sixteen years old. Sinners! You'll not become your ungrateful, selfish mother. You'll not shame the Belles' good name."

My breath started coming fast, as if it wasn't doing what it was supposed to do to keep my body alive. Maybe I was dying, just like Corinne had said I had. My chest tightened, but I didn't dare look away from my grandmother. I didn't know what most of she said meant; I wouldn't ask.

"Now come with me," she said, and yanked my arm again. "I was hoping you'd not have to learn things the hard way, but I suppose

you'll have to all the same." She glanced down at me. "There are many ways to apply the rod to a child without leaving marks. You're about to learn what happens to you when you disobey."

Panic made my breath come faster. "No, please," I begged. "I'm sorry! I won't do it again, I won't!" I didn't even know what the punishment was. Only that she terrified me.

"That's right. You won't."

Up the stairs we went, up to the third floor. The lights were off—all but one light on the wall, halfway down the corridor. It made strange shadows grow long against the floor in front of me. Where was she taking me? My breath came faster. My heartbeat quickened.

At the end of the corridor, a short, fat door with a black iron handle. We reached it, and Corinne Belle stood over me.

"Remove your fresh new clothes, this beautiful dress I purchased just for you, and hand them to me."

Stunned, I could do nothing but stare at her, eyes wide. I couldn't speak. I couldn't move. I was frozen. I didn't want to give her my clothes.

"Now!" she thundered.

Slowly, I pulled the new plum-colored dress over my head and handed it to Corinne. Next, my shiny black shoes. My skinny arms covered my bare chest.

Reaching down, she opened the small door. "Removing your clothes makes you vulnerable. It humbles you. Keeps you in perspective. Now get inside. Think about what you've done. And ask God to forgive you."

I paused. Inside the small room, it was pitch-dark. Blacker than black. I could see nothing. Nothing at all.

Her bony hand pushed the top of my head down and shoved me forward. "Get. In!"

47

With a gasp, I stumbled into the tiny room. A closet, really. The door slammed shut behind me, and a key turned. Only a thin line of light appeared at the bottom of the door.

"Do not scream, Harper. Do not call for help. Do not sob." Through the small crack, her shadow moved across the door, as though bending close. As though peering inside. "You'll not make a sound. If you do, your punishment will be twice as long."

The snapping of her heels against the floor as she walked away rung harshly in my ears. I wanted to scream out, but she'd warned me not to. I didn't want her to leave me. I didn't want her to come back. I just wanted to be…gone. I hugged myself tightly, sat down in the corner, and cried as quietly as I could. My breath hurt as it pushed in and out of my lungs, faster and faster, until I became dizzy—

"Hey, darlin'. Are you okay?"

I leapt as the stranger's voice penetrated my thoughts and dragged me back to the present. I was breathing hard. My chest was pounding. My eyes darted around me. Night had fallen while I'd drowned in my daymare of the past. I collected myself, cleared my throat, smiled, looked at the couple standing there, staring down at me. "Yes, yes," I said hurriedly. "I'm fine. Allergies. They always get me this time of year."

The man, probably in his mid-thirties, smiled warmly. "Okay, just checkin'." He reached for the hand of the woman he was with; pretty, with a long brown ponytail. Together, they jogged off.

I watched them for a while, until they'd nearly made it back around the pond. Before they passed by me, I got up, threw my wrapper and empty bottle in the trashcan, and hurried to my car. Full darkness had fallen, and already I felt the pings of anxiety hitting me. I hardly ever stayed out after dark. Not alone, anyway.

Back at Delta house I parked, locked the car, and just as I walked through the common room, Murphy stopped me. I forcibly pushed the unwanted daymare I'd just experienced out of my mind.

"Guess who has acquired a subject?" she said, her eyes glittering with a frightening sort of mischief.

"Who'd you find?" I asked.

"This is so brill," Murphy continued, and pushed her hair behind her ear. "Less than a handful of hours after our plan was executed and I've not only chosen my prey, but he's agreed to meet me at MacElvee's for drinks tomorrow night."

Curiosity bit at me. "Who?"

That Grinch grin spread over Murphy's face. The slow one. "Josh Collins."

My brow quirked in confusion. "He's dating someone, I thought."

"Freshly dumped," Murphy gloated. "Besides. Completely mental, that one. He's better off." Her hand darted out before her, like a fish swimming through the water. "I wasted no time, love. Slipped right on in." She elbowed me in the ribs. "Brilliant, yeah?"

I couldn't help but grin. "Definitely so, since he's like the go-to guy for the Kappas' Halloween bash every year. But Murphy—don't do anything, you know. Degrading."

Her eyes widened in mock-horror. "Are you off your trolley, Harper?" she grinned. "I wouldn't dare. So what about you? Have you made a final decision yet?"

"I'm still considering."

"You should def give it a whirl, love. He's perfect," she answered.

I shook my head in disbelief. "See you in the morning, Murphy."

"Hey, what's the rush?" She inclined her head toward the sofa, where the gas fireplace was lit. A few other sisters sat on the floor, books opened.

"I've a test to study for," I replied, and glanced toward the staircase. "You know I study better alone."

Murphy's gaze held mine for a few moments. "Yeah, love. I know. So, hey," she continued. "Are you headed home for the holidays? Or do you fancy spending them with me and the fam in a non-traditional British sort of way?" She tapped my nose with her long, delicate finger. "Roast and Yorkshire puddings are screaming for you."

I offered her a smile. "Thanks, Murphy, I appreciate the offer. But you know, my folks always have this big…thing on the holidays. Huge. I'm expected to be there." My laugh was light, jubilant. Fake. But only I knew it. "Big Belle celebrations."

Murphy nodded, but her eyes remained on mine. "Absolutely." She turned me toward the stairs. "Now chivvy along for your bit of swotting. Wouldn't want you getting anything less than an A."

I grinned. Swotting meant to cram or study hard—something she professed never, ever to do. "Thanks. And good job on your Dare subject." I headed up the steps, and in my room, I closed the door, closed my eyes and breathed. The daymare at the park had drained me. Kane for some reason plagued me. And now Thanksgiving and Christmas loomed. Every year was the same. So many offers to go home and celebrate the holidays. So many invitations to go home with someone. Murphy. Olivia.

So many refusals. I refused them all, every single year.

On the floor rested a handful of envelopes. My mail. Lifting them and setting them onto my bedside table, I shrugged out of my suit and hung it neatly on a hanger. Running the brush through my hair I pulled it into a ponytail and slipped into a freshly dry-cleaned pair of pajamas that smelled like lavender. Across the hall, the bathroom was blessedly empty for once and I went through my nightly face-washing, moisturizing, teeth-brushing routine. Then, I crossed over to my room, closed the door, and climbed into bed. No textbooks. No studying. Not tonight, anyway.

The light stayed on. Always on.

Soon, with the sounds of my sorority sisters' laughter wafting up the staircase, my eyelids grew heavy and I drifted off to sleep.

The moment my eyes popped open, Kane McCarthy was there. In my brain. Behind my eyelids, like a photograph. Five-thirty a.m. What was he doing in my thoughts so early? On my nightstand, I lifted the copy of *Sense and Sensibility* I'd purchased at a used book store in Covington and began reading. I'd read it a dozen times before, but it didn't matter. Jane Austen was by far a woman I admired, and I loved all of her works. Corinne Belle had insisted I read her novels as a child, swearing it would make me more well-rounded. Little did she know I honestly enjoyed it. *Sense and Sensibility* and *Emma* were two of my favorites, and I'd read them both many times. Austen's profound words seemed to stay with me for days on end, even after I'd closed the book.

Slipping out of bed, I hurried through my morning yoga routine, my full-body stretches, my sit-ups. Then before anyone else awakened, I pulled out the pair of trainers from beneath my bed, along with the running leggings and a light jacket, and set out for the second thing I did for sheer pleasure: run. It was something Corinne Belle would frown upon; it was something I hid from her, as well. As I eased out of Delta house, the chilled November morning greeted me, along with the still-darkened sky, and I set out to the parking lot. I didn't dare run on campus; the park was much safer. There, I left my car, eased out, did a few more stretches, and started my morning run. Slow at first, I picked up the pace, reveling in the burn of my muscles, the long stride of my legs, the ache in my lungs. It was the one thing that really made me feel alive. Made me feel like me. Rather, what was left of me.

No one else was about. Just me, the running path, and the pond. Unavoidably, my thoughts again landed on a pair of smoky brown eyes and flawless skin. Messy hair. And I had to shake my head to clear my thoughts of Kane McCarthy.

Why was he troubling me? Wasn't he a perfect subject for the Dare? Murphy thought he was the perfect choice. I ran harder, as if trying to put distance between me and his image, and by the time I succeeded the very hazy edge of daybreak cracked the sky. My lungs now burned, and I bent over at the waist, grabbed my knees, and sucked in volumes of crisp air. Sweat clung to my neck, and the cool air swept over it as I breathed—

"Running from something?"

Gasping, my heart leapt as I jumped. Kane leaned against the tree closest to the park bench I'd sat on the night before.

"What are you doing here?" I asked, surprised. "Are you following me?"

Those smoky eyes regarded me in silence. "Yeah. I guess I am."

My eyes darted through the barely-there haze of early morning. A few others had begun their morning run, so I wasn't alone. Still, he unnerved me, and I questioned him. "Why?"

Kane must've sensed my unease; he remained against the live oak. He shrugged. "I was out, saw you leave. Guess I wanted to know where you were going so early." He inspected me then, toe to head, then lifted one brow. I was utterly speechless, so I waited for him to speak. "Why do you drive twelve miles off campus to run?"

There it was again. Edgy. Caged in. I didn't like questions, and Kane McCarthy was full of them. "It's really none of your business." I breathed, forcing the adrenaline pulsing through me to settle. "And frankly I think it's pretty bizarre that you'd follow a total stranger—a girl no less."

There was that slow, easy smile. "There you go with that strangers thing again. I told you last night. We're not strangers anymore." Still, he stayed where he was, propped easily against that tree, arms crossed over his chest, that leather jacket opened and exposing a dark T-shirt beneath. He pinned me with a look. "It's safe out here? A girl like you?" His gaze held steady. "Alone?"

Wiping my damp brow with my forearm, I began edging my way to my car. "What do you mean, a girl like me?"

Now he pushed off the tree and his long legs stretched over the ground as he followed me. He shrugged. "Small. Easy target." He rubbed his chin. "Goody-goody. Beautiful."

That caught me off guard. It also angered me. "So only

small, beautiful girls get attacked? I don't think so. Besides, I can handle myself. And yes—this is a safe place." I inclined my head. "The Covington Deputy Sheriff jogs here every morning and stays until after daybreak." I glanced around and saw the sheriff on the opposite side of the lake. At the water's edge, an old lady fed the ducks. Perfectly safe.

At the car, he caught up with me. "I'm not trying to scare you," he said quietly. He stood close now—so much that I could smell the soap wafting off his skin. "I'd just...hate to see you get hurt."

I opened my car door and before I could close it, Kane was there. Keeping it opened with an easy grip. When I looked up in alarm, or surprise—whatever—he was staring down at me, and there was a gentleness about his features, in the relaxed lines around his eyes, the ease of his full lips that captivated me, banishing the fear that had sprung up inside of me. It was strange. Exhilarating. Terrifying. "All women are potential targets, Harper." His eyes grew solemn. "You just happen to be a beautiful one. Sometimes, that puts you at a higher risk." He turned my car door loose. "Be careful."

I barely knew what to say. I swallowed, felt the cagey feeling gnawing at me again, and I gave a nod. "Of course. Thanks." I closed the door then, and he stepped back. After I started the engine and put the car in reverse, I looked at him, and he offered an easy smile.

Again, the kind of male beauty that made one's eyes kaleidoscope.

As I backed out, he waved, and I nodded, and as I pulled away I glanced in my rearview mirror. Kane stood there, hands in his pocket, legs braced wide as he watched me leave.

Only when I passed a vintage truck, parked close to the exit, did I wonder how Kane had gotten to the park. I then questioned if it was his and figured it had to be.

Apprehension left me as soon as I pulled onto the road, yet my thoughts ran rampant through my mind as I drove back to Winston. Within two days Kane McCarthy had not only entered my life, uninvited, but he now knew one of my secrets—that I chose to drive twelve miles away from campus to run. I was positive he suspected I had motive, and I felt sure that he'd eventually ask questions. Yet somehow, I felt sure he'd keep it to himself.

Why, I had no idea. He was about as polar opposite of me as one could get. He wasn't the usual type of guy who even remotely showed an interest in me. And that caused me to pause and consider.

Later that afternoon, I was hurrying to Calculus when I noticed Brax and Olivia just ahead of me. As I caught up to them, my eyes scanned the area for Kane—he was nowhere to be seen. The closer I grew, though, Brax's distinct voice drifted back toward me.

"Gracie, he's runnin' fuckin' numbers again," Brax said. "Right out of the Kappas' frat house. Swear to God, I feel if he gets busted, it'll come down on me."

My skin prickled as I computed the words. Running numbers? Out of the Kappa house?

"Brax, you aren't your brother's keeper," Olivia comforted. "What he does isn't your fault."

"He's my fuckin' brother, Gracie. Damn, he's got a hard head!" Brax rubbed his head, the back of his neck, then halted so fast I slammed into the back of him.

"Oh!" I gasped. "Brax, I'm sorry—in such a hurry here I didn't see you!"

His strange blue eyes flashed over me, and he tossed me a grin. "No problem, half-pint. You okay?"

"Yes, of course," I assured him. "Hey, Olivia."

She smiled that warm smile that always made me feel a little at ease—much more than anyone else. "Hey back," she said. "We're going for pizza later. Wanna come along?"

"Oh," I said, and shifted my briefcase in my hand. "Thank you, but I can't. Huge test."

Olivia nodded. "Maybe next time?"

I forced my smile. "Yes. Definitely so."

Brax pulled Olivia to his side and he gave me a wink over the top of her head. "See ya 'round, Harper."

I smiled. The lines around Brax's eyes and mouth gave his worry away, and I couldn't help but wonder just how much trouble Kane was stirring up. I didn't know much about numbers and betting and gambling, but I could tell Brax wasn't taking it lightly. Not at all. "Bye, guys." I watched them for a moment, walking together, and Brax leaned close, pushing Olivia's braid off to one side and pressing his lips to her neck. Olivia shrugged and squealed, as if it tickled. Without thought, my hand lifted and grazed the side of my own neck. Wondering.

"Positively dreamy, don't you think?"

I jumped at the sound of Murphy's voice in my ear as she leaned over my shoulder and stared in the direction Brax and Olivia had taken. She puffed out a breath, and it tossed a few strands of my hair. "Damn, he's got a fetchin' backside." She cut her eyes at me. "Wickedly scrummy. Don't you think?"

Murphy was one of the few who could drag out a real smile in me, and she'd just done it. I shook my head as she oogled Brax. "You're shameless."

She gave me a light head-butt. "One of me best qualities. And you're going to be late to Cal."

"Oh, shoot!" I gasped, and took off to class.

The whole way there, though, as I darted through Winston's occupants as they milled about the quad and hurried to various parts of the school, my mind worked. Wheels turned. Kane McCarthy was running numbers out of the Kappa House. While he didn't exactly come across as a thug or a delinquent, despite his smoky stare and leather jacket—he actually looked more like a rough-around-the-edges Abercrombie model. Still, he was doing something illegal. Something Brax despised. Something he could get into serious trouble for, and Brax, too, more than likely.

Kane McCarthy needed reforming.

He needed a Bad Boy Makeover.

And by the time my Calculus professor ended the class with a reminder of a large pending quiz, I'd made my mind up.

I'd found my subject for the Dare. Actually, I was doing not only Brax a favor, but Kane, as well. It was a win-win, if I succeeded. And the Kappas would lose.

And I'd quite possibly lost my mind.

As I gathered my belongings and slid them neatly into my slim leather briefcase, ideas surged through my head. I couldn't deny that there was something alluring about Kane. He was beautiful, in a feral sort of way. At the same time, I felt edgy. Foreign. Vulnerable.

Scared.

For the first time in my life I decided to do something, despite all of those feelings pounding away at me. Warning me.

Besides. It was a reformation Dare. No harm could come of it except for hopefully saving not only Kane's hide but Brax's, too. He of all people didn't deserve to be caught up in the middle of it.

Best of all, though? Olivia and Macie and any other girl who'd suffered the Dare in the past would be privately vindicated. The Kappas would lose their numbers man. And hopefully gain some humility.

And we would possibly put an end to the Kappas' stupid dare for good.

4. Pursuit

ONCE MORE, I STOOD before my sisters in the common room in an unofficial meeting. I lifted my chin. "So our very own Dare is now officially on its way."

The girls all gave a light applause.

I looked first at Murphy. "Murphy Polk has somehow managed to secure the Kappas' own Josh Collins."

"Good luck reforming that one, Murph," Margie commented. "He's so full of himself."

"Yeah, Murphy, you have your hands full."

Murphy rose from the sofa and smoothed the front of her red plaid pajama bottoms. Then she daintily turned and poked out her bottom. Across the backside the word Queen was embroidered. She pointed at it. "There's a good stiff reason I wear these bloomers, loves," she said with a wicked grin.

She rose tall. "I've got Collins, no problem." She sighed. "He definitely needs polishing, though. Starting with a manicure."

We all laughed.

I scanned the room. "Leslie, how about you?"

Leslie remained sitting on the floor; legs crossed yoga-style, her blonde pixie hair tucked behind one ear. "Jake Soverinson? He's on the baseball team. Big buddies with the Kappas, but he's not in the fraternity."

Another light round of applause. I nodded. "Good job, Leslie."

"Alright, Ms. Belle," Murphy chided playfully. "Spill the proverbial beans. Who's your man?" She winked at me. She knew.

I drew a deep breath. "Well, you won't know him. I've only encountered him a time or two, actually."

Several *who's* filled the room as the sisters anxiously awaited more.

I pinned a smile to my face and drew courage from somewhere deep inside of me. Was I really committing to this? To say it out loud made it official. I inhaled. "His name is Kane McCarthy. He's...actually Brax Jenkins' older brother."

Murmuring became a low roar as the girls all gasped and commented and then looked at me for more explanation. I folded my hands together where I stood. "He's not a student. Actually, I've discovered he's possibly the Kappas' numbers man for the football season."

I watched Murphy's mouth pull into a grin, and she gave me an approving nod. She'd known I was on the fence about Kane, but seemed pleased I'd made up my mind.

"Isn't that...illegal?" Annie Hall asked. Her shoulder-length black bob flipped up on the ends.

I nodded. "Yes, it is. Which is why he needs reforming in a big way. It also puts Brax at risk, and as we all know he needs no provocation. Or further risks. So all of this information is for our ears only. It doesn't leave this room. I...aim to put a stop to Kane's numbers, for his sake and for Brax's." Everyone knew Brax Jenkins—especially on Olivia's behalf—would throw a punch at the blink of an eye. He'd been in trouble before and couldn't afford any more.

Murphy grinned. "Brilliant, my friend, I knew you'd choose wisely. By the by, I think that tops even Josh Collins."

"You're probably right," I agreed. "Okay, girls. Remember. This is a top Delta secret. If any of this gets leaked it'll go straight to the Kappas. Or to the campus police." I gave them all a stern look. "We don't want that. So let's begin. And don't forget about the Turkey Run this Saturday. Even if you're not actually running, please be prompt to hand out bottled water and snacks. Also, begin your lists for the bake sale. We'll vote for five different recipes."

Everyone agreed, and our un-official meeting adjourned. As usual, Murphy headed straight for me. She grasped my hands, felt me stiffen, and quickly released me.

It was a reaction I absolutely couldn't help. No matter what I did. I knew she never meant any harm—it was normal for friends to do that. Only I wasn't normal. And strangely enough, the only person who I ever thought suspected that about me, was Brax Jenkins. And, Murphy. I hid it well. Nothing less was expected of me.

And Murphy was extraordinary. Because she never, ever called me on it. Never judged. Like now, when I could see her eyes soften as she released my hands. Not out of pity, I didn't think. But because she saw my reaction was real, unavoidable, and she truly wanted to be my friend.

There were times—so many times—I'd wanted to just tell her everything. To let her in. To be real, true friends. But I hadn't. I didn't dare.

"So. You're going to relieve him of his wicked ways! What's your plan?"

My eyes lit on hers. "First, I'm going to march right over to the Kappa House," I grinned. "And place a bet. Let them know that I know."

Murphy cocked her head to the side, causing the dainty diamond embedded into the side of her nose to sparkle beneath the lamp light of the common room. "You don't know the first thing about numbers or betting, Harper Belle." Her gaze narrowed. "Besides. That's illegal."

I gave a light smile. "I'm not really placing a bet. It's just to get his attention again."

There was the Cheshire Cat grin. "I like you, Harper Belle. I really, really do."

*   *   *

I KNEW KANE WAS at the Kappa House; that vintage wagon truck was parked in their lot. I'd changed from my typical tailored suit that I wore during school hours to a form-fitting black dress, cream hose and black leather boots that zipped to my knees. A ginger colored silk scarf wrapped around my neck, and I'd pinned my bangs back with tortoise shell clips. Clutched beneath my arm was my black leather purse, and as I hastily crossed the street to Kappa House, I glanced over my shoulder.

Murphy watched me from her bedroom window. With a pair of binoculars.

The roar of music thumped from inside as I climbed the porch steps, rapped on the door, and waited. Moments later, the door opened, and the smell of beer and something else I cared not try and identify wafted out. Jason Willis stood there, elbow propping his body against the doorframe, and the smile he poured over me made me inwardly cringe. A big cow lick made his hair flip up at the part.

"Well now, Saint Harper," he crooned. "What do we owe this pleasure?"

I pasted on a wide, fake smile. "Hi, Jason. Can I come in?"

Josh Collins' head appeared over Jason's. He wore a Silverbacks baseball cap, turned around backwards. "Hell yeah, hot neighbor babe like you can come right on in." He held the door open. "Move your ass over, Jase." He grinned at me. "Welcome to the Kappa Kingdom. Want a brew?"

"Uh, no thank you." As I entered the dimly lit common room, scents and bodies and the feeling of being trapped singed my insides; I ignored it. Pushed it aside. In the living area, I turned around and faced Josh. He was there, smiling down at me. Not a bad looking guy. Just...well, I hoped Murphy could do a reformation job on him.

"So what do you want, gorgeous? We already signed up for the Turkey Run," he said, then smiled. His eyes gleamed as he dipped his head toward me. "We don't bake, darlin', so the bake sale is off."

Several of the guys laughed. One snorted.

"I'm actually here to see your new friend," I stated. "Kane McCarthy."

The expression on Josh's face shifted. Even more predatory, if possible. "Is that so?"

I nodded. "It is."

Josh stared at me a moment, then threw his head back and laughed. "Well, damn, girl." He inclined his head toward the stairs. "Follow me."

I did, and at the top of the stairs we turned right. Two doors down, Josh pushed open the door. The room contained no less than a half-dozen Kappas, and a half-dozen others I didn't recognize. In the center, at a desk, sat Kane. When we entered, he looked up. Those fathomless eyes lit on mine, and surprise widened them. He relaxed, though, and leaned back in the chair. Those expresso brown pools slowly inspected me, from the tips of my boots to the top of my head. Then, they settled on my eyes.

"You here to place a bet?" he asked in that smoky voice.

Dredging up as much confidence and courage as I could find, I slipped into an easy smile that surprised even me. I made sure my gaze didn't falter. "I am," I said slyly.

The guys all joked; whistled, wailed, and all the other immature things guys do to make fun of a situation. I stood straight, though, and didn't budge. I kept my gaze locked onto Kane's. And he kept his on mine, as well.

Then he surprised me. He rose and walked directly to me, grasped me by the elbow, and looked down at me. "Come on," he said in that quiet, controlled smoky voice that matched his eyes.

His fingers heated my skin as we walked, leaving a room full of laughing hyena Kappas behind. Confusion made me stutter. Made me almost forget he had ahold of me. I flinched. He didn't let go.

"W—what are you doing?" I demanded, trying to tamp down my rising panic. Wanting to keep up the farce of me wanting to place a bet. "Did you not hear me?"

He didn't look at me as he led me down the steps. "I heard you."

"Let me go," I urged. "Now, please."

He didn't, and as we passed Josh, he simply grinned and shrugged. "Nice try, Delta." He winked, and I wanted to kick him. "Save me some cookies, will ya? And tell Murph I said hi!"

Laughter trailed us as Kane hurried me outside, and it was only after we'd descended the steps that he turned me loose. I rounded on him, but at the same time backed up, keeping my distance. "How...dare you." I began to shake; I willed it to stop. It didn't. So I paced to hide it.

Kane braced his legs against the concrete, crossed his arms over his chest, and studied me. Silently. Thoroughly. Only his eyes spoke, a slight simmering flash noticeable only beneath the glow of the Kappas' yard light.

"What are you looking at?" I demanded.

He stared for a few more painful moments. "I just don't know yet."

I stiffened. "What does that mean?"

He shoved his hand through his already-messy hair. "I can't read you." He cocked his head, pushed his hands into his pockets, and stepped toward me. I stepped back. He acted as if he didn't notice the movement. "You look like a typical high society snob." His eyes moved over me, and I held my breath. "Fancy clothes. Expensive car." He rubbed his chin. "You have that air about you, like you're better than anyone."

Before I could breathe, he was there, in front of me, not touching me, but he might as well have been. His body heat enveloped me, as if invisible hands pulled us together. "I think you're bluffing." Then he did touch me; his knuckle caught my chin, lifting my gaze to his, and I was speechless. Breathless, as his wise eyes watched me. "If I know anything, Harper Belle, it's a bluff."

I could barely draw in a breath; it almost came out as a gasp. I felt my eyes tearing up, and as stupid as it was, I couldn't stop it. My skin broke out into tingles—exactly the feeling I'd had in the past before a panic attack. The feeling I'd get if trapped in a darkened place. I swallowed hard, pushed his hand from my chin, and stepped back. Distance helped, but I still breathed hard. I couldn't hide it, either. "You...you don't know me at all. I *am* better."

His laugh was surprisingly soft and void of mockery. "I know more than you think I do." He stepped toward me again, but didn't touch me. The light cast down behind and around him, causing his face to be cut into odd planes and shadows, with only glimpses of the pale skin of his face showing. "I know I'm making you nervous. Believe it or not, Harper—that's not my intention."

"I—I don't care what your intentions are," I said quietly. My voice shook as I spoke, and I knew he heard it. I moved backward, away from him, and in the next second I'd stepped off the paved walk and into the wintry-dead grass. My pointed boot heel sank, stuck, and before I knew what was happening my balance shifted and I was going down. My arms jutted out to catch myself, and my purse dropped—

Kane leapt, caught me, set me upright. So fast, I hardly

had time to realize most of my body was wrapped in his arms. My eyes widened as he looked down at me, and unavoidably, my entire self started shaking. He didn't let go of me. Not at first.

Those velvety brown eyes moved over mine. "I don't know why I can't stop staring at you," Kane said quietly. His easy-going voice, in complete contrast with that brusque Boston accent, sent shivers across my skin. Then he steadied me, and stepped back. He shoved his hands in his pockets and inclined his head. "Get out of here, Harper Belle," he said. But his mouth, those full lips that were tinged with just enough shade of rose to make them stand out against his alabaster skin, smiled that easy smile. "You don't want this," he inclined his head toward the Kappas' house. "Something else, maybe. But that's the part of you I can't quite read yet."

Back on the paved walk, I breathed, straightened my posture, raised my chin. Inside, I still shook. *Keep it hidden, Harper. At all costs, don't let them see you.*

"You don't know me or what I want," I answered weakly. Almost a whisper. I hated it. Couldn't help it.

Then I could do nothing more than turn on my heel and walk away as fast as I could.

As I marched back across the street, up the walk and back to Delta House, I knew his gaze stayed on me. I knew he didn't budge from where he stood beneath that yard light. And more than anything, as I climbed the steps to my own sorority house, I knew one thing with more certainty than I'd experienced in some time.

It wasn't the last time I'd see Kane McCarthy. No matter how much I wanted to back out of my very own Dare. Despite

how incredibly edgy and unnerved he made me, we'd be together again. Perhaps not taking or making bets, but
something. I felt it inside of me. Almost as if it'd been there
all along, only I'd ignored it.

The moment my hand lit on the doorknob, the door fell
open, and Murphy was there, eyes wide, a skully cap pulled
over her lob haircut. "*What* was *that* all about?" she asked
breathily. As usual, when she was exceptionally excited about
something, her North York accent fell heavy. "Come on, Harper. Spill!"

The common room was unusually empty, and we both
made our way to the sofa and sat down. Murphy waited, almost bouncing on the cushions. I fought the urge to close my
eyes, to purge the embarrassing scene of Kane dragging me
from the betting room in the Kappa house.

And his uncanny perception of me.

I breathed in. Out. Trying my best not to look as exhaust-
ed as I felt. "Well," I finally said, looking at Murphy's wide-
eyed gaze. "Kane McCarthy will not be as easy as I thought."

Her long lashes grazed her cheeks as she blinked, almost
in slow-motion. "Oy, why's that?"

I shook my head and stared into the low flame of the gas
fireplace. "Firstly, he's not your average Kappa. Rather, Kappa
affiliate. He's not even your average bad boy." I sighed and
looked at her. "He's arrogant and authoritative. He makes
assumptions and isn't afraid to voice them."

A smile leapt to Murphy's expressive mouth. "Really? What
else, Ms. Perceptive?"

I ignored her playful jab. "He's challenging me, Murphy.
But he doesn't quite know who he's messing with." Which was

a bold-faced lie. He knew all right. Knew all too well. I could see it in that profound stare of his.

There it was. That knowing grin on Murphy's face. "No, he doesn't indeed."

That night, I lay in bed, unable to sleep. I tossed. I turned. I rose, walked to the window and sat on the sill, watching the inky November night. I pushed up the old glass and allowed the chilled air to flow over me. Texas had a myriad of weather changes, and even in the dead of winter it could be hot as Hades. Not true this year. It'd been chilly ever since mid-October, and I liked it. It felt...clean. Fresh.

Kane McCarthy's truck was gone; back at Brax's, no doubt. I replayed every second of our earlier meeting. Every stare, every touch, every word. I could still even smell the scent of his worn leather jacket. More than anything, though, were his words. They'd affected me, more than I'd let on to Murphy. As a matter of fact, I'd hidden pretty much everything from Murphy. I hadn't told her I'd almost had a panic attack. It'd been almost a year since I'd had one, usually brought on by nightmares of things from my long-ago past. Usually, during a visit home. Things I'd spent years in therapy to forget. Corinne Belle had insisted on it. I'd lied there, too. To the therapist. To Corinne.

I hadn't forgotten anything at all about those terrifying days so long ago. When I was eight. What had happened to my parents. What I'd seen. I even remembered the police officer who'd found me that night.

What had happened, after. At my grandmother's.

I kept it all bottled up inside of me. Corinne Belle had warned me never to let anyone know of it. Not to let them know who I really was. There'd be consequences, she'd said. And there would be, too. Even now. I hadn't told a soul anything. The Harper Belle I'd become was a product of Corinne's fine grooming. If one would call what she'd done grooming.

And as long as it—as I—stayed that way, everything would be okay.

But then, Kane McCarthy happened. I felt as though his sultry eyes could see straight through my lies. The thought terrified me worse than the nightmares I'd grown up with. How could he, though? I barely knew him; had barely been around him. How could he know anything other than what I portrayed about me?

I brought to mind his face; his features. His flawless skin. His gestures. His voice. There was a perception about him that frightened me. But besides that, there was something mysterious about him. As though he, too, were hiding something. Keeping secrets. Funny, I sometimes got the same impression, on a much smaller scale, from his brother Brax.

There was no way out of this thing now. I'd thrown the gauntlet down with the Dare. The girls were completely onboard. To back out would inspire questions; demand answers. I wasn't prepared for either. So I'd have to figure out another way to get at Kane McCarthy.

Only I was going to have to learn to control the absolute terror he stirred within me.

If not, everyone would know. They'd be able to see me.

And that just simply could not happen.

Ever.

5. Masquerade

I'D DONE SOMETHING I almost never, ever did. Unless I was sick. Which I rarely was.

Skipped a morning run.

Kane would've been there, leaning against the tree. Or sitting on my park bench. I knew it like I breathed air. And somehow, that had intimidated me. Kept me prisoner. Kept me from doing the one thing that freed me. Even if for a short while.

It angered me, in the end. I was angry at Kane for, well, intimidating me. Angry at myself for allowing it.

I swiped the moisture from the bathroom mirror with my palm and glared at the face staring back at me. Corinne Belle had always said I had more eyes than face, and she was right; so wide that they had to tilt upward at the outer corners to fit properly. Almost like an alien. Watery bluish-green in color, I vaguely remember my father's eyes being the same. I fingered my wet hair—straight to just below my shoulders, blonde. I lifted my face, turned it side to side. Sharp features, like a bird, Corinne had said.

Just like my dad.

Corinne Belle had changed my name, but not my features. Something I'm sure she would've given her right arm to successfully do.

I hurried through my bathroom rituals before the others awakened, and slipped back into my room. With my towel wrapped around me, I searched through my closet and chose a dark brown cashmere cardigan that I layered with a cream silk undershirt and a pair of tan trousers. A pair of brown leather heeled Mary Jane's completed my outfit for the day. As I dried my hair, thoughts crowded my mind. Calculus. Literature. Bake sale. Turkey Run.

Kane McCarthy.

His words had stung, even though they were the exact impressions I'd purposely given people for as long as I could remember. Rich snob. Better than everyone else.

Both descriptions were far, far from the truth.

Flipping the blow dryer off, I set it on my bed and my eyes found the round vinyl hat box I kept on my dresser. Depicting vintage postcards of travel, like the Fiji Islands, Hawaii, London, Australia, it was where I kept every extra penny my grandmother had sent to me. For food. New clothes. Extracurricular expenses. Old fashioned, she'd insisted on sending me cash instead of a check, or directly depositing. I didn't have an account. I never would—not while in college, anyway.

I didn't deserve one, after all. Her money wasn't my money. One day, she'd said, I'd owe it all back to her. And back to her everything would go. Every stitch of clothing she'd insisted on me buying to keep up appearances. The Lexus. Every hand-bag. Every pair of leather shoes. Every single dime.

So I used as little as possible. I didn't want to owe her or anyone else for that matter. Ever. It was one reason why I didn't go out with Murphy on a regular basis. Or with Olivia and Brax for pizza. Or to the mall with the sisters—unless it was with money we'd earned with a fundraiser and we were using it for something other than ourselves.

No one knew who I really was. No one would.

I applied my make-up, smoothed my hair and tucked it behind my ears, and pulled on my clothes. I made sure every-thing looked just...so. Then, at my money box, I paused. Considered. Hunger pangs rumbled inside my stomach.

Breakfast it would be.

Sliding the lid over, I lifted three one-dollar bills from its belly, replaced the lid, and folded the bills neatly in half. Breakfast always was the cheapest meal of the day, especially with a student discount. Too bad it was a nearly-impossible task to keep food separate in the community kitchen down-stairs. I'd tried before, though, and no one ever seemed to remember whose food belonged to who. So I'd made the de-cision to select one meal a day to purchase, versus jockeying a loaf of bread and a package of turkey meat, or a box of oat-meal, in the Deltas' community kitchen.

Easing out of my room, I made my way down the hall, down the stairs, and out into the early morning. On the porch, I paused. Inhaled. Not quite six a.m., no one was yet about, and I reveled in the absolute stillness of late-fall air. Above, the sky blinked with stars over a blanket of inky velvet. It was so quiet. Peaceful. Morning darkness was somehow different than nighttime darkness. Not as threatening. Not as terrifying. The older I'd gotten, the less fearful I'd become of morning darkness. Especially at Winston. With lamp lights blazing the campus, I set out.

My heels thumped against the paved walk as I made my way to the café. A breeze wafted through and rustled the leaves on the flowering pear trees that lined the walk. Winston's buildings rose from the darkness like so many ancient fortresses; looming, protective, with Olivia's observatory as the beacon. I liked it here, really.

The café doors had just opened, and inside the warm air smelled like the gingerbread candle burning on the counter. The girl by the register wasn't a student, but we were familiar. She usually worked the morning shift and knew I'd always be her first customer.

"Hi, Lily," I said, quietly selecting my instant package of cinnamon raisin oatmeal and a small carton of whole milk. I handed both to her.

"Morning, Harper," she replied with a bright smile. She was a little older than me, with pale skin and strawberry blonde curls she kept piled high on her head. "That'll be a dollar fifty."

I handed her two dollars, she returned fifty cents and a cup and spoon for my oatmeal, and I then dropped the other bill I had into her tip jar. She grinned. "Thanks, as always."

I smiled and gave her a slight nod. "No problem." At the coffee bar I hastily prepared my oatmeal with hot water and a few pumps from the half n' half carafe. Then I headed back outside and started toward the fountain. Once there, I took the bench directly across from it, sat, and stirred my oatmeal.

"Do you always eat alone?"

I jumped at the sound of Kane's voice. He emerged from the darkness, his alabaster skin stark against his dark hair and the even darker morning. "Why are you following me?" I didn't look at him; I spooned a small bit of oatmeal into my mouth and chewed, biting into a raisin.

He moved closer, eased down onto the bench beside me, and the motion made the scent of his leather jacket and soapy skin reach my nostrils. It was a piney mint combination that I found I actually liked. In one hand, a steaming cup of coffee from the café, its bitter aroma rising in a cloud of steam through the little slotted spout in the lid. Leaning forward, resting his forearms against his knees, he looked straight ahead at the fountain. Sipped his coffee. I found it interesting, too, that I hadn't leapt off the bench, ready to bolt.

"I guess you sort of drive me crazy," he finally responded. "I wasn't following you, Harper. I saw you leaving the café." He looked at me over his shoulder, sipped his coffee, then shrugged. His mouth lifted in a half-grin, and his eyes simmered. "Then I followed you."

I continued eating my oatmeal, because I really didn't know what to say to any of that. I sipped my milk, took another bite. "I like the early morning. Before anyone else is awake." I slipped him a glance. "It's...peaceful."

"It is," he agreed. "Here, anyway. Back home? Never."

Nevah. His Boston accent was unique; heavy, sultry, soft all at once. Void of all *r's*. I liked it. And I kept it to myself.

My mind scrambled as I sifted around for something to say. *Don't forget the Dare, Harper. That's first and foremost, don't forget. He's running illegal bets out of the Kappa House. Stop him from gambling, hurt the Kappas, do a favor for Brax.* I spooned the remaining oatmeal into my mouth, chewed, swallowed, and then sipped my milk. Gathered my courage. "Would you like to help out with the Turkey Run tomorrow?"

Kane leaned back, his long legs sprawled in the way guys do, and looked at me. "What's that?"

"It's a benefit five-k run that we sponsor each year before Thanksgiving," I answered. "People pay a fee to enter, we provide bottled water and snacks, and two-thirds of the proceeds go to purchasing holiday turkeys for the shelters and soup kitchens in the surrounding counties."

He nodded. "We as in...?"

"My sorority."

He shoved a hand through his hair, leaving it even messier than before. "See, there you go again."

I blinked. "What?"

Kane ducked his dark head and searched my face. The inky morning had begun to lighten, and his faced seemed beautifully flawless and ghostly at the same time. Those eyes, though...wise beyond his years. I could tell, something stood behind them, something almost familiar. Something I recognized...but not quite. And that scared me.

"Like a masquerade," he said softly. "You seem one way on the outside—rich, perfect, better than everyone else. But then you eat a sparse meal alone on park benches at six in the morning. Meticulously separating yourself from everyone— even your own sorority sisters." His lip quirked in the corner.

"And you gather turkeys for the homeless." His eyes never left mine. "A severe contradiction, Ms. Belle."

I swallowed my fear at his articulate speech and all-too-accurate description. "Well," I said, my voice as quiet as the morning. "That's an amazing hypothesis of my character, having only encountered me a few days ago." I looked at him now, meeting his gaze and forcing myself to hold it. "Coming from a guy who wanders onto a college campus hundreds of miles from home to illegally run bets out of a frat house." I cocked my head. "Pretty well-spoken for a thug."

Those coffee colored eyes shined as he watched me closely, seemingly inspecting every one of my features as if trying to pick me apart, or trying to see through a seam, a hairline crack I might have left behind to show my true self. I'd been careful over the years. Yet...he seemed to get closer than anyone. And fast.

He didn't look offended by my words; how could he be? He certainly hadn't been shy about bluntly listing my supposed qualities. He might suspect some things, but he hadn't even cracked the surface.

"I guess we all have a few secrets, yeah?" he said, his voice husky and blending with the quiet morning air. His words caught me off guard, and so did the shift in his eyes. They always seemed soft, somehow, but now? A flash of something, almost undetectable, and almost too fast to notice. But I had. "What time?"

I blinked again. "Excuse me?"

His smile came easy. "Turkey Run? Or are you retracting your invitation? You know, being as I'm a thug and all."

I felt heat creep up my throat and fan at my cheeks as my accusations pinged back at me from Kane's mouth. I wasn't accustomed to insulting people—especially total strangers. It left a bad taste in my mouth. "Six a.m. At our house."

Kane rose. "What if I want to run?"

I also stood. "You'll have to pay the entry fee."

He faced me then, standing close, and the way his eyes moved over me? He might as well have been touching me. Never had I met someone who possessed such emotion in only their eyes. It stirred something inside of me. Something I couldn't decide if I liked, or feared. "Yeah? What kind of fee?"

"Thirty dollars." I couldn't seem to look away from him. Like I was trapped in a trance.

His body shifted closer. Hands stuffed into his jacket pockets. Seemingly harmless. But I knew better. "If I pay a hundred will that ensure me a place beside you?"

I drew in an inconspicuous breath, slowly released it. Steadied my voice so it didn't seem like he affected me as much as he did. "Not really," I replied. "It would depend on the kind of runner you are." I looked at him now, in the early hours of dawn, and he was even more beautiful than I'd once thought. How was that possible? Sounds invaded my thoughts; a hedge trimmer's motor hummed from somewhere on campus. A car door slammed. Voices floated on the wind. When had Winston awakened? And how had I been so oblivious to it?

My eyes fixed on his mouth as he spoke. I couldn't help it.

"I'll take my chances," he said in that husky, quiet Boston voice, then called over his shoulder as he lumbered away. "See ya in the morning."

I stared after Kane McCarthy as he disappeared across the quad and faded into the hazy morning light. Just like his voice, his stride was easy and effortless as those long, muscular legs carried his equally solid, tall frame. Like an ethereal be-ing, he simply...vanished. Like a ghost. A spirit. Was he even real? Was this situation I'd suddenly found myself in, real? It could've been a dream. Or a nightmare.

No, I'd had plenty of nightmares. Kane McCarthy definitely wasn't one of them.

This was a situation I'd promptly placed my own stupid self in. And it was one I'd need to fast get a grip on if I was going to pull off our private Dare against the Kappas. I couldn't let Kane get under my skin.

As I maneuvered throughout my day, surrounded by fel-low Winston students, sorority sisters, acquaintances, I realized that despite how many conversations I had, how many phony smiles I gave out, one thing was for certain.

I truly was alone. Alone, I understood. My back against a wall, enclosed, I felt safe. As long as I held people at a dis-tance, they wouldn't suspect the real me. Wouldn't ask questions. Wouldn't crack the code to my internal safe.

Safe. Safety. It meant as much to me as trust did to others. I knew why; always had known why.

When I thought hard about it, it really only came down to one thing.

A small, dank, smelly kitchen cabinet.

The rest of the day dragged by; so did I. My forced buoy-ancy was beginning to wear thin on me, for some reason. In the past, it'd been rather easy, that false persona. Why had it grown difficult? Like, overnight? What was wrong with me?

Later that afternoon, the Delta house was abuzz with activ-ity. Setting up the starting line for the Turkey Run, stretching the hand-made banner from our side of the street to the

Kappas'. I never did catch sight of Kane again, and somehow, that disappointed me. He may be a thug, but he was an intelligent one, well-versed and I sincerely enjoyed talking to him—when he wasn't busy pointing out my supposed flaws, that is. Something about his persona intrigued me. Interested me. The way he studied me so thoroughly, just before he spoke. No one had ever gained my attention in that way, ever. And he remained on my mind for the rest of the day.

After darkness fell, Delta sisters gathered in the common room to make the numbers that would be pinned to the participants' shirts. Crates of bottled water sat at our front door. I busied myself in our small kitchen making chocolate chip cookies for the participants as they crossed the finish line at the Killian fairgrounds entrance tomorrow. Murphy sat on the counter, the bag of semi-sweet chocolate chips opened and dangerously in her hands.

She popped one in her mouth. "What's up with you?" she asked. "You look like pure shite, you do."

I looked at her and almost smiled at the comical lines of concern pulling at her brows. I leveled the flour in the measuring cup with a knife and added it to the mixture. "I'm just tired, I guess." I mixed in the cup of flour, then turned off the beaters. "Kane is meeting me here in the morning. He's helping out with the run," I said, and leveled the second cup of flour. I gave Murphy a sideways glance.

Her mouth dropped open.

"And he's participating," I continued.

"Shut up," Murphy replied. She popped another chip in her mouth, her eyes narrowed to slits, and she elbowed me. "No wonder you look all wonky. You've been a busy bee, acquiring all of that out of him." She grinned. "I knew you had it in you." She popped another chip in her mouth. "Josh is helping, too. As a matter of fact, he's using that obnoxious bull of a pick-up truck to help deliver bottled water to the checkpoints." Her head cocked to the side. "So tell me about Kane. What's he like?"

I thought about it. "He's intelligent. Soft-spoken. And extraordinarily...perceptive."

Murphy edged closer. "How so?"

I shrugged, finished mixing the cookie dough and moved it to the pan I'd lined with parchment paper. I started dropping tablespoonful's of cookie dough in a row. "I don't know. He sort of hangs onto every single word I speak, every gesture and motion I make." I looked at her. "He seems to see inside of me."

Her eyes softened. "Is that so?" Her smile curved her lips. "Sounds like the dog's bollocks if you ask me. Except for the illegal activity, of course."

I smiled. "What about Josh? Is he as much of a..." I thought of an appropriate description.

"Useless shitfaced knob?" Murphy finished. She laughed. "Once you peel him away from his obnoxious mates, he's actually quite nice." Her eyes darted to the mixing bowl. "Christ, I'd sell one of my kidneys on eBay for one spoon of that dough."

I couldn't help but smile at Murphy's drama. "Go ahead. But just one spoon." I slid the pan into the oven.

"Yes!" She grabbed a spoon from the drawer, scooped up the dough, and pushed it into her mouth. Her eyes closed. "Oh my God, woman." She grinned at me. "You sincerely need to put pre-law behind you and just open a bloody bakery." Her eyes closed again as she chewed the dough. "Wicked and scrummy, all at once. I swear to God, it'll be your fault if my bum gets too big."

I smiled, shook my head, and set the cooling racks on the counter. I'd taught myself how to bake, and as old-fashioned as it sounded, I actually enjoyed it. The talent had come in handy with the sorority since we were always having bake sales.

"So about Kane," Murphy continued, her eyes on me. "You're diggin' him, aren't you?"

My thoughts scrambled for an appropriate response. I wasn't sure what I really, truly thought of Kane McCarthy. Other than that I couldn't get him out of my mind. I sighed. "He's...definitely interesting," I answered. "Not as much like Brax as you'd think. He's not loud. He's actually very articulate and soft-spoken."

"Well," Murphy said, leaping off the counter and peering into the oven. "I can't wait to meet him in person tomorrow." Turning, she leaned against the counter, and that infamous Cheshire cat grin returned. "Progress with Josh: We're going for curry Sunday." She wiggled her brows. "To Karma. I'm driving."

My eyes widened. "Really?"

She gave me a proud nod. "Guess what else?"

"There's more?"

Murphy batted her eyelashes. "He's accompanying me to an off-broadway show in Dallas."

Now, my eyes bugged. "You're kidding?"

"Positively so right!" she said. She licked her finger and swiped it through the air. "Score one for the Yorkie!"

"What in the world are you doing to get him to agree to all of these things?" I asked.

She looked at me and winked. "Just a bit of snogging is all."

I couldn't help it. I laughed. "You're off your trolley," I said, using the phrase she frequently used on me.

Murphy shrugged. "Let's just say it looks like we may have both hooked our prey." Her smile was slow. Wide. Wicked. "The how of it doesn't really matter, me thinks."

6. Falling

THE MOMENT I STEPPED out onto the porch of the Delta House, my eyes landed directly onto Kane McCarthy's tall, muscular frame, casually leaning against one of the pillars. I don't know why he surprised me, but he did.

"You said six o'clock, right?" he asked.

Easing the door closed behind me, I edged closer. "I did, yes." I inspected his running clothes; long-sleeved black T-shirt, black running shorts that hit just at his knees, and black trainers. When my gaze lifted to his, his eyes were there, searching mine for acceptance, or encouragement. I wasn't sure of either. He glanced at himself and shrugged. "Brax had extra."

"No doubt he has an entire room full of running gear." I smiled. "He and Olivia run all over campus. So you decided to enter," I said, and lit down the steps past him, and stopped at the paved walk. "Thanks for your help this morning. Josh Collins has already dropped most of the water off at the checkpoints. We'll load the rest into my car and—"

"I got more than enough room in my truck," he offered, and joined me on the walk. He threw his head toward the parking lot, and I realized just how much taller, bigger he was than me. "It's over there." He grinned, his all-knowing stare steady and boring right into me. "So you got Josh into this, too?"

I shook my head. "No, actually one of the other sisters did."

He rubbed his jaw with a big knuckled hand. "A conspiracy, yeah?"

My heart jumped. He couldn't possibly know. "Oh, no, not at—"

Kane gave me a lazy smile. "Just messing with you." He inclined his head to his truck. "Ready to load?"

"Oh, yes," I answered, and turned back to the porch. "Thanks. Let's...definitely load the water then." I jogged the steps, and at the top I spun around. "Oh, you might—"

He was right there, as close as two people can be while sharing the same breathing space, and his eyes immediately found mine. His frosty breath trailed out of his mouth as it blended with the chilly air. So close, I could feel the heat of his skin brush mine. Standing one step below me, we almost stared eye-to-eye, and a sly smile pulled at his lips. The air froze in my lungs, so trapped in the moment. I found myself completely and utterly speechless. Unable to move. Chained to the porch.

"Right. Girls' sorority house. Six a.m. I'll…stay right here," he said softly, and there was amusement in his voice. "No problem." He leaned a little closer. "You can breathe now, Harper." That came out quiet, meant only for my ears.

I did breathe then, and my warm breath met the cool November morning air and puffed out white before me. "I'll be right back." Hastily, I let myself back into the house. More than half the sisters still ran around in their night clothes. Or less. Still getting ready for the Turkey Run.

Inside, I cringed. Murphy and the other sisters stood clustered around the window. Murphy, guilt smeared all over her creamy features, jumped back.

"We were watching," she admitted shamelessly with a grin. "I fancy an introduction."

"Me, too," said Leslie. Followed by several others.

With a resigned sigh, I turned and opened the door. Kane stood as he had before, leaning against the pillar. "Kane?" I said. "These are the sisters of Delta house. Girls, this is Kane McCarthy."

He glanced past me, at the girls piled up behind me at the door, and gave them a wide, flawless smile. "Ladies."

Murphy pushed passed me, still in her plaid pajama bottoms and her favorite Union Jack tee shirt, her hair in pigtails, and I said a silent prayer she'd try her best and contain herself.

"My name's Murphy, love," she said, introducing herself, and they shook hands. "Harper's best mate. Are you ready for the run?"

Kane's eyes found mine, where they smoldered. Turned soft. A smile tipped his mouth up in one corner. "Been looking forward to it all night."

Murphy's gaze shot to mine, and pure deviltry made them twinkle in the porch light. "Fancy a good challenge then, do ya?"

Kane didn't stop staring at me. "Yeah. I do."

Inside, I shivered a little. His words, his stare, sunk deeper than anyone I'd ever encountered. With an embarrassed smile I left the two of them chatting as a few other girls and I gathered the remaining flats of bottled water and carried them to the porch.

It was going to be a long, long day. I knew at the end of it, Murphy Polk would be filled to her North York gills with questions. I braced myself ahead of time. For now, though, I had to deal with my Dare project. To let the girls see me affected by him would not do. Not at all.

Over the next hour Kane, Murphy and I rode to the checkpoints along the Turkey's route and set out the extra water that had been donated, and plastic-wrapped platters of the chocolate chip cookies I'd made. Murphy kept Kane busy with questions, asking him about Boston, making fun of his accent. Which, in turn, made Kane laugh and do nothing except make fun of hers. And at each checkpoint sat an assigned Delta, to keep the wolves, i.e. fraternities and other obnoxious guys with bottomless stomachs and no manners, out of the cookies. Kane registered for the run and to my surprise he in fact did pay the hundred he'd threatened to pay in order to run beside me.

My thoughts bumped off one another as I wondered how many frat boys had lost their parents' money to him. The idea made me mad. Not that the fraternity boys had lost their money. That was their own fault. It angered me that Kane chose to make a living that way. It frightened me a little. It could be dangerous. Couldn't it?

By the time the race was about to begin, Brax and Olivia had joined us at the starting line, between our house and the Kappas'. Katie Mulligan pinned our numbers to our chest and back. Brax was in full-Brax mode.

"Gracie!" he danced around her. "You know I'm gonna win, right?" Brax teased. He wore the same thing as Kane, except a Silverbacks skully was pulled snug over his head. His unique features seemed harsher in the cool early morning, but by the softened expression in Olivia's eyes, she didn't think so.

"Brax Jenkins, this isn't a race," she chided, and play-punched his arm. "It's for charity."

"I'm still gonna win!" he laughed. Then inclined his head. "I'm at least gonna beat my lunkhead big brother over there." Like his features, his Boston accent seemed harsher, louder than Kane's.

"Yeah, you might." Kane grinned back at him. Then, his gaze found mine. "Guess we'll just have to see."

"How'd you con him into runnin' anyway, half-pint?" Brax asked me. "I didn't even know you two had met." He jogged closer, ducked his dark head, and locked those crazy pale-blue eyes onto mine. "You put a fuckin' spell on him or somethin'?"

"Brax, stop it," Olivia crooned. "Harper, he's just jealous because he'd asked Kane earlier," she grinned a wicked grin. "He'd said he was too busy. Didn't you, Kane?"

When my gaze found Kane's, he wasn't embarrassed by Olivia's words. He wasn't looking away from me. It was dead on me, that mysterious, somber, sexy smolder only he possessed. "Something like that."

"Yeah, whatever," Brax said, and pushed his brother. He began bouncing from foot to foot as though preparing for a boxing match. Brax glanced over his shoulder at me. "Half-pint, you stay away from this guy, you hear?" He punched Kane in the shoulder, then his eyes found me again. He cocked his head. "Dorchester boys are bad news."

I gave him a hesitant smile, and nodded. My gaze caught Olivia's, and although Brax didn't seem aware, she did. I could tell. I had to wonder to what extent Brax really did know Kane. And did he know how his brother had pursued me? Followed me to the lake? The cafeteria? Brax seemed to be joking, but was he really?

Soon, we were all lined up awaiting the announcer's horn, and true to his words, Kane stood right beside me.

"You'd asked before if you could place a bet," he said, leaning close to my ear. "You still up for it?"

I stiffened, unsure how to answer. I didn't want to take part in his illegal dealings. Part of his reformation was to get him to quit it altogether. Only now was too early to let him know that. Luckily, though, I didn't have to answer.

"If I beat you, you go out with me," he said in that charming accent. When my eyes widened, his smile did also. "My choice where."

Once again I watched his warm breath blend with the cold air and turn white and puffy, his skin so clear save for the shadow of dark stubble. And eyes so endless that I had a difficult time saying no.

"And if I beat you?" I asked instead.

His wide, full mouth tilted. "You won't."

The horn sounded then, and as my heart leapt, so did the other runners around me. Including Kane. He ran beside me for some time; I sped up, so would he. Occasionally, I'd slip a glance at him. Sometimes, he'd already be looking at me, and a victorious grin would be present. It wasn't that I didn't want to go out with him; that was the purpose of the Dare, after all. To get the subject to fall for the Darer. In order for the reformation to take place, of course. It almost sounded silly, when said aloud in my head. What was I doing?

I settled into my run, allowed the air to ease in, out of my lungs at my own controlled rate. I reveled in the feel of my muscles burning beneath my black Nike leggings and matching long sleeved black fitted nylon top, and my skin. Then, something dawned on me. I didn't mind going out with Kane, not because of the Dare, but because...I wanted to. He intrigued me. He made my skin tingle, my heart race. I found it hard to breathe around him. All things I'd never experienced before. Not even once.

It'd never been allowed. It was forbidden. Not with Corinne Belle keeping an eye on me. I had attended an all-girls school and was never allowed to attend the dances that would sometimes pop up. I'd been too scared to notice boys before, even when I first came to Winston. But Kane was different, somehow. He bothered me. Lingered in my head. Wouldn't go away.

What would Corinne think of that?

The one thing I knew for sure: She absolutely couldn't find out. I'd do what I had to do to keep it a total and complete secret.

Soon, the pack of runners began to thin. I stretched my gait, but so did Kane. He did so with complete ease, as though running came second nature to him. He wasn't winded; quite the opposite. He'd pulled a beanie over his head and seemed to be…simply loping along, those long legs eating up the pavement as if it took no effort whatsoever. Who was he, really? Not a potential student. Didn't have a regular job. Halfway across the country from his home, running illegal bets out of a fraternity house.

He baffled me as much as he terrified me. Without having told him a single secret, he suspected. Saw through me. Knew. I could feel it.

I'd have to be very cautious with Kane McCarthy. No matter how much he piqued my interest.

Time flew by as the Turkey Run wound down. Murphy and Josh had greeted us at a checkpoint with a bottle of water, and neither of us had slowed much to grab it from her as we passed by. Josh was beside her, wearing a Turkey Run T-shirt, and he'd given Kane a slight nod. Murphy wiggled her brows in a comical way as she'd looked at me, and a smile twisted my mouth. I pushed it back and continued on. I had to wonder, though, what might be running through Josh's mind. Seeing his numbers man running the race beside me.

The moment the sign for Killian's fairgrounds came into view, Kane threw an easy smile my way and took off. Ahead, Brax and Olivia ran side by side, but as soon as Kane flew by them, Brax took off. I eased up closer to Olivia, her long messy braid bouncing off her backside with each step. She looked at me and rolled her eyes.

"They both seem to think there's some sort of prize if they win," she said, slightly breathy.

She wore a pair of black tights, similar to mine, but paired with a long sleeved Star Wars themed T-shirt. I nodded. "Well, I suppose there is."

"What do you mean?" She quirked a brow.

I almost internally slapped myself for telling Olivia anything. Not that she wasn't nice, or trustworthy. It was just...I didn't tell people things. But since she was Brax's girlfriend, she'd find out soon enough. So better to hear from me first.

"Kane sort of bet me that if he 'beat me', I'd have to go out with him," I answered.

A slow smile spread over Olivia's face, pulling at the scar she had on her lip. "I see." Her gaze remained ahead, at the finish line. She just kept on smiling. "Warning." She threw a look my way. "Brax won't like it one little bit." She smiled. "He likes you. And he's very skeptical of his brother right now."

I caught my breath. "So why are you smiling?"

She let out a light chuckle. "Because I really like Kane," she said. "He's a very caring guy. And I think he has even more potential than he's aware of. Especially with the right person in his life."

Olivia and I crossed the finish line together. Ahead, Brax and Kane were both hunched over, grasping their knees and sucking in air. Kane turned his head, eyed me, and his eyes sort of smiled. The gesture didn't escape Olivia.

"See what I mean?" she said breathily.

And I was hesitant to acknowledge that maybe, I saw it too.

"Boy, you can tell those two are brothers," she said in her slight drawl. When I didn't answer, she looked at me and grinned. "Their confidence can be slightly overwhelming at times."

I didn't say anything, only nodded, and I thought then that Olivia Beaumont had to be one of the most sincere people I'd ever encountered. Like Murphy, she didn't pry, didn't poke, or dig. There wasn't a mean bone in Olivia's body, I suspected. Strength radiated from her, like a beacon from a lighthouse. I remembered the pain she'd suffered from the last Dare. How she'd held her head high, didn't let any of it get her down. Even after the loss of her grandfather, she'd remained steady as a rock. I also remembered how Brax had fought for her.

Something I strongly admired in her. In him.

If only I could be like that...

"I'll...see you around, Olivia," I said quietly.

"Hey, if you're not doing anything later on—"

"I—I can't," I stammered. Then I looked at her. "Thank you for always inviting me." I almost felt compelled to give her a reason. I almost felt compelled to actually accept her invite, for once. But I didn't.

A gentle smile tugged at the scar on her lip. "Anytime, Harper."

I ran over to the tables at the finish line, where a few of my sorority sisters were busy handing out the chocolate chip cookies. I grabbed a half-full platter and started helping, and soon I had nothing but crumbs. Murphy joined me. Her lob was pulled into two tight pigtails, and she wore winter-white shorts, crazy-striped knee socks, and a long-sleeved Turkey Run T-shirt.

"Would you care to know how much we collected?" she asked in a whispery, excited voice? She wiggled her brows. "A damn pretty shilling or two, that's what."

I knew how much we'd collected because I'd collected all of the entry money for the race. I gave her a puzzled look. "How much?"

The Cheshire Cat was back and smiling. "Nearly three thousand quid!"

My eyes bugged out. At least, it felt like they did. "Say what?"

She leaned close, and I could smell the flowery lotion she used. "Three. Thousand. American. Dollars."

I blinked. Quickly did the math. "But seventy-five people entered the run. Last I counted we had two thousand three hundred and fifty dollars." And that was because Kane had donated a hundred dollars.

"Well, apparently there was a last-minute donation." She grinned. "Fancy that." She looked at me and sighed. "You're all sweaty, love. Want a lift back to campus?" She threw a look over her shoulder. "We've got this." Another smile. "Josh is picking up the tables and taking down the banners. We're going for drinks tonight." Brows wiggled. "I'm determined to get him to the salon in Covington for a mani-pedi. I'll save details."

"Please do," I agreed, smiling. "And…no. I'm going to run back." I waved. "See ya later."

I started jogging back to campus. By taking a few shortcuts I could make it back in probably twenty minutes, if I kept up my pace. And I could. If I could do anything, it was run.

No sooner had I left the fairgrounds did Kane sidle up next to me, keeping pace with his long stride. "Trying to duck out on me?" he asked.

I slipped him a look. "Perhaps. I don't like mingling with criminals."

"I'm not a criminal. I'm a businessman. And the winner of our bet."

I didn't answer him, and we continued running in silence. The sun hadn't really emerged; it looked more wintry than it actually was. A gray gloom hung over everything. The temperature had warmed up to the mid-sixties, and the long shirt I wore now started to suffocate me.

At least, I thought it was the shirt.

"Are you afraid to go out with me?"

At the traffic light we were forced to stop. I looked at him, a little breathless. Either from his beautiful features, or the way his eyes spoke so heavily at times.

"I'm more afraid of what that will do to my reputation," I answered.

He stared at me, that deep, searching stare. "I'll pick you up tomorrow at six p.m. sharp." His smile was sly, confident. And he ignored my jab. "Dress warm."

When the light changed, Kane took off, turning down the street and heading to where I now knew was probably Brax's apartment. I watched him for a second, his easy trot, and wondered at my reaction when he glanced over his shoulder and threw me a wave.

Heat crept up my neck. My heart fluttered. And as I crossed the street and passed through Winston's main entrance, I dared only admit to myself that I could barely wait for tomorrow night at six p.m. to arrive.

7. Chances

NERVES CLAWED AT MY insides. All the sisters were out, Murphy and Josh had already left for curry, and I was alone. Almost as if I felt as though I were doing something wrong, I paced as I waited for six p.m. to arrive. I had a bad case of the jitters. For the hundredth time, I glanced at the clock on the wall in the common room. The minute hand tick-ticked so loudly, I almost wanted to cover my ears. Five forty. A little longer. *If Corinne Belle finds out about this...*

It had rained during the night, and this morning when I'd awakened the temperature had dropped. A cold front was moving through and the high for the next several days would be in the low fifties. Lows at night in the mid thirties.

Kane must've checked the weather when he'd advised me to dress warmly.

Kane McCarthy. Businessman. From Boston. *Are you out of your mind, Harper? You've never even been on a date in your life and this is who you choose to be your first? A shady numbers man? All for a dare?*

I passed by the entryway mirror, and glanced at myself. I didn't really know what I was doing. A first for me, actually. Everything was usually so well-planned out—whether I planned it, or someone else did. The latter was usually the case.

I didn't own fun clothes. I owned...Belle clothes. Sophisticated, successful, tailored clothes. They'd been chosen for me and purchased for me by my grandmother. So the best I could do was a pair of olive fleece-lined leggings that I'd borrowed from Murphy, my tall black leather Frye boots, and a ribbed black turtleneck. My designer black wool pea coat lay draped over the hall tree, along with a light tartan scarf and black gloves. I glanced at the clock again. Pulled on my coat, scarf. Grabbed my gloves and shoved them into the pockets.

Hopefully, warm enough.

I'd twisted my straight hair into a single French braid, and out of nervousness applied one more swipe of lip balm. Paced. Waited. Something in my gut warped; I knew deep down that just being with Kane wasn't going to get me into any sort of trouble. I'd have to actually be physically caught gambling to be in jeopardy. Was it that I knew I was doing something completely forbidden in Corinne Belle's eyes? What if I got caught? I cringed at the myriad of punishments running through my mind.

Maybe it was the fact that Kane was doing something illegal that frightened me? Somehow, I wished he was...better than that. To have more integrity.

Maybe I could convince him.

A knock at the door sounded and startled me from my thoughts. My boots clicked against the hardwood floor as I pulled open the door. Standing there, wearing that smoky gaze, was Kane. He regarded me silently, intimately, completely, without barely a shift in his facial expression. Behind him, the sky had turned dark, and the light from the porch cast a ginger glow against his skin.

With his legs braced wide, he held out his hand; easy, inviting. Tempting. "Do you trust me?"

My breath caught in my throat. "Not exactly," I answered. Hesitantly, unused to physical touch, even with my friends, I placed my hand in his. It was big, callused, warm, and he tugged me through the door. A completely foreign feeling, I found I sort of liked it. We descended the porch steps and crossed the yard to the parking lot in silence. At his vintage truck, he stopped, unlocked the door and looked down at me. His usual leather jacket covered a dark plaid undershirt, a pair of dark jeans, and boots a shade lighter than his jacket. He looked comfortable. Beautiful. Like something out of an outdoor catalogue.

"Hop in," he urged softly.

Strangely enough, I did just that. I hadn't even ridden for weeks with Murphy until we'd gone to Karma. With my chin held high and my shoulders straight, I eased into the driver's side and scooted across the bench seat. The vinyl was cool through my leggings. I buckled up, crossed my ankles and folded my hands in my lap. I couldn't help scanning the parking lot, searching for anyone who might be watching. Who would tell on me.

Kane slid in behind the larger-than-average steering wheel, pulled the door shut, and looked at me. Shadows from the yard light cut across his face, making him look even more mysterious than I thought he was. His eyes softened. Turned liquid.

"Relax, Harper," he said in that unique, oddly soothing voice. "I'm not dangerous, you know."

I drew in a deep breath. Eased it back out. "Maybe." I looked at him. "Does Brax know you're taking me out?"

His smile was crooked. "He warned me to leave you alone," he confessed. Then his eyes softened again, seemingly drinking me in. "I just couldn't seem to help myself."

My skin flushed at his words, and I barely knew what to say. I twisted my hands together in my lap. "But you're not even from here," I offered. "How do you know where to go?" I looked at him then. "Where *are* we going, anyway?"

His laugh was gentle, easy. "You'll see." He started the truck, and it roared to life. "Olivia told me about this place," his smile was crooked. "Thought I needed to see it at least once."

"Oh." I glanced out the window. "Why with me?"

Kane was silent for a moment. "Why not with you?"

I pondered that for several seconds. Maybe minutes. My gaze hung onto the passing signs as we faded out of Killian and headed north. Trees were dark, lurking giants crouched just out of reach. Cars were few; Sunday evenings, things were slow on the road. I couldn't help but wonder if Kane could tell I'd never actually been out on a date before. Twenty years old, on my first official date, and I had to keep it to myself. Hide it. Prayed it didn't get out that I'd been lying all those other times. Made up dates. Made up guys. Made up loves. A big fat made up life.

"Okay, I'll answer for you," Kane volunteered. I peeked over at him, and his gaze stayed straight ahead on the road, and I watched the angles and planes of his face shift in and out of the lights that we passed. It fascinated me.

He fascinated me.

It was definitely a new experience.

"Ever since that first day, when I asked you for directions?" He kind of smiled, half-laughed, soft and barely there. "Then when I saw you talking to Olivia and my brother, and every other time I've seen you since?" He shrugged. "I can't stop thinkin' about you, Harper." He let out a sigh. "Something about you I identify with." He looked at me. "Something that reminds me of me. Something broken. Something no one else sees. And it draws me to you."

That shocked me. "But I'm not a criminal," I said. "How can I remind you of, well, you?"

Again, he didn't seem affronted. Just…factual. "There's actually a little more to me than numbers," he said, then glanced at me. Liquid pools of coffee grazed my eyes. "Believe it or not."

I knew there was something because every time we were in the same breathing space, something like a current hummed beneath my skin. I wasn't stupid, or naïve. Just because I'd never been on a date before, or had sex before, didn't mean I was blind to the signs of attraction. I knew how things worked. Murphy was a walking, breathing Wikipedia of dating, snogging, and sex and all things in between. She inadvertently taught me plenty. Maybe not everything, but plenty.

"How do you know I'm not already in a relationship?" I asked.

"I asked."

"Oh." I had nothing to say after that. All of my big Dare plans seemed to be getting tossed right back at me by a quiet, strange beautiful guy with liquid eyes, wise beyond his years. I glanced out the window, watched the dark figures pass by.

Some time passed before Kane turned down a long, dark road. "Don't worry," he said. "I know this looks creepy, but it's really not. I promise."

"I believe you only because I know Brax Jenkins," I said with confidence. "He'd punch your eye out if you did anything shifty."

A faint rumble of laughter spilled from Kane's throat. "Yeah, he's already warned me to keep away from you and you can believe he'd be madder than hell if he knew I'd taken you out here." He winked. "But I'm the older brother, see? Where do you think he learned everything from?" Then, as he slowed the truck, his gaze found mine. "I might be fast with the numbers, Harper, but I don't swindle hearts. It's not my MO."

I somehow believed that about him. "That's...good to know."

It wasn't long after that when Kane pulled to a stop at a crossgate. He looked at me. "Ready?"

Inside, my nerves jittered. It was dark. I didn't like the dark, and immediately, my breath hitched. I tried to stifle it, the panic I felt creeping up along my spine. I didn't want Kane to see it. "I suppose."

Out of the truck, with a blanket he'd grabbed from somewhere behind his seat, Kane extended his hand and helped me out. From his pocket he pulled out a small flashlight, flipped it on, and some of the tension eased from me as soon as the light arced through the blackness. Grasping my hand firmly, he tugged me toward the crossgate. A sign read KEEP OUT. TRESSPASSERS WILL BE PROSECUTED. My feet braked, and Kane jerked. He looked down at me.

"What's wrong?"

"This…is trespassing," I stammered. "See that word, Kane? *Prosecuted?* We could get into trouble."

He rounded on me, sort of creating an enclave around us with his broad shoulders. He invaded my space; it made me feel protected, somehow. He didn't even need to assure me with his hands. His eyes, his voice did the same maneuvers. "Haven't you ever done anything daring, Harper?" he asked gently. "Anything that made your adrenaline kick in?"

"Of course not," I said quickly. "Especially if it means going to jail!"

The lines around his eyes and mouth eased as he smiled. "It's okay, Harper. Olivia knows the owner and I called ahead. Besides, Brax just brought Olivia out here the other night." In the darkness, he tilted his head, ducked it to get a better view of me. "Your face is hidden in the shadows," he said quietly. "But I know you're tense. I can feel it. I asked you to trust me. Is it so hard?"

If he only knew. "Okay. Lead the way."

We ducked under the crossgate and followed a hard-packed dirt path up a slight incline. Up and up we climbed, until our breath puffed out white with moisture.

"Notice anything yet?" he asked.

"No," I answered breathily.

Kane laughed softly and we continued on, the narrow beam of light slicing through the darkness.

Finally, we plateaued, the trees cleared and we stood perched on a bluff.

An engine roared overhead, and when I craned my neck to look, I gasped as a commercial jet seemingly skimmed the top of my head.

"Oh!" I gasped again. "Kane!"

His laugh was husky and cut through the night air. Under his arm, he unrolled the blanket and set it on the ground at our feet. "Sit."

I did, trying to keep my boots off the edge. "Where are we?"

Kane flung himself beside me, shoulder to shoulder. The moment he turned off the flashlight, the panic rose again in my throat and I gasped.

He looked at me. "What's wrong?"

I tried to calm my breathing. "I, uh," I stammered, "I don't really like the dark." I didn't want to admit it, but there it was. I had no choice. My body fought the urge to take off and run. "Hate it, actually."

"Hey," he said. "I'm right here. I won't let anything happen to you. I promise."

I nodded, breathed. "It's not you. It's the darkness."

Suddenly, he pushed the flashlight into my hand. "Tell you what. If you get nervous, turn it back on. But I'm right here."

I squeezed the flashlight, and somehow just having it in my hand, in my control, eased my panic. "Thank you," I said softly. I glanced around. "Where are we?"

Only a thumbnail moon illuminated the bluff, but I could see Kane's profile as he spoke. "Would you believe we're on a farm behind the airport?" He inclined his head in a direction behind us. "The main runway extension is back there," he said, then looked at me. We were close—too close, almost, for comfort. "You have to lie back to get the full effect."

He spun around then, stretched his long body out over the blanket, crossed his boots at the ankles, and tucked his hands behind his head. In the moonlight I could see his those liquidy pools staring at me. He smiled. "Take a chance for once. I won't bite. Promise."

Another plane zoomed overhead, and again, I gasped. Kane laughed. "Hurry up and lay back before you miss the next one," he said.

With a hefty sigh, I kicked my boots over the blanket and stretched out beside him. Our shoulders touched; our heads were close. The flashlight gripped tightly in my hand.

"I never see this many stars back home." His feathery voice drifted in the darkness. "I guess you're used to it."

My eyes were glued overhead. Sure, I'd seen stars. I'd seen blankets of them. But had I really noticed? "The sky. It's so…big," I said. My eyes roved from one end to the other. "It seems endless."

He was quiet for a moment. "Here comes one," he said.

We both held our breath as a jet seemingly skimmed the sky above our noses.

"Are you warm enough?" he asked.

Heat radiated off his body, so close to mine, and the sensation was new. Exciting. Frightening. "I am," I said, even though I shivered.

He laughed lightly, then grew quiet. "Who are you, Harper Belle?"

I kept my gaze trained at the sky, but my insides froze. "What do you mean?"

"You're the president of a sorority, yet you have no friends. You attend meetings, but are never seen anywhere other than sorority events. Class. The library." The shift in air made me know he'd turned to me, so I looked at him. "You don't go out for pizza. You don't go out to movies. And you don't go to the local pubs."

I tried to keep my mask in place. "Seems like you've been doing some research."

Those brown eyes, as fathomless as the inky sky, searched mine. "No. I just recognize myself in you, is all." He turned on his side, propping his head with his palm. "Fear is our common factor, Harper," he said, and his words washed over me like warm, honeyed breath. "Broken recognizes broken. It's also what sets us apart."

I now turned on my side to face him. My heart thumped at his perceptiveness. "A criminal philosopher. Interesting," I said, forcing my voice to stay strong. Not crack. Not let him know how close to the truth he probably was. "I've said this before, Kane McCarthy. You don't know anything about me."

"I'm trying," his voice was soft, and a crooked smile tilted his mouth. A mouth I had a difficult time looking away from. "I've found out a few things, though."

Fear and panic instantly gripped me. Made my spine stiffen, and my skin prickle. Had he found out about my past? Who I really was? "Like what?" I asked slowly. I tried not to overreact. Did he know what had happened? What was inside of me?

What I could become?

His gaze moved over my face, so slow and painfully thorough he might as well have been dragging those full lips over it. "That you come from a rich, affluent family. You're pre-law. You date, but you don't date lowly college students. And that you never, ever break rules." His gaze settled on my mouth. "And that you eat turkey sandwiches alone. Jog alone, away from campus so no one can see you. Interact with you. You eat oatmeal alone. And you trust no one." His eyes returned to mine. "Yet you came out here with a near-total stranger." He grinned. "Who may or may not be a thug. Why?"

I thought about it for a moment. "I'm even surprising myself, coming out here with you," I answered. "Trust is a powerful gift that I bestow very, very lightly Kane McCarthy. If I were to give it to anyone, though," I thought more. "It'd go to Olivia Beaumont. Which is why I'm here with you now. She seems to trust you." That was a partial truth. The other reason was of course to gain footage with Kane on the Dare. "As far as the other accusations?" I sighed. Some weird part of me wanted to just…let it all out. Tell Kane the truth. I was so, so weary of keeping secrets. Tired of being scared. "Only half-truths of course. Murphy is my friend. And I do occasionally go out. I just happen to not want to waste a single dime of my family's money partying it up versus getting my solid education." I watched him watching me, and that did make me a bit more antsy. "I'm on the fence about pre-law, actually." I'd blurted that part out, and I wasn't sure why.

"What then?" he asked, and returned to his back, facing the plane jetting overhead. "If you didn't have your family pushing you into pre-law," his gaze found mine in the moonlight, "and I'd be willing to bet a grand that's the case, then what would Harper Belle want to do with her life?"

That he'd guessed that didn't sit well with me, either. But for some reason I didn't think anything I said to Kane McCarthy would get back to Winston University. "I really like taking pictures," I finally said, and thought about the used camera I'd saved up to buy. The pictures I'd secretly driven hours away to capture. I kept it to myself, though. No one knew but me. I looked at him. "I'm a novice, though. Just learning." I studied him. "And if Kane McCarthy wasn't busy taking illegal bets for the Kappas, what would he want to do?"

Kane joined me on his back, staring skyward. "Hmm. Honestly?" He was silent for a moment as he thought. "You won't believe it."

"Tell me," I urged.

"A cop."

We were both silent after that. Until Kane's voice broke through the night.

"Funny," he said softly, and kind of surprised. "I have a feeling we both just did something completely out of the ordinary for either of us."

He didn't even have to explain, because I was thinking it myself.

And only then did I realize we'd been in the dark this whole time, and I'd actually forgotten the terror of it.

I had the light in my hand. In my power. My control.

But with Kane beside me, it hadn't seemed to matter so much.

8. Kane

SHE KNEW AS LITTLE about me as I did about her. Well, almost. I had done a little research, asked some questions—although Olivia Beaumont had been tight-lipped about almost everything. *Ask her yourself,* she'd said. Brax, of course, had said, *Leave her the fuck alone, Kane, and I fuckin' mean it.* But I couldn't. She'd burned my brain from the moment I'd asked her for directions. I had a strong feeling Harper and I both could read into the masks we each wore. The shields we each locked in place. The reason I knew this was because people who did that—shielded and masked—could almost always spot another kindred spirit. It was a gift, I supposed. Sort of how I could immediately spot another product of the foster system.

Harper Belle was a complex soul. She hid something behind that broken smile, and it wasn't pretty. She had a lot of people fooled, no doubt. But not me. I recognized it as clearly as I recognized my own demons. All that richy-rich, affluent family shit? Yeah, she might have been raised in that environment, but that's not who she was. She was something else entirely.

And she completely fascinated me.

It wasn't so much her looks—which were beyond beautiful to me. It was the beauty that lay behind the perfect skin, the striking eyes, and the lithe runner's body. It was…something I almost couldn't put my finger on. Strange, though, when it came down to it, I'd label it as pain. The pain that lay just below the surface of the beauty. It intrigued me. Made me want to step in, stop that pain, and kick anyone's ass who had caused it.

"You're very different from your brother," she said in that delicate Texas drawl. Which also fascinated me. I could see now why Brax was so crazy about Olivia's.

"I am?" I asked.

"Yes," she said. She pushed her hair behind her ear, and I balled my fingers together to keep from doing it for her.

"How am I then?" I prodded, curious.

"Well," Harper continued. I noticed the way her brows bunched together in the middle when she thought about something. "Brax is loud. Obnoxious. Swears profusely, although it seems like since he met Olivia, it's a little less." She looked at me. "Don't get me wrong—I think he's a really great, really intelligent guy. He's just…so much harsher than you."

I watched her, intrigued by the movement of her mouth, and the way her teeth pulled at her lips when she wasn't sure

109

about something. I wanted to kiss her. In a bad, bad way. But I didn't dare. Not now. So I lightened the mood. "You sayin' I'm a wimp?"

She laughed, and for once it sounded sincere. "No. You're more like a silent storm. You have a quiet sort of strength," she said, and I watched her profile beneath the watery moonlight. "Even your accent doesn't sound as harsh as Brax's. I don't know, you kind of have a sort of wisdom that is extraordinary, I guess. Brax is loud. Uses his fists. You actually look like you use your fists, but you don't. Or…" She gave me a quick look, and her widened eyes nearly made me laugh. "Do you?"

"It's rare that I have to," I assured her.

"I thought so," she said on an exhale. "You…think things through. Demand respect through your silence. Using only your eyes." She looked at me, and the way her face scrunched up as she peered at me in the moonlight, inspecting me closely, sank straight through me. She was incredibly perceptive. "You speak a lot through your eyes. That's sincere power." She stared at the darkened sky. "Impressive."

So she had me semi-pegged. That, to me, was impressive. "Well, while I'm running around being all silently powerful," I said, turning to her. "You're putting on a front that I have a feeling isn't fitting you all too well anymore, Ms. Belle."

Even in the darkness, her eyes flashed something familiar.

Fear.

Hell, I knew it well.

"You said we all have secrets. Why can't it just stay that way?" she said.

Her diplomacy eased my mouth up at the corners. "Because I seem to want to know everything about you."

"Oh," she breathed. "Well…I'd prefer it if you stopped illegal betting activity with the Kappas. It not only puts yourself at risk, but your brother, too. And that's selfish. So I guess we both want something we can't have."

"Why do you care so much what I do there?" I had to ask because no one other than Brax had ever cared. And even he didn't know my true reasons.

She sat up and tucked her slender legs beneath her. With my head propped against my palm, I stayed stretched out on my side, watching her. She reminded me of a fawn—one that would startle and take off with any sudden movement or sound, so I just…listened. "For one, it's illegal. Where's the integrity in that kind of lifestyle? I mean, do you plan on having a family one day? Children? Is that your legacy? *I was a damn fine criminal, kids. The best around.* I mean—" She now looked exasperated, as though trying to get me to see a point I'd never, ever see. Her pretty little brows bunched together again, and I found it endearing. "Does that employment come with a 401K? Medical and dental benefits?"

I couldn't help but smile at her rant. It was a justifiable one. And I'd heard similar from Brax, just the other day.

If either of them knew why I actually did what I did, maybe they wouldn't judge me so harshly. I rubbed my jaw, felt the unshaven stubble there that had grown back since I'd shaved earlier. "I have my reasons, Harper."

"I see," she said, and sat ram-rod stiff. "Well, I suppose you wouldn't need all those benefits in prison."

I sat up then. No, I didn't want to go to prison. I wouldn't, either, because as soon as I was finished at Winston, I'd hit the road and be on my way. "I'm not going to prison," I said with

111

a light laugh that sounded acerbic in the night air. "Ever." I pulled one knee up, rested my forearm against it, and she watched my movements as closely as I did hers. "But your concern for my retirement and future is…touching."

She cocked her head. "How is it you on one hand run illegal bets, but on the other secretly wish to be a police officer?"

My mind went there, due to her prodding probably. "Scumbags fill the world, Harper. Not the kind like me, who run numbers for money. I'm talking about the ones who hurt people." I stared at her, almost willing her to see the truth without actually having to say it out loud, confess it to her. That was a first for me. "The ones who need to pay for their crimes in the worst possible way."

"I see," she said softly. Her eyes cast down to her lap, and she brushed at something on her coat. "Did you donate extra money to the Turkey Run?" Her eyes flashed at me then, wide and incredible and alluring. Waiting for an answer.

"I had a good payday," I said. It wasn't a lie; I had.

"It was generous of you," she continued. "It will feed a lot of families."

I nodded, and couldn't help leaning toward her. Almost as if by getting closer I could sap some of her warmth. Infuse some of her fears and flush them out. "I'm glad." We were close, not facing each other but sort of catty-corner, shoulder-to-shoulder, and it would be so easy to lean in, take just one small taste. Just to see.

She felt it, too; I could sense it. She seemed confused, though. As if she was unsure what the sensation between us was. I knew—had sensed it the very first time we were within eye-shot of each other. I couldn't explain it. It had nothing to do with her physical beauty—although at first, sure. I noticed that. Who wouldn't? She was elegant, delicate, with faultless skin and plump lips that begged to be savored.

It was her eyes, though, that dug into my brain. Wide, almond shaped and the strangest blue-green I'd ever seen, they held something in their depths that probably no one else saw but me. Sadness. Pain. Loneliness. And of course, fear. Broken, but maybe not hopeless.

Kindred spirit.

She cleared her throat. "I have an idea. Sort of."

I glanced down at our hands, so close on the blanket they were almost reaching. Touching. Not quite, though. I looked at her. "And what is that?"

She shifted her position; seemingly closer. Yet her eyes fluttered, glanced off mine to stare into the darkness. I watched her draw a long breath in, as though she was preparing for something frightening. After she released it, she let her gaze settle on mine again. "It's something of a challenge for us both, I think. You'll probably enjoy it because it is along the lines of a bet."

I did lean toward her this time, but not too invasive. I grinned. "I'm dying already. Tell me."

A faint smile paused her words, and she glanced at her boots, shy and awkward and engaging. Then she breathed, gathered courage, it seemed, and the mask was back in place when she looked at me. "I propose a challenge of truths and confessions." She folded her hands, lacing her fingers together and sitting them properly in her lap. Every movement fascinated me. She was...so oddly different. "You tell me something. I in turn tell you something." One of her eyebrows rose. "We have to solemnly swear to say the truth and only the truth, so help us God. And it stays between us. Only us."

I searched her eyes; studied her features in the moonlight. She suspected I hid just as many secrets as she did. And for some reason, she was interested in knowing my truths. I'd confess a few. Not all, but some. I smiled. Nodded.

"You're on, Ms. Belle," I agreed.

"Good. You go first," she said hurriedly.

I leaned a little closer. She smelled good—not perfume good, but something else. Maybe it was the scent of pine that surrounded us. Definitely something I wasn't used to in Boston. I waited. Wondered what made her tick. What would make her buckle. Sigh with pleasure. Or content.

"Well?" she finally prodded.

"I've wanted to kiss you since that day in the park."

Her eyes rounded, making them even wider than they naturally were. "Really?" Her tongue slipped out, wetting those full lips that I couldn't stop staring at. She had no idea what it did to me.

"Yeah. Really." I searched her eyes. She hadn't run away, and that was a good thing. "Now you."

Then, I saw it. Fear. And I watched as it flared, rose in her like something alive, and she shifted uncomfortably on the blanket. My hand reached for hers, and I noticed she'd never put on her gloves. Her fingers were cold. "Hey," I said as gently as I could. "Don't say anything that makes you want to run."

Her eyes softened then, like pools of water as they searched mine. "Okay." She swallowed, glanced away, staring at another plane passing just over our heads. She didn't look at me now, and that's how I realized she spoke the truth.

"I've never kissed anyone before."

I couldn't keep the shock off my face. I tried, but I couldn't. I believed her.

How, at twenty years old, had she never kissed anyone? *How?*

"Do you trust me?" I said softly. I wanted her to, so bad.

She said nothing; only nodded. Vulnerability rolled off her in such harsh waves, I almost felt it.

Right or wrong, I couldn't help myself. It might make me a bastard, but swear to God, I couldn't help it.

I leaned in and kissed her.

9. Consumed

I FORCED MY EYES TO stay open as Kane's head tilted, grew close, and in the moonlight I watched his long dark lashes brush his pale skin. The moment his cool, firm lips pressed against mine, I closed my eyes and exhaled. Kane seemed to swallow it, breathed in as I breathed out, barely moved against my mouth. It was gentle. Soft. And when he shifted his lips to taste the corner of my mouth with the slightest swipe of his tongue, I gasped, and he swallowed that, too.

He pulled back then, his eyes on mine, and mine unavoidably on his. What seemed like surprise filled the liquid coffee pools as they stared at me, speaking volumes without uttering a single word. I was speechless; I could barely breathe.

"Are you okay?" he finally asked. He hadn't moved away from me. Just out of reach. There, in my space, but not terrifying.

"My heart is beating fast," I confessed. "Like I've been running. And my lips are numb."

That coaxed a smile to touch his lips. His teeth gleamed white in the odd light of night that we sat in. "Is that a good thing?"

"I'm not sure," she answered. I looked at him, watching his eyes closely. "I...guess you think that's pretty weird? Twenty years old and never been kissed?"

He didn't falter. Not once. His eyes only softened as they did. He wore sincerity in those lush brown orbs like some wore their heart on their sleeve.

"Weird, no," he answered. "Surprised, hell yes." His fingers found mine, and I allowed his touch as he twined our hands together. "Privileged, more than anything."

I tilted my head, curious. "Why?"

"To be the first."

I nodded, understanding. "Oh." The current between us that was there earlier still existed; it hadn't evaporated. "Was the kiss an experiment?"

"It was a strong desire." His fingers squeezed mine. "I'll want to do it again."

I nodded. "Me, too."

A jet soared overhead, and we simultaneously glanced upward as it passed.

"I should go," I finally said. "The week before Thanksgiving is always so busy. And I have a test—"

Kane's mouth covered mine, swallowing my words, surprising and thrilling and scaring me at the same time. Not as light, not as feathery as before, this kiss felt...different. Intoxicating. I tasted the faintest trace of spearmint. His knuckles grazed my jaw, held my mouth still as he explored, and my heart raced harder than it had before. I felt as though I was sinking straight into him. Then, he pulled back, his eyes on mine. "I couldn't help myself." His easy words washed over me. "But I'm not sorry for it."

Breathless, I couldn't take my eyes off him. "I'm not, either," I answered.

A smile claimed his beautiful face, and wordlessly he rose and pulled me with him. I stretched my legs as he shook out the blanket and folded it, then with it tucked beneath one arm, and my hand grasped in his, we headed back down the bluff.

"Funny how, now that we're used to the moonlight we can see perfectly fine without the flashlight," I noticed.

Kane looked down at me as we walked. "Why don't you like the dark?"

My mind flew to the memory of that cramped, wet, dank kitchen cabinet. A pitch-black closet. Alone. What had driven me to both places. Inside, I involuntarily shook at the memory. I knew that was something I couldn't share with Kane. Not now or ever. "I think I had nightmares as a little girl." It wasn't a lie; it was the exact truth. I simply left out a few critical points out. "Just never got over it, I suppose." I wanted to know more about Kane, and that surprised me. Never had someone intrigued me enough to ask questions. Want to know things of their past. With him? I was drawn to him like...well, like I'd never been in my whole life. I slipped a glance his way as we walked; his knowing gaze already there, waiting. Almost anticipating.

"Go ahead," he crooned. "Ask."

"Wow." I smiled.

Kane jerked to a stop, and I jerked with him. My eyes flew around us, to the ground. "What is it?" I asked. "A snake? I don't like snakes."

"It's rare that I see you genuinely smile." His knuckles found my cheek, and brushed across my skin. "It's stunning."

I didn't know what to say. Heat crawled up my neck and onto my cheeks, and I was glad for the nighttime concealer. I wasn't used to compliments. Not from guys. Not real ones, anyway.

Kane's compliments were real. Weren't they? I felt they were, but...still. "Is that the kiss talking?" I couldn't help but ask. Why it suddenly mattered surprised me, too. Almost as much as my reaction to his kiss. My first kiss.

"I can't say for sure," Kane confessed. His voice had a lilt to it, though, and when I looked at him, I could see his eyes shimmering with laughter. "Might have to experiment more. You know. Kiss. Smile. Repeat."

A shiver raced through me at the thought of that.

Fear replaced the shiver, though. "Kane?"

"Yeah?"

"Don't take this the wrong way," I started. "I suppose by now you've guessed that the whole *she never dates lowly college guys* is really *she's never dated anyone.*" I ducked under the crossgate, and he followed, and at his truck we stopped. He was quiet as he waited for me to continue. "I have my reasons for keeping up the persona I portray at Winston, and I'd like to keep it that way. You asked if I trusted you?"

His brown eyes seemed like two dark caves against his pale skin. "I did."

I lifted my chin. "Then I trust you to trust me," I continued. "I don't want people knowing about us."

He nodded, but his eyes said something else I wasn't able to pinpoint. "President of a sorority definitely doesn't need to be seen kissing a known criminal."

"Yes," I admitted. "That's right. Not to mention I don't want it creating other suspicions. More questions I'm not willing to answer. For anyone." I searched his eyes. "Do you understand?" I said this gently. I wasn't trying to hurt his feelings. It was nothing more than simple matter-of-fact with me. It had to be. If Corinne Belle found out...

He was quiet for a moment as he tried to see behind my eyes; to see what other secrets I might be keeping locked away. No matter how hard he searched, he'd only see what I wanted him to. His hand lifted then, traced my jaw, slipped over my braid and pulled it over my shoulder. "Can I see you again? Away from campus?"

I had to wonder what this was—this thing between Kane and I. A fling? He certainly didn't live here, so...what next? In a very short period of time, I'd allowed him to get closer to the real me as I'd ever let anyone. In my life. Yet he was as unstable as any I could imagine. I looked at him. "How long do you plan on being here? At Winston, I mean. With your brother?"

"I guess that all depends," he stated. "On a lot of things."

I nodded. "Yes. You can see me again. Away from campus." I eyed him. "Unless it's a campus charity event." Then I offered him another smile.

His lips pulled. "You're on." We climbed inside the truck, he started the engine. "Do you have a cell? I never see you with one."

I nodded. "I do. It's just not glued to my hands like most people."

"Another like in your favor." He reached into the ashtray, retrieved his cell phone, and handed it to me. "How about putting your number in there for me?"

And that brought another uninvited smile to my face.

The ride back to Winston, on the darkened, single-lane highway wasn't nearly as unsettling as the ride earlier. We didn't say much; didn't have to. Kane held my hand, and I was acutely aware that *he* was acutely aware of the attraction that lay between us. Had I struck a match, the inside of Kane's truck would have burst into flames, I believed. I liked the roughened skin of his knuckles, his fingers against mine. The warmth the two created together. I wondered, briefly, if this was how Brax and Olivia had started out? Was this how normal couples reacted to each other? This attraction? Corinne Belle had called it pure sin. Was it? I thought about the feelings Kane stirred inside of me. So new. So untested. How could something that felt so good be sinful?

I wondered just how much trust I would bestow upon Kane McCarthy.

The moment we pulled down the lane leading to Delta House, I saw a figure in the parking lot, close to my car.

"Oh, hell," Kane muttered.

It was Brax, straddling his motorcycle. I tensed; I knew the encounter wouldn't be pleasant.

"Hey," Kane said softly. He glanced at me. "Don't worry, Harper. Nothing will happen here, okay? I promise. Just go inside, and I'll text you later."

I met his gaze. "Thank you," I said quietly. "For tonight." I set the flashlight on the seat beside me. "For this."

Kane's eyes softened. "My pleasure. 'Night, Harper Belle."

I studied him, smiled. "Goodnight, Kane McCarthy."

He walked me to the porch, gave me an assuring smile, and then turned and headed to his brother. At the door, I paused, and looked over my shoulder. Brax was off the bike, his hands on his hips. Even from across the yard I could feel his anger. Hear his harsh words. His scarred face made him look even fiercer.

"What the fuck, bro?" Brax said angrily. "You fuckin' crazy? *Harper?*"

If Brax's anger was vivid from across the yard, Kane's was twice as furious. All rolled into a silent, raging storm.

Kane ducked his head, looked Brax in the eye; stern. Quiet. Authoritative. "Not here, bro. Not here."

Brax rubbed his head, swore, and climbed on his bike. I could feel the tension in the air between the two brothers; heavy, like a sopping wet blanket. Kane glanced my way once more, gave me a nod and a smile, and headed for his truck. In seconds, both had disappeared.

I swiped the card through the key pad and let myself in. Delta house was still dark; no one had made it home yet. All the while I hurried through my nightly routine of getting ready for bed, Kane claimed my thoughts. Had he and Brax resolved their differences? Why was Brax so concerned about me? Was Kane really dangerous, and just a master of disguises? I was. Why not he?

As I climbed into bed, I stared at the ceiling and the shadows caused by the lamp I kept burning on my nightstand. Every sensation, every moment with Kane from the bluff came rushing back to me. The way his lips brushed mine, lingered, and how his tongue had felt like velvet. My skin tingled even now, thinking about it. How had he managed to stir so many feelings in me at once?

Just then, my cell phone buzzed where it sat on my nightstand. I reached over and picked it up, and while I didn't recognize the number, the text was very familiar.

KANE: HEY, ARE YOU ASLEEP YET?

My heart leapt as I read his words.

ME: NOT YET. ARE YOU AND BRAX OK?

KANE: YEAH, HE'LL GET OVER IT. SO ARE YOU BUSY TOMORROW AFTERNOON?

I thought about my hectic pre-Thanksgiving schedule.

ME: UNTIL FOUR, YES. WHY?

KANE: MEET ME AT YOUR FAVORITE PARK. AND BRING YOUR CAMERA.

My breath quickened at the thought of Kane wanting to see me again.

ME: OK. WHY?

KANE: YOU'LL SEE. HEY—I REALLY LIKED TONIGHT.

A smile fought its way past my lips, and even though no one was around to see it, a blush crept up my throat and warmed my cheeks.

ME: WHY?

KANE: BECAUSE I REALLY LIKE KISSING YOU.

Again, heat caught me off guard. Another smile. Two things I was unused to.

ME: I LIKED IT, TOO.

No sooner did I send the text, my phone rang. It was Kane.

"I just had to hear that adorable accent of yours again," he said.

I gave an embarrassed laugh. "You're crazy."

"'Night, Harper."

"Goodnight, Kane."

"Don't forget," he said, just before I hung up. "Four tomorrow. At the park."

"And bring my camera," I added. "I'll be there."

We hung up, and the smile on my face felt foreign; surreal. When had the Dare backfired on me so drastically? Actually, if I could get Kane to end the bets at Kappa house, it'd be a surefire win. But I hadn't counted on actually liking him.

And I did. Surprisingly, I really did.

The next day, my usual schedule kept me pretty busy. I had one meeting in preparation for the Dash-n-Date, and one for the holiday bake sale. And, I studied two hours for upcoming exams in Calculus and Literature. All the while, though, the memory of Kane's mouth against mine, his lips hungry, unfamiliar, tasting mine for the first time assaulted me, bringing a dreamy smile to my face that Murphy had caught more than once. At the bake sale prep my mind drifted to the night before on the bluff with Kane, with planes soaring over our heads, the night air draped over us like a blanket, and his lips exploring mine. My skin tingled. My heart sped up. I fought a smile.

"Jesus, Mary and Joseph," Murphy whispered next to me. "The expression on your face is filling me with sheer terror." She looked at me, peering close into my eyes. "Have you fallen ill?"

My lips quirked "I have not."

"Well tickety-boo, can we get on with this, then?" She shoved a list under my nose. "What do you think about these for the bake sale?"

My eyes scanned the list. Chocolate chip cookies. A definite must. I placed a check with my red marker. Mint brownies. Check. Snowballs. Check. Ginger snaps. Check. Rum. *Rum?* I looked up at Murphy and she gave me a sly smile. "Just making sure you're in there," she said, and tapped my head with her finger. "You seem to be off in Neverland." Then her eyes widened. "Blimey, you like him!"

"Minus the rum, yes, I agree with all of these," I answered. "What are you talking about?"

"You've fallen for your Dare," she said quietly. "You little tart."

I could do nothing but look at her. Blink. Keep silent.

"Gotcha," she conceded. "Tight-lipped as usual. Right. Well I don't know about you, but I've got a Dare-Meister to meet for drinks at MacElvee's." She cocked her head. "So, besides the nauseating grin on your face all the time now, how're things coming along with Kane?" She wagged her brows. "Reforming?"

"Um, yes," I stammered. "He's...surprisingly moving faster than I thought."

"Josh is picking me up after six," she announced. "Talk about surprising. I even got him to quit dipping that hideous worm dirt the other baseball players do."

We laughed, and she tilted her head. "Something in you has changed, Ms. Belle." The Grinch smile returned. "I find I quite like it on you."

"Keep it to yourself, why don't ya?" I teased. "Wouldn't want to ruin my reputation."

Murphy twisted a pretend key at her lips. "Safe with me, love." She studied me. "So, are you still bound for Belle

House?" she asked, and ducked her head to look at me. "You can always come home with me, you know."

I smiled, and it felt genuine. Murphy was indeed a kind soul. "Thanks, Murph, but yes. I'm expected home for Thanksgiving. Lots to prepare and set up for Christmas." I grinned, and this time it was fake. It felt fake, and it was. I hated it, too. "Family tradition."

"Gotcha," Murphy answered. "You know the offer remains open."

"Thanks, Murphy," I replied. Then I glanced at my watch. "Oh, I've got to run."

Murphy, who had braided her long lob bangs and had them pinned back, grinned. "I bet you do, love. Where are you off to?"

I turned and headed for the exit. "See you later, Murphy." I waved.

"Bollocks," she said behind me.

I wasn't about to divulge all of my goings-on with Kane just yet. Everything was too new for me. Too fantastic. I wasn't even sure I was doing the right thing. But as I pulled on the only casual garments I had—my running gear—my thoughts raced at how much I couldn't wait to get to that park to see him. Just the anticipation of...well, I didn't know, had me on edge. Pulling on my trainers, I slipped into my running jacket, pulled my hair into a ponytail, and grabbed my camera. Then I was out the door.

Kane was already at the park when I arrived. To my surprise, though, he kept his engine running, leaning against his door with his arms folded over his chest and his legs crossed at the ankles. With my camera strapped over my shoulder, I locked my car and started toward him. He wore a pair of mirrored shades, so I couldn't see his eyes. But the lines around his full mouth shifted into a smile that was more than contagious. He pushed off then, and started toward me.

As we grew closer, I couldn't help but smile back. "Hey—"

He walked straight up to me, steadied my head with his big hands, turned it to just the right angle, and covered my mouth with his. Swallowing my greeting. Tasting my lips. Making my knees feel gummy and loose. His tall frame engulfed me, crowded me, and his unique scent of pine and soap and leather swept over me.

"Hey back," he said once he'd lifted his head from mine. "I've been dying to do that all day."

"Oh," I said a little breathless. He was still close, and I could see myself in his shades. I glanced down and noticed he wore a small round silver medallion. I lifted it, and it felt cool beneath my fingertips. I looked at him. "A compass?"

Looking down at me, he nodded. "Brax gave it to me for my twenty-first birthday," he answered. "So I'll always know how to find my way." He laughed lightly. "I suppose he's still waiting on me to do that."

Such a profound gift between two brothers. I didn't know what else to say, so I just nodded. "Why is your engine running?"

That smile took over his face again, and he inclined his head. "It's a surprise. Let's go before we lose light."

He walked me around, helped me up into the truck, and then closed the door once I'd buckled in. He jogged around the front and hopped behind the wheel.

As he pulled out of the park, I half-turned in my seat. "How is it you know so many places around here and you're not even from the area?"

127

Kane laughed, and I found I really liked how smooth the sound was. "Olivia knows all the great places," he answered. "It's not far."

"I like it better when you're not wearing glasses," I confessed.

Kane immediately slid his shades off and looked at me. "And why's that?"

I shrugged, a little embarrassed. "Like I said before. You speak with your eyes." I gave him a smile. "When they're covered up I feel like I'm not really seeing you."

A slow sly smile captured Kane's mouth as he looked straight ahead. "You like my eyes, don't you?"

Heat burned my cheeks. "Well, of course I do."

Kane chuckled and in the next second we were turning down a long dirt drive. A small sign was nailed to a tall pine that read HANCOCK PRESERVE.

"Olivia said there is a nice lake back here. Wildlife." He slid me a glance. "Thought you might find some good subjects to photograph."

"I didn't even know this was back here," I said slowly, taking in the scenery that literally popped into view. Tall pears still retained most of their leaves, and they were every shade of red and yellow and ginger and in between. A nice-sized lake set down the hill from a narrow walk path.

"Well let's see what you can find," Kane said, and together we started down the path toward the lake. He held my hand as we ambled down the dirt path, and at the bottom, I immediately saw several subjects.

Wordlessly, I squatted close to the water and shot several of an old boat that had been turned upside down on the bank. A bird. A squirrel. At the far end of the lake, two men fished off the bank. I took several shots of them, as the waning after-noon sun caught them in just the right light.

"Can I try?" Kane asked.

I handed him the camera. "It's an older model, and I've got it on manual focus," I said. "And, well, you know how to focus. Then you press this to shoot." I showed him the button, and he nodded. He held the camera up and looked at several views before pointing the camera at me.

"Hold still," he said, and I hid my face. "Harper."

I sighed and removed my hands and looked at him, and he focused and took the picture. Then he smiled. "Even more beautiful in person."

"Stop it," I said, and retrieved my camera.

We walked until the sun dropped behind the tree line, and I took several pictures—including one of Kane that he hadn't known I'd taken until the camera motor clicked. He just looked at me and grinned. Shook his head.

"Well if that didn't break the lens nothing will," he said with a grin, and threaded his long fingers through mine. "Why don't you pursue photography if you love it so much?"

"Well," I said, and that cagey feeling fell on me. The one that occurred when anything ever came up about my family. "Law is...sort of expected of me. The family business, I guess."

Kane looked down at me, and his eyes seemed pure black in the waning light. "Do you always do exactly what your family tells you to do?"

"Yes," I answered. Didn't even hesitate. "I mean, it's a good career choice."

"Hmm." He studied me as we walked now. "Remember our betting game?"

"Yes," I answered again.

"Okay, here goes. Was Winston your idea, or your family's?" he asked.

We continued climbing the path, back to where we left the truck. Kane now walked behind me. "Well," I said, trying to figure out a way to phrase my choice of Winston without flat out lying. I just couldn't. "Collectively both," I finally said. "It...was the right choice." We reached the top, and he rounded on me, and I looked up to him. "But I'm really glad," I said. And I truly was. "I like Winston. It's a good school." *And far, far away from Belle House.*

Kane's dark gaze studied me for some time. "Now that part I believe," he said softly. His knuckles lifted to graze my jaw, and he lowered his mouth and brushed his lips against mine. He lingered there, stilling against me, just breathing. When he pulled back, his eyes sought mine. "I feel that there's something hiding inside of you," he said gently. "And that someone else put it there."

I could do nothing but look at him, breathless. His alabaster skin, void of all blemishes—just those long, long eyelashes and coffee colored eyes.

"I aim to set it free, Harper," he said, then kissed me again.

I exhaled, and he swallowed it in, drew me into him, and for once in my life I wished to God he really, truly could.

Rescue me.

It wasn't until later that night, after Kane had dropped me off at the park and he'd gone about his business, and I was lying in bed, that I scrolled through the pictures I'd taken that afternoon at the reserve. When I came to the one Kane took of me, I stopped, amazed. Wide eyes stared into the lens.

Wide, soft, and shimmering. Not quite as alien as I'd thought in the past. A small tilt to the corners of my mouth eased my features. I knew the transformation was because of who was taking the picture. It stunned me.

I scrolled some more, until I came across the ones I'd captured of Kane. Those smoky eyes stared back at me in a way no one else ever had.

And when I set my camera aside, and closed my eyes, I still saw him. Saw those eyes. And recognized in him just what he said he recognized in me.

Fear.

10. Alone

IT WAS THE DAY before classes let out, and Kane's words from the reserve had haunted me ever since they'd left his mouth. Just as his kisses had. His touch. His sincerity. And his perception. I couldn't stop thinking about him. Was he real? And would I ever trust him enough to let him know the truth about me? It was all so confusing. So...frightening. Why would I trust someone who was planning on leaving? Why was I setting myself up for a hurt I'd never experienced?

I stretched my legs at the Covington recreational park as I did nearly every morning of my life. This morning was cold; my breath floated out of my body in white puffs. I snugged the knit hat over my ears, did a few body twists. The air sank into the fibers of my fleece jacket and stung my skin. I shoved my hands deep into my pockets.

"You're not starting without me, are you?"

I jumped at Kane's voice, but it was quickly replaced by the slamming of my heart and sharp intake of my breath. He'd parked on the other side of the pond and had jogged to me. Right now, his steady gait carried his long legs and muscular frame directly to me, and he didn't stop until his hands had cupped my face on either side, and his mouth had found mine. I couldn't get used to his kissing; I wasn't getting enough. His hands moved from my face, to my waist, and as his lips warmed against mine, he pulled me closer. My arms had escaped my pockets and now encircled his neck.

Almost like I knew what I was doing.

I didn't.

He suckled my bottom lip, and the sensuality of it had adrenaline humming in my ears. When I looked up at him, into that flawless face and coffee eyes, my knees felt soft. I was glad he still had ahold of me.

"I'm pretty sure I'm going to go insane over the holidays. Are you sure you won't come home with us to Olivia's for Thanksgiving?" he asked. His dark brows, perfectly arched, peeped out just below the black beanie he'd pulled over his head. "You know your secrets are safe there." He wagged those dark brows. "Endless kissing."

A smile tugged at my mouth. "Tempting. But," I sighed, stared away from his wise eyes before he saw something else I didn't want him to. "I have to go home, Kane."

For the very first time since, well, as long as I could remember, I felt compelled *not* to go home. It was scary, admitting that I'd rather be with Kane. We hadn't known each other for long— we really didn't know each other at all. Yet I couldn't deny the attraction, the pull I felt toward him. Instinctive and raw, I felt it just as strongly as I felt my own heart beating.

Again, his temporary status, not to mention his sketchy occupation, dropped a dose of reality back in my lap. I couldn't not go home, though. I was expected. I had no choice in the matter, really.

His mouth swept mine once more, and I breathed him in. Piney soap and clean shampoo. He made me lose my train of thought.

"All right, well, can I call you?" he asked.

We began to lope, making our first lap around the pond. "I would like that."

"Can I see you before you go?" he asked.

I threw him a glance, and noticed we both puffed out white clouds of air as our warm breath mingled. "I'd like that even more."

We finished our run, and it was easy for me to imagine Kane McCarthy existed on a different plane than he really did. One where I didn't have to hide seeing him. One where he didn't have a shady occupation. And one where we spent the holidays together. It was a novel idea. Novel and very, very dangerous to engage in. He held my jaw with his hand, tilted my head, and claimed my lips with his. His mouth settled over mine, and its sensation was addictive; I wanted it all the time. Another danger, I thought.

"Not to scare you away or anything," he said, "but I'm going to really miss you, Harper Belle."

I felt the blush creep over my skin. "I'm going to miss you, too, Kane McCarthy."

And I wished like anything that I didn't have to leave.

*   *   *

I'D JUST FINISHED PACKING my overnight bag when my cell phone vibrated on my nightstand. It was a text from Kane.

KANE: WHERE/WHEN TO MEET? I'M DYIN OVER HERE. AND STARVED.

I grinned and sighed. I could hear his accent, even in text message. He seemed so genuine. So sincere. Dangerous, yet…not. I thought about it.

ME: RIDGEVIEW RESTAURANT. JUST PAST COVINGTON. LOOK FOR THE SIGN ON THE RIGHT. YOU CAN'T MISS IT.

KANE: IN 30?

ME: RACE YA THERE ☺

KANE: YOU SMILED AGAIN. I LIKE THAT. SEE YA IN 30.

I dropped my phone in my small leather bag, inspected my room one last time. I counted the money I'd taken from my money box to be sure I had enough, and smoothed my tailored suit before shouldering my meager overnight bag, locking my door, and descending the steps from Delta House. The other girls had already gone; Murphy left the evening before. There was always an eerie silence about campus prior to holidays, when all of the students had left. A deafening calm that almost made my ears ring. Ghostly almost.

Sometimes, I wished I could just stay behind and enjoy it.

Setting my bags in the back seat of the Lexus, I started the engine, glanced once at Kappa House, and headed to the main gate. Soon I was halfway to Covington.

Kane had beaten me to the restaurant, and when I pulled into the mostly-vacant parking lot, he was leaning against his truck. Shades covering his eyes. Leather jacket. Worn jeans.

Boots. His hair switched every which way with the wind.

Perfect.

A slow smile crept over his face as I pulled up next to him, and although I couldn't see his eyes, I knew he watched me close. I stepped out of my car and he was there, my face in his hands, his mouth descending on mine. I drank him in.

I was getting way too used to it.

He pulled back, though, and kissed my forehead. Took off his shades. While his mood was buoyant, his eyes seemed heavier. Sad. "Let's eat."

Inside, one older couple sat close to the hearth at a small table. Kane led me over to a booth overlooking the ridge and pines and cottonwoods, and I scooted into my seat. Surprisingly, he slid in beside me. He draped an arm over my shoulders.

"Is this okay?" he asked.

I nodded.

The waitress came over—a thin, middle-aged woman with pale blonde hair. Kane ordered hot chocolate, and he looked at me. "Do you want some, Harper?"

I hesitated. I wasn't used to having things bought for me. But the waitress, well, waited, and I didn't want to seem like a weirdo. "Yes, please."

"Gotcha. You look over the menu and I'll come back with your drinks." She walked off, Kane thanked her, and he ducked his head to look at me closer. "Something's bothering you?"

Suddenly, that wary feeling returned. I usually ate once a day. Sparingly, to save money. I kept bananas and apples—anything that didn't need refrigeration, in my room, and I'd make them last all week. I didn't splurge on café lattes and hot cocoa. My routine seemed rather average and normal...until someone else got a glimpse into my private life.

Then it seemed strange. Very, very abnormal. Not average at all.

I pasted a smile. "I'm fine, really."

Silently, he studied me. The guy with more perception than I'd ever given him credit for. I didn't think he bought my lie, but he didn't call me out on it. For that I was thankful.

He opened the plastic menu in front of us and we looked over it together. When he chose a burger, I chose a small bowl of house soup. His gaze slipped to mine.

"Harper," he said softly after the waitress left. In his eyes, worry. Another thing I wasn't used to. "You eat like a bird. Aren't you hungry?"

"This will be just enough to tide me over until I get home," I answered quickly. "They'll have so much food prepared, I'll want to make sure I have plenty of room in my stomach." I smiled. "Besides. Soup is good. It's nice and warm." I sipped my cocoa. "I'm fine, really."

"Is it because you hate where my money comes from?" he asked.

I considered that. "Yes. And also I'm not a big eater, is all."

His smile warmed me. "Guess I'm just used to Olivia. God, that girl can eat."

I remembered that she could.

I remembered envying it at some point, too.

When our food came, we ate in not-too-uncomfortable silence. I sensed Kane was thinking about me and my awkward ways. About Thanksgiving. About him being with Brax and

Olivia, and me being, well. In my own direction. Soon, though, we were finished, and on our way out he grabbed two mints at the hostess' desk from a small wicker basket. He handed me one, and we both peeled the wrappers off and popped the mint in our mouths. As we left the restaurant, he draped his arm over my shoulders and pulled me against him. I liked the way it felt; warm, protective even. I fought the urge to sink into him. Sag against him. Tell him everything. To stay with him. Go to Olivia's folks for Thanksgiving. To see what it would be like to be…normal.

I didn't. Didn't do any of that.

At the car, he turned me to him, his arms sliding down my waist. Kane's touch stirred something inside of me: a heat, a fire, a desire I was brand new to. I understood it; I didn't know how to handle it. He lowered his head and kissed me, and the taste of the mint he'd just eaten lingered on my tongue.

"I hadn't counted on you, Harper Belle," he said quietly. "You came out of nowhere."

I simply looked at him, surprised by his words.

In his eyes, I heard more; could see he wanted to say a lot more to me, but didn't. Wouldn't. Maybe it was too soon? Maybe he was unsure of me. Just as I was of him. Either way, he swiped his lips across mine once more, and this time I allowed myself to breathe him in, sink into Kane. He groaned, deepened the kiss, and I was alarmed at how the fire inside of me flamed.

"Call me when you get to your folks' place, okay?" he said, then kissed the tip of my nose. "Drive safe. Watch out for idiots."

My face cracked as I smiled against the cold air. "I will. You do the same."

"Olivia's driving, thank God," he teased. "Queen of safe."

As I pulled away from the Ridgeview, I watched Kane as he watched me leave. Legs braced wide, hands shoved in his leather jacket pockets, hair sticking up every which way. He stood that way until I turned out of the little causeway leading from the restaurant. When I turned onto the main road, my breath eased from me. I'd been holding it for what reason? Hoping to keep hidden the things I wished to hide from Kane? Why did he matter so much?

Never did I expect the feelings I was experiencing. Had I kissed some random stranger, would I still be experiencing the same sensations? That fiery desire that, even now, miles down the road from him, still burned inside of me? Or was it happening because of him? Because we connected in a way I was too scared to explore. Too scared to admit.

I had too much old, bitter, baggage. I had that…thing inside of me that I wanted no one to ever see. Too much pain accompanied me. I was consumed with it. It'd never go away and I wouldn't wish it upon anyone.

As I drove, and got to that half-way mark between Winston and Belle House, my anxiety leveled out. I knew it wouldn't last; it was only because here, I was in the middle. Nothing was expected of me. I was not at school, where everyone thought I was a pampered upper-crust socialite who'd been born with a silver spoon in my mouth. And I wasn't at Belle House, where I wasn't really a Belle at all, and where I was more like an unwanted pregnancy; an orphan. A mistake. A reject.

In the middle, I could be me. No one cared if I was pretty. No one cared if I had money. Not one soul cared if my parents had been drug addicts, or if I'd been caught in the middle. That'd it all been because of me. My fault.

Here, I simply was me, and I breathed.

11. Home

ALMOST SEVEN HOURS FROM Winston, when the very last rays of dusk reached over the dense pines and cotton-woods and flowering pear trees, the lane leading to Belle House emerged from the shadows. I didn't need to put on my turn signal. No one ventured out here. Ever. Not anymore.

I turned up the lane and began my ascent, climbing the narrow lane now overgrown with underbrush. The wayward branches swiped at the side of my car, like fingers trying to grab at me, pull me into the dark depths of the woods. My breathing became harsh, fast, and I hit the accelerator. Gravel, pine needles and dirt spat out behind me as I climbed faster. I always hated this drive. Hated it.

Finally, I crested the hill and the darkened halls of Belle House greeted me once again. It reminded me of a toothless old man, grinning at me from the darkness. My headlight beams arced over the pillars of the entrance; dark, curtains drawn, lights extinguished. The cast iron lamp posts lay void of their flames; the circle drive empty. Remnants of the past year's storms lay strewn all over the lawn, the verandas; pine branches, old straw, pinecones and debris. I parked close to the veranda and with a heavy sigh, killed the engine and climbed out. Grabbing my overnight bag and my flashlight, I eased the door closed and headed to the entrance.

Who would've ever thought that, in a grand magnificent mansion such as Belle House, the key would be kept beneath the doormat? It almost made me laugh, but when I kicked the corner of the mat up with the toe of my pump, there it was, just where I'd left it. I bent down, grasped the copper key, and slipped it into the lock. For the first time in almost a year, I let myself in.

My hand slipped inside first, reaching for the light switch, and when I found it and flipped it, light flooded the breezeway. I stepped inside and closed the door behind me. Turned my flashlight off.

Home.

As I made my way to the living room, I flipped on every switch in the house until it blazed with light. Furniture sat like old ghosts, shrouded in sheets, awaiting life to enter once again. It never would. I hurried through the rest of Belle House, opening every door, turning on every single light and lamp—except for the third floor. I stood there, on the platform of the second floor, looking up. Instantly, my heart began to pound. Voices began to whisper in my head, and I slapped my hands over my ears to make them stop. Never,

ever did I venture up there. Where that room was. That cramped little closet no better than the dank kitchen cabinet I'd once hidden in. No, never again. Unwanted images began to streak across my memory, and my breathing increased. "No!" I yelled out. "Stop it!"

I turned and ran back downstairs as fast as I could.

After the lights were all ablaze I headed straight for the hearth in the hall. I dropped my overnight bag, and quickly stacked a few leftover logs across the grate. Poking shards of fat lighter beneath, I grasped a long match from the canister, struck it, and set the flame. Soon the aged wood began to crackle, pop, and I sat back and watched it spark to life. The smoky woodsy scent soothed me, in a way.

Outside, the wind picked up, and it creaked against the windows and doors, and my thoughts swarmed in my head. Thoughts of Kane, especially, and how much I'd wished he was here with me. But he couldn't be. He never could be. For him to be here would mean he'd learn my secrets. Learn of the nightmares. And I didn't want him to know that. Then, they shifted, my thoughts. To this big empty mansion, how there wasn't anyone here but me. Never would be. I'd called a few days before, knowing I'd be making the journey here and knowing I couldn't tolerate staying the night in the dark. So I had the electricity turned on, and although it'd just be for a few days, it was better than letting anyone at Winston see who the real Harper Belle was. A crazy orphan with a dead family. Dead, all except Corinne Belle, who'd been in Oakview Nursing Home for the past year and a half, wearing adult diapers and having to be fed through a tube in her stomach. She still had me, though. Kept me prisoner. Belle House? All the staff had been let go. The place deserted, left to me upon the death of my grandmother. I didn't want it; I wanted nothing from her. But she'd made sure otherwise.

Despite Corinne's stroke and fading health, there was nothing left. Nothing now but an enormous bank account and the good Belle name, according to whom you spoke to. This was my punishment. My legacy. And tomorrow, Thanksgiving, I'd dutifully go to Oakview and visit Corinne Belle. She'd pounded it into my head, from the very first day I'd arrived at Belle House, that I was privileged to live under her care, and under the Belle name. She'd enforced it in me that, no matter how rich she was, I hadn't earned a penny of it and that I'd best plan to pay her back for everything, one day. She'd supplied the best-tailored clothes, for Belle appearances, of course. The Lexus. Nothing more.

So for as long as I remembered, I saved every extra penny I had. To pay her back. Otherwise, she'd lock me away, she said. In a dark room with no clothes and no food where no one could ever, ever rescue me. She said I was mentally insane, an orphaned child with psychological problems no one would ever want. And if I wanted to make it in life, I'd keep it all quiet. Hide my psychosis or someone would see. And if that happened, she'd have me committed to an asylum. One far, far away so no one would ever suspect anything. So, I had hidden it all very well. Even after her stroke. Because somehow, she still scared the living hell out of me. Somehow, she could still see everything I did. And if it was something she disapproved of? If she thought sinful? There would be *consequences.*

Opening my overnight bag, I pulled out my cell phone. A missed call and two texts from Kane. *There'd certainly be a consequence if Corinne found out about him.*

She never would. I'd make sure of it.

KANE: DID YOU MAKE IT OK? LET ME KNOW YOU MADE IT OK?

KANE: HARPER? LET ME KNOW YOU'RE SAFE, OK?

My heart flipped at his words, and I wanted to call him back. I wanted to hear his voice. Instead, I sent him a text, explaining my lack of signal but yes, I'd made it safely. Then I powered off my phone before he could text me back, and shoved it into my bag. I pulled out the pair of thin blankets I'd rolled tightly and brought with me, opened one before the fire on the floor, and set the other close to it. Then I pulled out a bottle of water. A sandwich I'd bought earlier from the café. And my copy of *Sense and Sensibility*. I sat, read by the fire, and ate my meal.

As I lay on the floor later, book face-down against my chest, I turned and stared into the fire before letting my eyes drift shut. Kane's face appeared; chiseled, handsome, perfect. I certainly hadn't counted on him. His beautiful, flawless skin; rich, coffee eyes that knew way too much. He'd gotten to me, and I'd allowed it. How? So careful, all these years. Yet all it took was...him. I felt his lips on mine, and I found myself craving it, his scent, his touch—even his voice. Is this what it would feel like when he finally left Winston? Would I crave him like this? As I wavered off into what would surely be a restless night of sleep, I sighed, and kind of wished I hadn't met Kane McCarthy at all.

The next morning came faster than I'd expected, which was a good thing after all. The dark room on the third floor usually haunted me all night, every night, but this time, it hadn't. But my bones and joints were stiff from lying on the floor. The fire had nearly burned out, and I dragged myself from beneath the blanket and threw a couple more logs on to get the heat generating again.

I didn't waste the apple and banana I'd brought; I was expected to eat with Corinne, a traditional Thanksgiving dinner served by the nursing home staff. So instead I ignored the pangs in my stomach and tidied up in the bathroom just off the kitchen. A half-bath, it was big enough for my needs. I washed my face, reapplied my make-up, and swept my hair back in a sleek ponytail.

I inspected myself. No one would be able to tell I'd slept on a floor in a deserted, derelict old mansion.

By nine I was on my way to Oakview. My nerves didn't really kick in until I pulled into the parking lot. Once the one-story brick building's entrance caught my eye, I knew what lay just beyond it. To the left, down the first corridor.

I had to make myself breathe several deep, long steadying breaths before I got out of the car. Closing my eyes briefly, I gathered myself. My thoughts. My composure. Then I stepped out into the brisk November air and strode to the entrance.

The moment I opened the door, the inevitable scent of age, urine and bleach hit me square in the nose. I pasted my smile on, waved to the ladies at the front desk, and made my way down the corridor to Corinne's room. Number thirty-eight. The door was ajar, and I swallowed, breathed, stepped inside.

"Hello, Grandmother Belle," I said with a strong voice. Her eyes fluttered open at the sound of it, and they soon found me by the door. I noticed her pure white hair had been recently brushed and pulled up into a small knot on the top of her head. Deep lines cut into the skin of her powdery white face. Only the thin line of red lips marked any other color in her skin. I walked closer, and those cold blue orbs followed me the entire time. They were the only body parts she had control over, those eyes. They looked like ice as I sat in the chair beside her bed. "Happy Thanksgiving," I said quietly. And then I didn't say anything else at all.

Corinne Belle's stare bore into me, and I knew she loathed my being there. Loathed her own condition; once a proud, strong, controlling woman, she now had to rely on attendants for her each and every need. I knew my being there irritated her; or perhaps my appearance didn't suit her, because her breathing picked up. My eyes watched her chest rise and fall, faster and faster, until little grunts escaped her lips.

Immediately, as though she'd stricken me, I sat up. Folded my hands in my lap. And forced myself to look into those icy blue eyes. "Just so you know, I'm making all A's this semester again," I told her. "My GPA remains a 4.0. And our sorority just raised three thousand dollars at the Turkey Run for the homeless."

Still, she puffed. Breathed. Grunted. Glared.

Panic began to rise in my throat. I had no idea what she wanted. I know what I wanted. To run. Escape. To never ever set foot inside Oakview ever again.

Or to have to look into those frigid eyes of the woman who hated me. Who locked me in the dark room. Who humiliated me.

Hated me, yet had given me every Belle heir dime.

It made no sense. Not three months ago, Corinne's attorney had contacted me, telling me that just prior to her stroke, she'd made changes to her will, leaving everything to her only living relative. Me. I wanted so badly to tell Corinne Belle that I wasn't going to ever take her money. That I'd pay back every dime she sent. Every nickel she'd sank into my education, I'd give back. Somehow. Someday. It was dark money. And it wasn't mine.

Why was I still so terrified of her?

"There you are! Ms. Belle, you're looking just as beautiful as ever!"

I leapt in my seat at the sound of Corinne's nurse, Ms. Baker. A sweet woman in her fifties, she'd been caring for Corinne ever since her stroke. She had a cleft chin, which had somehow always fascinated me. And she always greeted me as though I was a slice of buttered bread. If she only knew.

Still, I smiled. "Happy Thanksgiving, Ms. Baker," I said.

"You visit a while and I'll bring your tray in once dinner is served," she said, and her eyes glowed with a certain spark of joy that I found myself envying. "It's exceptionally tasty this year!"

"Yes, ma'am," I replied. She'd said the same thing last year. "Thank you."

Ms. Baker hurried out but left the door slightly ajar; that left a slice of relief, a way of escape if needed. I slid my gaze to Corinne; those screaming eyes blazed at me, and I sat in silence, staring at my hands. Inside, my stomach knotted; part of me wanted to tell her things. Tell her about Kane. But I knew I dared not. It didn't matter that she was stricken with silence and immobility. She had power over me and she knew it. She had people watching me. At the first sign of my disobedience, she'd send them for me. To be taken to the asylum. God, I didn't want to go there.

I felt her gaze bear a hole in the side of my head, and I forced myself to turn and look at her. Tears gathered in my eyes, and I hated that I couldn't stop them. I said nothing. I'd told her about school. About the sorority. My grades. What more did she need to know?

Blessedly, Ms. Baker returned soon with a plastic sectioned tray of turkey and gravy, stuffing, yellow squash, and cranberry sauce. On the side, a slice of pumpkin pie and a cup of sweet iced tea. "Thank you," I offered, accepting the tray and setting in my lap.

"Oh, you'll need these," she grinned, handing me a plastic bag of silverware and a napkin. "Enjoy!" She checked Corinne's feeding pump that made a click-click sound every so often as it dumped a thick tan liquid into her stomach. At the door, Ms. Baker stopped and threw me a warm smile. "You're such a sweet granddaughter, you know? Coming here every holiday to sit with your grandmother." She turned her cheerful gaze to Corinne. "Isn't that right, Mrs. Belle?"

My grandmother's fiery glaze darkened as it shot toward Ms. Baker, who only laughed. Corinne starting grunting again, her chest rising and falling with her aggravated breath. "Oh, don't get yourself worked up in a tizzy over there. Enjoy your visit!"

My gaze shot to my grandmother. Fury poured out of her eyes like lava streams. Before the stroke, had anyone dared say something like that to her? Ms. Baker left the room, but Corinne's stare remained at the door, her anger reflecting onto someone else other than me. I nibbled at my tray—barely a bite from each except the squash, which was just too rubbery for my stomach to tolerate. After a sip or two of tea, I set the tray aside, rose, and smoothed my suit.

"I should be getting back," I said quietly, and Corinne's gaze fell on me once more. Icy blue fire shot forth, and she began to pant. Grunt. Breathe hard. With my hand shaking, I reached for hers and grasped it. It was cold, thin, veiny. "I'll see you in a few weeks," I said softly.

Then I lifted my tray and left Corinne Belle's room.

As I deposited my barely-touched meal to the kitchen, I noticed the staff was cheery and singing carols in the main hall, putting up their artificial Christmas tree. Boxes lay about, some opened with ornaments and red fuzzy bows spilling out the top. Ms. Baker waved goodbye as I headed to the lobby, and I didn't catch a full breath until I'd stepped outside and closed the doors behind me.

Hurriedly, I crossed the parking lot, but it wasn't until I'd managed to climb into the Lexus and close the door tightly behind me that I allowed myself to cry. With tears falling, I started the engine, backed out of my space, then left Oakview Nursing Home behind. At least for a few more weeks. One more visit. Then I'd have another break where I could just be at school, pretending I was someone entirely different than who I was.

I made it back to Belle House in record time, set another fire in the hearth, kicked off my pumps and changed into a pair of warm fleece pajamas. Beneath the blanket, I made it halfway through *Sense and Sensibility* before the last rays of daylight fell across the hall. Then I dug a banana out of my bag, sat cross-legged by the fire, and ate it. The moment my eyes drifted shut, the nightmares returned. I fought them all night. Those demons that hounded me. I woke up sweating, achey. I'd drift back into a restless sleep. By the time light shone through the drapes in the hall, I'd already been awake for an hour. I rose, dressed, and washed my face.

I spent the day preparing for my December visit, which basically included chopping more wood so that I'd have a fire to lay in front of when I came up for Christmas. I chopped for two solid hours. I didn't even realize blisters had formed on my hands until I stopped—and they'd begun to sting. After I loaded the wood inside, I ran cold water over my palms. I supposed they'd just have to heal on their own.

The Christmas visit would be more lengthy, as we had nearly three weeks before the new semester started back up after New Year's Day. It was a visit I dreaded, but I'd make sure I had enough to read. Enough to eat. I'd make it through, just like I always did. I called the electric company, deciding to keep the power on since it was just a few weeks away. At least then I wouldn't have to run through the place, switching on lights. I'd leave them on. Every single one of them.

That night, I laid by the fire on the floor in the gathering hall, and as the wind beat at the walls of Belle House, and the noises of an old decrepit mansion made frightening grunts and groans similar to the lady of the house who once ruled with an iron fist, I pulled the blankets up to my chin, squeezed my eyes shut. Fear stabbed at me—my old room was up there, after all, and the dark room on the third floor, and the memories that came with both chewed and clawed and pawed at the door like some wild beast. But I thought of Kane, the soothing softness of his husky voice, his all-knowing eyes, and his beautiful face. For once, the demons stayed away.

12. Savior

BY THE TIME MORNING cracked through the drapes in the gathering hall, I'd decided it was probably the longest I'd ever slept in Belle House. Ever. I credited it to thoughts of Kane, which had somehow soothed me. It frightened me, how many thoughts of him invaded me now. What would happen when he left? I hated thinking about it and refused to do so. I'd deal with it when it happened. And it would undoubtedly happen.

After stacking more wood by the hearth, and making sure the fire was properly extinguished, I gathered my things, closed the front door and locked it. Dropping the copper key back under the mat, I hurried to my car, climbed in, and left. Driving away from Belle House always felt like a double-edged sword; glad to be leaving, yet feeling as though a rabid dog was bounding after me, chasing me down the lane, down the bluff, until I'd safely reached the highway. Only then did I breathe easy. The drive was long. Quiet. Overcast. The blisters on my palms stung. I tried to fill my thoughts with anything other than my return Christmas visit to Belle House. So I thought of Kane. Of every moment we'd spent together since he first asked me directions to the observatory.

"It's not possible that Corinne Belle still has spies keeping an eye out on me," I said out loud. "Is it? She can't give commands anymore. How can she? She only has her mean cold eyes left." I watched the scenery pass by, and signs of winter clung to the half-bare limbs and browned grass. "No one stayed behind at the house. The attorney said there was no one else left, except me." I chewed my lip. "Only me."

I pulled through Winston's front gates just before dark. The campus was still quiet; most of the students would start straggling back through the gates late tomorrow afternoon, and that was fine by me. But when I turned down my street I noticed someone sitting on the front porch of Delta House. And it wasn't a Delta.

Kane sat in one of the rocking chairs, and the moment he noticed my car, he leapt up and jogged down the steps. Before I could turn off the engine he was reaching for my door handle. Surprised, I looked at his face; wrought with worry, lines pulled around his eyes, and his brows gathered together. I put the car in park, my doors unlocked, and he opened it.

"Hi," I said cautiously, and climbed out. He stood over me, close but not touching, although I wanted him to. His vibe was different; worrisome? Anger?

"You turned your phone off."

"Are you angry at me?" I asked. "I...you know I don't keep my phone on me like most girls."

His features shifted, eased, and those eyes searched mine, so deep, emotions raw. Then he sighed. "I'm not used to worrying—" he closed his eyes, sighed again. "I missed you."

That brought a smile to my face. A real, genuine smile. "I missed you, too." I glanced around the parking lot, just in case someone was watching. The thought made me a little edgy. "But I thought you rode with Olivia and Brax to her place?"

"I decided at the last minute to follow them instead," he answered, and his eyes dropped to my mouth. "Something in my gut told me I might want to come back a little early."

"Something other than the Thanksgiving Day football game?"

His eyes smiled. "I didn't need to be here for the game."

"Oh," I answered. My fingers itched to touch his soft, messy hair. I inspected him, and realized I'd missed everything about him. "Your nose is red." I grinned.

"So's yours," he replied. "And your lips are, too."

I glanced at the house. "Do you want to come inside?"

His gaze followed mine, then returned to me. "I thought you wanted to keep us a secret."

"Well, no one's around yet," I answered. "And it's not that I *want* to keep you a secret, Kane." That wasn't entirely true. I just didn't want him knowing about me.

He shifted his weight, and it moved him closer to me, crowding me against my car, and I found I liked it very much. "I thought maybe you'd want to have dinner with me. At Brax's place. Olivia's mom sent a ton of food with me and no way can I eat all of it by myself." He ducked his head, watching me.

"You've no meetings. No homework. No fundraisers to attend. Right?"

A smile tugged at my mouth. "Right." My body leaned closer to him. "Can I meet you over there in an hour? I'd like to clean up a little."

Kane's eyes smiled, and he bent over and sniffed my head. "You do smell a little smoky." The corners of his mouth lifted. "I like it. Even your cheeks are rosy. You must've had a good visit home." He winked. "I'll see you in an hour."

"See ya in a few," I said, and watched Kane as he shoved his hands in his pockets and started the walk back to Brax's apartment off campus. He glanced over his shoulder at me once, and I saw the whites of his teeth as he flashed me a smile. I waved and headed inside.

Quickly, I shed my clothes and showered, washing the wood smoke from my hair and body. Something was making me ache inside; it was an unfamiliar feeling, accompanied by dread. I knew what it was, actually. Only I didn't know what to do about it.

The Dare. I wanted no part of it now. Kane was not Dare material. Other than the fact that I wished like crazy he'd stop wasting his life running numbers. I still planned on convincing him to do something else with himself. But the Dare? Now that I knew him? He was above that. Above fraternity and sorority pranks and humiliation. It was stupid. And I was stuck. And despite the humility Olivia and Macie had endured, did I really, truly care a lick about the Kappas? I didn't. And it all seemed so childish now.

Part of me wondered if I should just tell him. But I quickly squashed that idea. He'd think I was an idiot for not only participating in it, but for thinking it up.

I'd have to figure out something else.

After I dried my hair and applied light make-up, I pulled my cream cashmere sweater dress from my closet and slipped it on, along with a pair of matching socks to wear beneath my black leather boots. Wearing my hair down, I tucked it behind my ears, gathered my coat, keys and purse, and headed to Brax's apartment. For a change, my mood felt light. Never had I returned from Belle House after Thanksgiving, or any time, really, to be greeted by someone like Kane. Never. I was usually filled with terror. Guilt. Now? My heart raced at the thought of being alone with Kane McCarthy, shaded from view, just the two of us. Worry niggled my brain, though. Would he see things I didn't want him to see? See me with those dark, wise eyes? I almost wondered if they contained super human powers. I shook the feeling off, deciding to treat myself for once to something I'd never had: companionship.

I parked in front of Brax's studio apartment, and before I made it to his front door, Kane had stepped out, grabbed my arm, and pulled me inside. The door hadn't even shut before his mouth was there against mine, seeking and tasting, and his hands loosened my coat and purse and dropped them onto the table by the door. Then his arms went around me, slid down to my waist, and pulled me against him as his lips moved over mine. My hands eased up his chest and found their way around his neck. I couldn't help the groan that escaped my throat, and he swallowed it down and deepened the kiss. Sensations rocked me, heated my insides, and I thought I'd melt into a puddle right there on the spot.

Then, with a final sweep of his tongue, his lips over mine, he pulled back. His coffee eyes were shining, deep pools of liquid glass. "Hey there," he said, smiling.

I smiled back. "Hey yourself."

"You wanna sit?" he asked, inkling his head toward the sofa.

"Sure," I answered, and Kane laced his fingers through mine and tugged. I couldn't help the gasp of pain when his big hand squeezed my palm.

"What is it?" he asked, then looked at my hand. Turned it over. Then he grabbed my other hand and did the same. "Harper," he said softly, and he gently ran his thumb gently over my blisters. He looked at me. "What did you do?"

Panic. Fear. "I um," I hesitated. "I helped chop some firewood." I gave a soft laugh. "Kind of a Belle family tradition." I found his gaze, and it watched me closely. "We all take turns."

Silently, he led me over to the sofa. A single candle in a mason jar sat on a big square coffee table, and the scent of maple and apples rose in the air. I sniffed, liking it. We sat down. He gathered my hands in his. "Next time wear gloves," he said. "Do you want me to doctor them?"

I smiled. "They're just blisters, Kane. I'll be fine." I sniffed the air, trying to push his attention away from my injured palms. "That candle smells so nice."

"Olivia's touch," Kane said. "She's good for my brother. Real good."

I looked around. I'd been in the apartment a couple of times before. "I think the trophy count is doubled since the last time I was in here," I noticed. "He really loves it."

"Lives it and breathes it," Kane answered. "Ever since we were kids." He laughed lightly. "The first thing he ever said to me, when we met, was, *Do you like baseball?*"

I looked at him. "When you met?"

157

Kane's eyes softened. "Yeah." He drew back a little. "You didn't know we were foster brothers?"

Fosta brothas. "I did, yes. Olivia told me. But I didn't know how old you were when you met." My mind whirled then, full of questions I had no right asking. Especially since I avoided my own. Somehow, I couldn't help myself. "What happened to your parents?"

Kane studied me for a moment, those profound eyes searching mine. Seeking trust? Avoiding fear? I thought for a moment he wouldn't answer me, and I regretted putting him on the spot. I'd have hated it. I'd have balked. Instead, he held my hand, stroked the top of my knuckles with his thumb. He looked down, then back at me, and I knew then he'd decided to trust me. I couldn't decide if I cherished that, or despised myself for it.

"Are we still playing the question game?" he asked, surprising me. "I answer one, you answer one? The truth and only the truth?"

Slowly, I nodded. And prayed he asked the right things.

His gaze dropped to our hands again, and he breathed. "You know how some kids turn out exactly like their dad or mom?" He looked at me. "I vaguely remember my mom. She…left us. A long time ago, before I was five. But one thing I know for damn sure. I'm nothing like my father."

The resentment in his voice shifted his features into something harsh, something much, much older. Something I wasn't used to seeing in gentle Kane McCarthy. I waited for him to continue. Squeezed his hand, sank closer to him.

"My father was a drunk, evil bastard," he continued. "The kind of scumbag who should've never fathered children." He

158

shook his head, wouldn't look at me. "Any excuse he could find to beat me or my sister, he was all over it."

My heart started slamming in my chest. "You have a sister?" I asked quietly.

His eyes sought mine. "Katy."

I swallowed past the lump in my throat. "Do you get to see her very much?"

A soft sigh escaped Kane's throat, and the smile he turned on me was sad, winsome, and vague. "As often as I can."

"What about your father?" I dared ask. I couldn't seem to help myself. I wanted to know more. All. Everything.

"Prison." He breathed again, squeezed my hand. Another winsome smile. "Your turn. And I get to ask four to your four. Fair enough?"

I nodded, fearful. But fair was fair. "Yes."

He half-turned, resting his back against the arm rest of the sofa. Outside, the light began to fade, and the candle burning on the coffee table flickered, making the shadows dance across Kane's handsome face. "Are you an only child?"

"Yes."

He nodded. "Where are your parents?"

"Dead, when I was eight. My grandmother raised me."

I'd even offered that one up on my own. It seemed relatively harmless enough. Didn't it?

"Why are you afraid of the dark?" he asked in that soft, buttery voice.

I glanced down, staring at our entwined hands. My breath caught in my throat, and I found the next breath even harder to draw. Kane's knuckle tucked beneath my chin and lifted my gaze back to his. "What are you so afraid of, Harper?"

In the depths of his brown eyes I saw mine reflected there; wide, fearful, unsure. "What is it you're hiding from everyone?" he asked quietly. His thumb grazed my jaw, my lips. "What's behind all this broken beauty? Tell me."

13. Lost

*D*EMONS ARE IN THE *dark, that's what. Blood. And they want to hurt me like they hurt my parents. Horrible noises that humans shouldn't make. Footsteps, creaking boards, and smelly kitchen sponges. Dark rooms with locks on the outside and asylums for girls who have psychological problems. That's what I'm afraid of. But I can't tell you any of that.*

Panic began to close my throat, and although I wanted to hide it from Kane, I couldn't keep my breath from trying to force its way out of my lungs. My eyes grew wider, and my skin flushed; hot and cold at once. My lips became tingly, numb, and I pushed away, tried to stand, but my knees gave way and I buckled back down.

"Harper, Harper, take it easy," Kane said, his gentle voice edged with concern. His hand wouldn't let go of mine; he pulled me to him, but I squirmed back.

"Hey, hey, I'm sorry," he crooned. "It's okay, you don't have to go there," he ducked his head, making me see his eyes. "Look at me, Harper. Focus. Breathe slower, honey. Nice and slow."

I couldn't; the breath wanted come fast, faster, but then Kane took my hand, placed it against his chest, and he again ducked his head until our gazes connected. "Feel me breathing, Harper? Feel my nice slow breaths?"

I did, and although I couldn't say anything, I nodded.

"Good. Make yours do the same as mine. Nice and slow. Be just like me."

With his hand pressing mine against his chest, I focused on the slow rise and fall as his air moved through. A heavy, faster thump-thump against my palm made me know his heart pounded. His eyes wouldn't leave mine, though. With him, I slowed my breathing. The panic began to fade. And the second he saw me relax, Kane pulled me into his arms. I went readily, and sagged against him. Tears leaked from my eyes, and shimmers wracked my body.

"Shh, Harper," he whispered against the top of my head. "I'm sorry, honey. It's okay, I promise."

"You can't say that," I said, and the sound muffled against the flannel button-up plaid shirt he wore. "You can't say that. You don't know."

For a while, Kane simply sat, with me resting against his chest, his hand stroking my hair. It soothed me, calmed me, and I was surprised by it. No one had ever been able to chase away a panic attack. No one.

"How long have you had them?" he asked gently. He knew I knew what he meant. The attacks. We were that in sync. Maybe he'd had them, too.

"Since I was eight," I answered. Finally, I sat up, and before I could dry my eyes with the backs of my hand, Kane's thumb was brushing the tears away. He lifted my chin. "I've been able to keep them away because," I looked away, although he kept my chin in his hand. "No one knows me." I closed my eyes, then looked at him. "Please don't tell." It was only a small facet of my life that Kane had accidentally seen. He didn't know the rest. *Jesus, please don't let him know...*

"Of course I won't tell anyone," he assured me. His thumb smoothed my brow. "You're safe with me, you know?"

Somehow, I really wanted to believe that. There was something incredibly protective about Kane McCarthy. Something, I imagine, from his past that he kept from me. Secrets. So very many secrets. Between the two of us, a bottomless trunk full of them.

"Do you want to get some air?" he asked, inclining his head to the front door. "We could take a walk?"

I shook my head. "I'm okay now."

His eyes sought mine, and he laced our fingers together once more. "You're such a contradiction." His lips moved like feathers against my temple. "You have to trust someone, at some point, Harper." He kissed the side of my eye. "Take my word for it. If you keep it all bottled up, you'll combust. And it might be something you can't control no matter how hard you try. No matter what persona you portray."

He was right and I knew it, and at that very moment, I wanted to tell him everything. Starting with the Dare. I opened my mouth, but no words would come. Not the right ones, anyway. Only dancing words. Those that danced around the true subject. I'd grown good at that. An expert. "You know how recovering addicts are always instructed never, ever to become involved with another addict?"

I looked at him then, and he was staring back at me, and those brown eyes pulled me in and swamped me.

"Is that us?" I asked. "Do we both have such traumatic childhood issues and secrets that we're too toxic to be together?"

Kane watched me in silence, and I was entranced by the way his Adam's apple moved when he swallowed. The way his chocolate colored hair shot out in so many directions. And the contrast of his eyes, brows and stubble against that pale skin. "I think my fears and secrets cancel yours out," he finally said. "And that leaves us reborn. New. Whole."

I gave a soft laugh. "I'm not sure what we are. Are you?"

He pulled me to his chest then, and the warmth of his body seeped into mine. "No, I'm not," he admitted. "But it's the realest thing I've ever had."

Those words struck me; almost as much as the mouth they came out of.

I felt the same way. Only, I didn't know how to show it. Wasn't sure if trusting Kane with all of my secrets was the smartest thing to do yet.

"Let's play it by ear, yeah?" he mouthed against my cheek, and that warm, slightly harsh Boston accent blended with the somber, easy tone of his voice.

I looked up at him. "Will you consider getting a non-illegal job? Or maybe even applying for classes—"

"Harper," he interrupted, but gently. "Trust me when I tell you this, okay?" He ducked his head again, forcing our gazes to meet. "When I say I can't quit the numbers, I want you know that I mean it. I'm not just some shady, lazy guy trying to get out of hard day's work and fair pay. I'm good at the numbers. I'm good at reading people. I make a lot of money doing it. More than I could doing anything else right now. And I need that."

Before I could say anything else, he stood, dragging me up with him. "Let's put all this gloomy talk behind us for now and eat. Olivia's mom—she's like a food fairy or something. It's amazing."

I laughed, and he stopped on his way to pulling me toward Brax's small kitchen and turned me around to face him. With his big hands, he framed my face, tilted my head, and lowered his mouth to mine. In his kiss I felt urgency; hunger. Desperation. Or maybe I was confusing his reactions with mine? I clung to him, learned how to taste, learned how to savor. Learned. It was all so new. Exciting.

And I knew there was much, much more.

As if he'd read my thoughts, Kane pulled back, breathless, and rested his brow against mine. His mouth moved to my ear. "It would be so damn easy not to stop," he whispered, and kissed my jaw. "So damn easy."

I breathed in. Out. "Then don't," I said quietly.

Kane shifted just enough to look at me, and his smile was warm, inviting, and oh so genuine. "I have to live with myself, Harper," he said. Smiled. Kissed me again. "I can't believe I'm saying this, but...when the time is right."

Without words ever being spoken, Kane knew I was a virgin. Of course he did. If I'd never been kissed before, odds were I'd never had sex before, either. I felt pretty positive Kane had lost his virginity a long while back. Yet he was willing to wait. For me? The feelings I had were a myriad of fears and hopes and desires. But one thing I'd come to recognize.

I liked the person I was with Kane. I felt like I wanted to laugh. Wanted to make jokes. I felt like eating a pizza, watching a movie. I actually felt…normal.

As long as no one else found out about my attacks. About my shady past.

About who I truly, truly was.

"Can there be lots of practice kissing while we wait?" I asked shyly.

In those profound eyes, I recognized desire. Laughter. And he pulled me against him, kissed my jaw, my lips, the end of my nose. Then he moved that sensual mouth to the soft outer shell of my ear.

"I'll kiss you anytime you want," he whispered.

And then he did just that.

And I knew then, without a doubt in my abnormal, warped mind, that I was lost.

Lost, forever.

14. Regrets

THE LAST DAY OF November came and went; only two and a half more weeks of the fall semester. Two and a half more weeks before the Dare would be revealed. Two and a half more weeks before I'd have to make the trip back to Belle House. For Christmas. To Oakview.

Alone.

I had regrets. Mainly, the Dare. I'd decided to talk to Murphy about it, see what she thought without giving too much away.

In my haze of budding romance with Kane, I'd forgotten how cunningly sharp Murphy Polk was.

"Hey," I said, walking up to her in the library. I draped my satchel over the back of the chair, pulled it out and sat beside her.

Tucking her lob behind her ears, her eyes assessed me, and she furrowed her brows. "Oh, I don't fancy that look. Not one bit."

"What look?" I asked. "How do you see a look?"

"Oh, I see one," she said. She pointed with her finger. "I can tell by that wee little wrinkle betwixt your brows there." She winked. "It's a definite look. And a dodgy one at that."

I sighed, studied the wooden tabletop for a second or two, then looked at her. "Kane isn't right for the Dare. The Dare isn't right, and I was stupid for suggesting it. I want to stop it."

That profound stare—similar, sometimes, to Kane's—eyed me long. Hard. And with such precision, I'd thought she had the super power of seeing straight through me. Me, and my façade.

Then, the Cheshire Cat smile.

"You *do* like him," she stated, matter-of-factly. One brow lifted. "Mayhap even love." Then her eyes rounded, and white showed completely around the hazel part. "Bugger me—you've had sex with him! You little minx!"

My face paled. "I—no! Murphy, be quiet!"

She laughed. "Bloody hell, Harper ol' girl, I didn't realize you were on the pull," she continued to grin. Shake her head. "Damn me."

I didn't know what *on the pull* meant, but she had it all wrong. "No, Murphy," I insisted. "We have not had sex. And I've not...pulled anything."

Her face screwed up before she burst out laughing. She slapped her hand over her mouth. "Well, why not? There's not a thing wrong with a good rumpy-pumpy," she winked, "or a bit o' slap and tickle—"

I couldn't help it. I laughed, then caught myself. "Murphy! Stop it!" I hissed.

A slow, wide smile captured her face. "Well now. There's something I don't see too often enough." She leaned closer, her knowing eyes roving my face. "Me thinks you've been a poser all this time, Ms. Belle. I rather fancy this new you."

I sighed. "I don't know what to do," I confessed. "I didn't think I'd, you know…"

"Fall for him?"

I didn't want to completely confess it, so I just sort of shrugged. Gave a wan smile. Murphy pulled me into a hug, timid, at first, because she was used to me backing away. But I allowed it. And she hugged harder.

"Right. Well, what shall we do, hmm?" she looked at me. "Damn Josh, all he worries over are his twig and berries. I mean he's totally fit and all, but," she blew out a breath. "He's been a challenge, I'll say." She shrugged. "But I sort of like him, too. And Leslie? She's got Jason eating out of her hand like a bloody dog searching for treats. I personally think that one's off his trolley, but that's neither here nor there."

"Maybe I should call a meeting? Discuss cancelling the Dare?"

A sly grin pulled at her mouth. "I second that motion, Ms. Belle. Well done."

The rest of the day flew by, and I'd felt somewhat lighter than I had in a long time. Just knowing the whole Dare thing was going to come to an end eased my mind. Truly, it hadn't set right with me for some time—even before I'd kinda started falling for Kane. I'd just been so angry about the Kappas' latest Dare victim, what they'd done to Olivia, that I hadn't given

169

much thought to what it truly meant. Despite the secrets I kept, I still had pride in the Deltas and what we stood for.

I'd let my anger lead me to an action that was irrational, and that made me little better than the Kappas.

I still wanted to keep a low profile with Kane—mainly because of his dealings with gambling. I'd wished I could try and convince him that there had to be something else he could do for income. He was intelligent—anyone could tell that just by talking to him. He was well-versed in so many subjects. Yet anytime I brought it up, he'd strategically shift gears. Change topics.

And, Kane had a way about him. A certain way that made me forget all about things like illegal gambling and betting on football games and taking money. The way he touched me with his eyes; how he held me in his arms? The way that profound stare never actually would leave mine?

It made me feel something I'd never, ever felt. In my life. Cherished.

I hardly knew what to do about it.

The Christmas Bake Sale had gone well. We'd raised nearly a thousand dollars, which we split between the local Toys-for-Tots Christmas organization and the local soup kitchen for holiday dinners. Brax, although not completely convinced Kane should pursue me, had eased up on his brother and he and Kane had both helped pass out toys, and had worn red and white striped elf caps with bells on the end. Olivia and I had laughed, and for the first time in my life, everything seemed…real. Part of something other than a nightmare. And the more Kane was in my life, the more faded the ugly part of my past became.

My phone buzzed in my purse on my way out of Psych, and I stopped beneath the magnolia tree in the quad to answer it.

KANE: I HAVE A SURPRISE. DRESS WARM. DOUBLE WARM. MEET ME AT BRAX'S AT 6.

My mind flashed. I'd decided to call a meeting tonight, to disclose my reservations about the Dare. To bring it to an end. I suppose it could wait one more day.

ME: HINT? ☺

KANE: NICE TRY. SEE YA THEN.

When I got to Delta house, Murphy was just leaving. Friday night, she was no doubt heading to meet up with Josh. "Hey, can I borrow those fleece leggings again?" I asked.

She smiled and waved. "Second drawer, love. Right next to me knickers. And grab that black wooly jumper in the closet, too. It'll look scrummy on you."

"Thanks." I shook my head, ran inside, and hurried through a shower. Pulling on the olive fleece leggings, I matched my Nordic winter boot socks, and a black turtle neck. I searched through Murphy's closet. I knew a jumper was a sweater, only because she'd informed me of that British adjective not that long ago. It was baggy, hanging to my mid-thighs, but comfy and warm. Quickly, I dried my hair, applied a little make-up, pulled one of Murphy's winter beanies over my head and zipped up my boots. Grabbing my bag, I headed out the door.

To Brax's.

For some unknown surprise that left butterflies tickling my stomach.

15. Kane

"WHY, BRO? I DON'T fuckin' understand you, man!"

I stared calmly at Brax. He paced back and forth in his living room like a caged big cat. He'd stop. Rub his head. Put his hands on his hips, stare at the ceiling a moment. Swear. Pace more. I just waited.

"After everything we've been through, since we were kids," Brax continued. "I don't get why you have to do this." He stopped and squatted down in front of where I sat on his sofa. "You're better than this. I know you are. If I can escape it, brother, so can you."

Brax didn't know just how deep into the numbers I was.

How, no matter even if I did want out, I couldn't get out. Not now. I looked at him, those crazy blue eyes pleading with me. I studied the scars he bore, and I remembered when they

172

were fresh. Raw.

"I'll be gone soon," was all I could manage to say. "I won't bring anything down on you, Brax—"

"Jesus, man, it's not about that!" he growled. "You can't keep up this life, Kane. The boys at the frat house might not be dangerous," he pointed at me. "But I know you. You're not playing with college boys. You're using them as cover for the big boys."

I eyed him quietly. Yeah, he knew me pretty well. "I'm not you, Brax," I said. "I don't have a golden arm. All I have is my perception and a way with numbers." I gave him a stern look. "Let this go."

"And let you what? Leave tread marks on Harper as you skid out of town?" he said harshly. "That ain't you, either."

He was definitely right about that. "I won't hurt Harper," I said.

"How can you make that promise when you know good and fuck well you'll leave here. Leave her. You don't think that's hurting her?" He rubbed his head and stood. "She's not like most girls here, man. There's something about her. Something that reminds me of us." He returned a hot glare at me. "I don't think she's the one you want to fuck over."

"I'm not gonna fuck her over. Christ, Brax," I said angrily.

"Leaving her behind? You're gonna break her fuckin' heart," he said. "And you goddamn well know it."

I stood, paced, found myself in the kitchen where I leaned against the counter. "I really like her, Brax. You're right. She is different. She is like us." With my hand I scrubbed the back of my neck. "It's all I can think about."

Some of the tension eased out of the harsh lines in Brax's face. "So. What are you going to do about it?"

I shoved my fingers through my hair. "Hell if I know." I looked at him. "I'll talk to her."

"I'm serious, Kane," Brax said. "Something's off with her. I've felt it ever since I first met her." He looked at me. "I think she's been through some serious shit. She doesn't need you making things worse."

I nodded, pushed out a sigh. "I recognize it, too. And I fuckin' hate it."

"Think about it," Brax said. "Think about quitting the numbers, okay? Before you get in over your hard fuckin' head." He walked to me, draped an arm over my shoulder. "I love you, man. I don't want to see you get hurt. Or Harper."

I wished I could tell him. How I'd managed to keep it from him all these years, I didn't know. But I didn't want him to know. Didn't want to put him or Olivia at any risk, and knowing Brax, he'd react in a way that would be unpredictable. "Can I borrow your bike?"

Brax looked at me with a hooded gaze. "Why?"

"I'd like to take Harper out on it. I don't think she's ever been on one before." I nodded. "And I'll talk to her."

Brax rubbed his hand over his head. "I don't fuckin' like this, Kane. I don't."

"I'm going to see her whether you like it or not," I informed. "I'm not asking permission. It'll just be with your bike, or without."

My brother glared at me for several moments. "All right. But talk to her. Don't just brush her off or you'll have me to fuckin' deal with. And figure out about the numbers, Kane. I don't want you getting into shit, then bringing that shit back here. Around Olivia." His face grew tight. "We'd have a problem, then."

I didn't want to get his hopes up. But I didn't want to leave my brother on bad terms. Before long, my time here would be up. My welcome worn. And I'd have to go. "You got it," I half-lied.

It was one of the hardest things I'd ever done, not telling Brax. But it was for his own good.

My phone buzzed in my pocket, and I glanced at the screen. "I gotta take this, man," I said. Brax's face grew tense, but he gave a nod, and I headed outside.

The cool air whisked against my face as I walked to my truck and leaned against it. "Yeah, well, that's what I wanted to hear," I said into the phone. "I don't care that they're going to be pissed. That's the name of the game, man. It's the chance you take when you place a bet. It's why it's called a bet."

I listened for a moment, unworried. I'd had unhappy customers before. Plenty of times. Most people knew when they played numbers, there was always a crap chance they might win, or one where I would win. This time, I won.

"Make the pick-up," I said. "I'll deal with them tomorrow if they have a problem."

I hung up, shoved my phone in my pocket, and craned my neck to look up at the sky. The late afternoon sun touched the lazy white clouds streaking overhead, burning the edges as dusk approached. I knew that once night fell, billions of stars would blink, linger. I understood Olivia's fascination of them.

Just like I understood Brax's fascination of Olivia.

Rather, his love. Damn. My baby brother was in serious, serious love.

Would I ever be free to do the same?

16. Scars

"**Y**OU'RE JOKING."

Kane's soft laugh made his eyes dance. "I'm not." His head dipped, and firm, slightly cool lips pressed against mine, swiped once more, then opened his eyes and looked at me. Mine were open and now they crossed.

"Do you trust me?" he asked.

"I do." I didn't even hesitate. It was frightening, yet there it was. "But I've never been on a motorcycle before."

Kane drew his brows together. "You live in Texas and don't own a pair of jeans, either," he accused, and leaned close so that his lips hovered over mine. "And until recently, you've never been kissed." He pressed his mouth to mine. "New experiences, Ms. Belle. There's a million of them, just waiting for you."

He was right about that. I looked skeptically at Brax's bike. I knew who it belonged to. I'd seen Brax riding Olivia around on it before. "It looks dangerous."

Kane stood back, held his arms out, and shrugged. "Do I?"

I tapped my chin. "Hmm. Let's see. Leather jacket. Check. Rugged jeans. Check. Rugged boots. Check. Slightly scruffy jaw. Check." I inspected him further. "Smoky eyes that make my knees all wobbly."

"Check?" he grinned. "Point made. But you know I'm not." He dipped his head. "So come on already. Looks can be deceiving and you know it."

"Go on, Harper," Olivia said, as she and Brax joined us in the lot by his apartment. "It's really a lot of fun."

I quirked a brow. "That's coming from a girl who likes getting thrown from a horse."

Brax burst out laughing. "She gotcha there, Gracie."

Olivia smiled. "It'll give you a valid opportunity to hold onto his muscular stomach."

I slipped a glance at Kane. He wagged his brows. I sighed and smiled. "Okay, okay. I'll do it."

Kane clapped his hands together. "Let's go!"

Brax leaned close, speaking words only meant for Kane, and Olivia pulled me aside. "He really likes you, you know," she said softly. "I've seen a change in him since meeting you. I can't explain it, really. He's always pretty even-keeled." She smiled. "Just...changed. Like he's been searching for something and has finally found it."

I met her gaze; knowing, wise, a lot like Kane. "For me, too."

Her smile widened, pulling at the scar on her lip. "That's good to hear." She sighed. "I know you have family, but you're more than welcome to come spend Christmas with us. We'd love to have you."

That familiar ping of uncertainty, of fear, of absolute dread that was so easy to ignore when fun and Kane and kisses stood in front of it, hit me in the stomach. "Thank you, really," I answered. "But yes, I'll be going to my family's."

She nodded. "You know to call if you ever change your mind?"

I smiled. "I do. Thank you."

"All right Ms. Belle," Kane's voice sounded beside me. "Time to ride out."

I blew out a nervous breath, walked over to the bike. "Whatever you say."

Kane straddled the seat, bracing the bike with his muscular legs. Brax helped me on. His strange eyes found mine, and by his brusque attitude I could tell he still wasn't liking Kane seeing me. "Don't lean against the turn, and don't try to stand and shift on the pegs." He reached down, grasped both of my arms and circled them around Kane's waist. His blue eyes stood in stark contrast to his scarred face. "Hold on, lean with Kane." He tapped my nose. "You'll love it. Promise." He helped me into my helmet, tucked my chin strap, bumped fists with his brother, and Kane started the engine. It rumbled beneath my backside, a tingling feeling that made me want to laugh out loud.

With a wave, Kane took off, and I tightened my arms around him, snuggling my hands beneath his leather jacket. The ridges of his abdomen pressed like stone against my palms, and I was intrigued by his body. How it might look without a shirt or a jacket on. Nothing but skin and muscle.

Daylight sat at the edge of dusk; it looked wintry out, with the sky streaked with gray and white and darker gray and ginger, and the trees now barren of leaves. We drove along, toward Covington, and I still had no idea where Kane was taking me. At the moment, I didn't care. This *was* fun! I liked how the sun dappled through the trees and flashed against my face shield, and I found myself wanting to go faster, faster. The bike rumbled beneath me. The wind whipped at me. And Kane's warmth seeped into mine as I hugged him close. I watched the scenery pass by, cars, trees, farmhouses, as though on an old-fashioned movie reel. It seemed...surreal. As though I was peering into someone else's life. A life where monsters and grandmothers and dead parents didn't exist. I liked this life. I wanted to keep it.

We'd just reached the next town past Covington, a small little two-horse town called Manna. The sun had dropped, the sky had grown darker, and the temperature had grown colder. Kane pulled into a tiny gas station; empty, save the two pumps on the side of the brick building. Knocking the kickstand with his boot, he propped the bike and raised his shield. "Gotta fill up the tank. Be right back," he promised, and I sat there and waited. I waited for what seemed like a long, long time. A big truck roared past, then slowed and backed up. It pulled in behind the station. The owners, maybe? The engine shut off, and I sat and waited on Kane to return from paying for the gas. What was taking so long?

I looked around me, at the single lane road running past the little gas station that sat on a bluff. Then I heard shouts coming from somewhere close. Behind the station, maybe? The voices grew louder, and I worried something might be wrong. I threw my leg over the bike's seat and slowly walked toward the station's entrance. The voices grew louder; I thought I heard Kane's. Peeking inside the gas station, I saw no one there except the clerk. A college aged guy, maybe my age. He spared me a quick glance, then a nod, before he went back to whatever he was doing by the register. Kane wasn't inside the station. Where could he be?

Confused, I eased out the door, and the voices caught my attention again.

"No goddamn Yankee's gonna take my fuckin' money," a gruff, older male's voice rose in anger. "You fuckin' hear me? I'll take that fuckin' jacket, too, bitch! And that bike!"

"Yeah, you fuckin' rigged them numbers, boy," another man's voice accused. "You might fuck those pussies at the frat house over, but we ain't frat boys!"

Grunts. More swears. More than one voice. More like, four. Oh, God, Kane was in trouble from those stupid bets he was running. Fear for Kane propelled me to step closer, look down the embankment of pine needles. There, in the creek. A shirtless, white body, clad only in jeans and boots. Dark hair.

My insides froze as fear stabbed me. Kane was getting a beating. A bad one. He was down, and every time he'd try to rise, another would kick him in the ribs.

"Stop it!" I suddenly yelled, and my cracked voice shot out over the creek bed. "I'm calling the police right now!"

"Go fuckin' shut her up, will ya?" one said.

"Get out of here, Harper!" Kane growled and surged to his feet then, threw his bare arms around the one closest to him, the one headed toward me, and dragged him down to the ground. In seconds, Kane had straddled him, and his fist was pounding into the stranger. Another guy headed straight for me; older, not a student. None of them looked like students. I turned and ran into the store.

"Hurry, lock the door!" I yelled, and the kid surprisingly jumped up and did just that. "Do you have a cell phone?" I'd left mine at Brax's.

As he locked the door, he handed me his phone. I paused. If I called the cops, Kane might get arrested. Quickly, I dialed my own number. It rang. Rang. I prayed someone would pick it up and answer it.

"Hello?" It was Olivia.

"Olivia! It's Harper! I'm just outside of Covington at a gas station. Some guys—they're beating Kane bad." I looked at the store's door, and the guy had gone. "I didn't call the cops. Please tell Brax to hurry!"

"Okay, stay away from them, Harper! Brax will be there as soon as he can." She hung up, and I handed the phone back.

When I went to the door, the truck was speeding out of the store's lot. I watched it crest the hill and disappear. Brax's bike was just where I'd left it. They hadn't stolen it after all.

Then I twisted the lock and took off outside.

"Should I call the cops?" the guy asked behind me.

"No! No, don't! Please," I begged. I ran. Skidded down the embankment in my heeled boots. Kane was lying in the creek bed; motionless, half on his side. I stumbled until I was next to him. The shadows had grown long, so long I could barely see. But I could, though. I could see enough. And what I saw made me cringe. Made my heart beat faster.

My hand went to his arm. It was cold, and I gave it a shake. "Kane?"

A low groan escaped his throat. I sighed with relief.

And then my eyes inspected him for injuries. His ribs were red where he'd been kicked. His face was already turning purple, his lip was cut, and his knuckles were raw and bleeding.

Then, I saw his back. And I couldn't help the sharp intake of air as I gasped in shock. Disbelief.

I nearly fell backwards. It felt as though I'd been punched in the stomach.

Just as I reached for him, for the puckered skin across his shoulder blades, his eyes fluttered open.

"Don't," he said hoarsely. "Please, Harper, don't." He pushed up on his elbows, fell back down.

It was done, though. I'd already seen what he didn't want me to. Another of Kane's secrets.

I reached for his face instead, and those profound coffee eyes regarded me. Filled with pain. With shame. With Fear.

"Sorry," he mumbled, then coughed. "They came out of nowhere. I'm so sorry," he grunted. "No cops, Harper. Please." He pushed up again, fell.

"Shh, no cops," I crooned. "I only called Brax. He's on his way." I smoothed his hair from his eyes. He was shivering now, his bare skin lying in the two inches of cold creek water. I took my black wool coat off, draped it across him, but he pushed up. This time, he made it out of the creek. I helped him up, and he leaned on me, but I could feel his sagging weight. "I think you need medical attention, Kane—"

"No," he said. "I'm okay." He wheezed that last part, and I didn't think he was okay at all. My coat barely draped across his broad shoulders, but I held it there, covering his back best

I could. When he looked at me, he looked with his entire soul. He said nothing. His eyes screamed. I just laid my head against his shoulder, holding him as steady as I could.

The sound of a rumbling motor roared close by, and at first, I thought the men who'd attacked Kane had returned. Fear froze my insides, and my gaze shot around the creek bed. Then doors slammed, and Brax's distinct voice called out.

"Harper! Kane!" he yelled.

"We're down here!" I yelled back, and in moments, Brax appeared. Another big guy was with him. Cory Maxwell, his friend and another Silverbacks baseball player. They both skidded down the bluff. Brax's face was drawn in worry, in anger; frightening, terrifying.

"I got this, Harper," Brax said, and he and Cory grabbed Kane by the arms and helped him back up the embankment.

My coat slipped off. My eyes darted to Kane's back, and my stomach nose-dived again as though I'd been punched. Seeing it once had been enough. Seeing it again was even worse than the first time.

Cut into Kane's skin, in what couldn't have been done without incredible pain involved, was the word *Stupid*.

It was at that moment when I felt like my life hadn't been quite as bad as I'd once thought.

17. Truths

OLIVIA SAT BESIDE ME on Brax's sofa, waiting. Brax was in the bedroom, out of sight, wrapping Kane's ribs with tape; something Kane had apparently taught Brax growing up in foster care. Every so often I'd hear the hiss of pain pushing past Kane's lips. Olivia grasped my hands, already clenched together in my lap.

"Brax will take good care of him," she said. "He won't let anything happen to him."

I nodded, and couldn't help but wonder if Olivia knew what I knew. What was inscribed by either a knife blade or some other sharp object, into Kane's back. Purplish-pink and puckered, it glared from his otherwise pale, flawless skin.

Stupid.

Who would've done something so horrible?

Heavy footsteps fell toward us, and Brax lumbered up to the sofa. His face was grave, but those strange blue eyes looked kindly down at me. I rose, but he placed his big hand on my shoulder. "He's sleeping right now, Harper," he said.

"I know," I answered, and looked toward the bedroom. The door was cracked, but I couldn't see anything. "Maybe I can just sit by him?"

"Actually," Brax said. "I need to talk to you."

I met his odd gaze. "All right." I sat back down.

"I'm going to make some hot tea," Olivia said, rising. "Harper?"

I shook my head, and she offered me a smile and moved across the studio, to the sink. Brax sat down beside me, his muscular forearms resting on his big thighs.

"Kane and me, we learned things the hard way growin' up. I met him in a pretty decent foster home. Nice people. But the good ones never last." He looked at me. "We were split up after that, but stayed in the same district." He smiled. "Kane was always lookin' out for me, and would beat the holy fuck out of any wise ass who tried to bother me." He ducked his head, much in the same gesture Kane did with me, and captured my gaze. "To this day, I'd die for him. But, to this day there are things I still don't know. About his past." He clasped his hands together. "I know he had a little sister, younger than me. Used to take her beatings for her. That was his real dad who did that shit to his back." He rubbed his head with his hand. "I don't know much else, other than the prick is in prison."

I drank it all in, every horrible word. Guilt rushed over me, for ever feeling sorry for myself. I wanted to go to him, so badly. But Brax kept me beside him.

"See, I don't know why Kane stays in the numbers," he continued. "He's wicked smart. But I do know one thing about my brother," he said, and I looked at Brax Jenkins then. Waited. "He's strong. And he's honorable. And when he's got your back, he's got it for life." He cocked his head. "So what I'm sayin' is, he's got your back. Make sure you have his, too."

My heart was in my throat. I couldn't say anything. Only breathe. Soak in every word. Every unbelievable word.

"Give him some time, Harper. For you to see his scars? It might seem like something small to you, or to anyone. But it's not. He's ashamed of them, and he'd have done anything to keep you from seeing them."

I nodded, understanding. "He doesn't want to see me, does he?"

Brax's strong hand grasped my shoulder and squeezed. "It's not you, sweetheart. It's something he's got to deal with. Let him. It's shitty, I know—but it's just our way." He leaned close. "You know, us Southie boys do things a little different."

He tried to lighten my mood, but it didn't really work. "I know," I replied, and part of me did understand. I rose, and turned to Kane's brother. "Thanks, Brax," I said quietly. "Please…let me know if I can do anything. And tell him," I looked up, into Brax's startling eyes, and words failed me, "that I'm thinking of him."

Brax's face relaxed as he smiled, and it was like some magical transformation. Harsh turned to handsome. No wonder Olivia had fallen so hard for him. "You know I will, half-pint."

Olivia walked me outside, and darkness shrouded us both. She'd pulled a red slouchy beanie over her head, and her long sun-kissed braid hung loose and messy over her shoulder. The yard light beamed around her like a halo.

"I'm sure he'll come around, Harper," she said. "Those two." She shook her head. "Their stories are unbelievable. The ones they share, anyway." She sighed. "I'm sure there are some things they'll always keep to themselves. It's a rough life they led."

I nodded. I didn't know what to say.

She smiled and hugged me, and I was so stunned that I didn't even flinch. "There are a lot of us who've had things happen that we'd rather forget," she said against my hair, then looked at me. "I'm here if you need a friend," she said sweetly.

"Thank you, Olivia," I returned.

And I left.

I laid in my bed that night, my mind filled with the drastic events of the day. The brutality of Kane's anger as he'd surged up and attacked had stunned me. I knew he'd been capable. He was just…always so gentle, so soft spoken. So in control. It was a shock to see him pound into someone with such fury.

I had cheered him on, though. I'd wanted him to beat the hell out of those guys. The way it'd taken three men to finally put Kane down? There was physical strength, yes, but it also took mental strength to get back up after a beating like that.

In my mind's eye, the ragged letters cut into his back anchored there, and no matter what else I tried thinking about, that came to the forefront. I don't know why I needed to know more, but I did. Brax didn't even know all the details. What made me think I ever would?

The next evening, I called a meeting with the Deltas.

"Ladies," I began. Back at the podium, usually tucked neatly against the wall in the corner of the common room, I once again gripped the wood with my palms. "After giving careful thought, I feel that I was perhaps too hasty for vengeance with the Kappas and their Dare." I glanced at the sisters. "I won't beat around the bush," I continued. "I feel the need to call off our Dare."

Several questioning *what?*'s filled the common room, so I continued.

"Morally, it's just not right," I urged. "We as Deltas are better than that, aren't we?"

"Well, what about teaching the Kappas a lesson?" Anna Conners called out. Her voice was edgy and frustrated, and I could tell she was not on board with my decision.

"The best lesson is to set by example," I encouraged. Several groans, mostly from the younger sisters, filled the room. I continued. "Sure, the Kappas might laugh at us. And they probably will continue to exploit their Dare victims. But we aren't responsible for their reformation. Or their punishment." I looked out over the crowd, catching several sisters' gazes. "It's not right to play with someone's emotions, no matter who they are."

"I second the motion," Murphy called out.

I gave her a smile.

"I agree, too," Leslie added. "Plus, I really like Jason!"

Several girls giggled.

"I think it's a mistake," Anna replied. "I think they shouldn't get away with what they do."

"You're right," I agreed. "But it's not our place to dish out their consequences."

Consequences. The word nearly made my stomach queasy.

Several moans still filled the common room. They didn't dissuade me.

"Is everyone clear on this matter?" I said clearly. "The Dare is officially off."

The sisters clapped, a sign that the majority agreed.

And I was glad at least one thing was off my conscience.

Over the next several days, I heard nothing from Kane. Olivia texted me each day, letting me know of his condition. Broken ribs, most likely, and contusions to the face and anywhere else those idiots had kicked and punched. Kane had played hardball with some older guys in Covington, and they hadn't particularly liked their outcome. Cory Maxwell had found out one of the Kappas had not only tipped the guys off, but had told them where Kane would be. They'd followed us that afternoon, and had beaten Kane for his involvement in their bets. Olivia said Brax went nuts, but Kane convinced him to let it go. He wasn't saying much else. And he wasn't calling or texting me. The depth of sadness that created inside of me left a gap. A hole. How had I let my emotions get so far gone with Kane McCarthy? And so fast? Each day that passed, I felt more hollow. More cold. I felt like I just wanted to crawl back inside myself. Hide. But I couldn't. I had to keep up the façade I'd always had.

The next afternoon, my art appreciation class dragged on and on until finally, it ended. I gathered my briefcase, my bag, and started across campus to the café. No one stopped to talk to me. No one smiled, waved, or said hello. I suppose I'd always preferred it that way. Only now, I noticed it more. Kane was right in his assessment of me. I really didn't have any friends. Other than Murphy and Olivia. I moved through the crowd unnoticed. Invisible. And for the first time since arriving at Winston, it bothered me.

At the café, I bought my usual turkey sandwich, a bottle of apple juice, and quickly headed to my car. In minutes I was at the park in Covington, and I'd claimed my bench. The crisp breeze wasn't overbearing, but it was chilled. The sun edged closer to the tree line behind the lake, and I peeled the plastic wrap off the sandwich and took a small bite. My appetite had fled completely, so I sat with the plastic container in my hand, watching the joggers on the running path. Kane filled my thoughts.

The image of his scarred back flashed before me. What had he truly endured? What kind of torment had he gone through in his young life? It had to have been a never-ending nightmare. How had he turned out to be so caring? So gentle? I knew he still carried his demons, though. Just like I did. The difference was, he had courage. He had the strength to put his horrors behind him and carry on with his life. Why couldn't I be more like that? Instead, I kept right on hiding with my monsters, behind my grandmother's money and the affluent Belle name. I was a coward. Plain and simple. What made me think Kane deserved to be strapped by someone as damaged as me? What made me think I deserved a guy like Kane?

"Pardon me," a brittle voice said beside me. "Is this seat taken?"

So deep in my thoughts, I was taken off guard. When I looked, a thin, petite elderly woman stood close to the bench. Her hair was white and cut in a jaw-length bob. She wore a pair of black sweatpants, a pair of sneakers, and a Texans sweatshirt. On her head, a white flowered skully with pink flowers.

"Oh," I answered. "No, please," I offered. I fought the urge to bolt; I preferred to sit alone, and until now no one had ever asked to sit with me. Not wanting to be rude, I stilled my legs, though, and gave her a smile. The one she returned came easily to her lips, and created lines around her mouth and eyes.

"Thank you," she said sweetly, with her little tinny old voice. She sat down.

I was unsure what to do then, so I took another tiny bite of sandwich and continued staring at the lake. Small shuffles beside me had my curiosity up, and after sliding a side glance toward the old woman, I saw she'd retrieved a small plastic bag containing three slices of bread. She took one out, ripped off a few pieces, and threw them on the ground in front of us.

"Quack-quack-quack," she mimicked, calling out to the handful of ducks at the lake's edge. Just that fast, they began to waddle toward us, returning the quack with gusto and excitement. Like they knew her. I remembered her then, always standing at the water, throwing bread. Quacking to the ducks. I hadn't given her much thought.

A familiar, uncomfortable feeling settled over me, and I started to stand. Escape.

"Oh, please," the woman said. "Stay for a while longer, won't you? And watch the ducks with me."

Stunned, I just looked at her, and her smile was soft and warm.

"I miss the company of another person, sometimes," she said. Her green eyes, somber and soft, pleaded. "Won't you stay?"

Somehow, she'd convinced me with those kind eyes. "All right," I answered, and settled back down. When I noticed she was watching me close, I gave her a hesitant smile.

"I see you here sometimes," I said quietly. "With the ducks."

She nodded, and her bob bouncing along her jaw. She smiled. "I see you, too."

The ducks had made it to the bench, and were gobbling the bread up as fast as the woman could break it off and toss it down. She handed me a piece, and I took it. Eyeing her, I did what she did: broke the bread into small pieces and threw it down. A fat white duck hurried over, scooped the bread up with his orange bill, tilted his head back, and chugged it down. My mouth tugged, and I grinned. When I glanced at the woman, she was watching me.

"Why are you so sad?" she asked. "I've noticed. Pretty girl like you, coming out here alone all the time. Eating alone." She snugged her hat down, and I noticed how frail and bony her hands were. "I wish every day that I wasn't alone. So what's bothering you, dear?"

I envisioned what it would've been like had Grandmother Belle been as sweet as this old lady. It was hard to imagine. Dare I talk to her? Tell her things? I threw a few more pieces of bread down, the ducks now gathered at my feet. The woman waited patiently for my answer.

I smiled. "I've always been alone," I said. "Until recently."

A slow grin pulled at her mouth. "You met a boy," she stated. "I saw him, too. Devilishly handsome, I'd say." She giggled, and the sound came out squeaky. "Cute tushie."

I gave a light laugh and nodded. "Yes." I looked at her. "We both have rough pasts," I admitted. "Something…happened recently. I think I may have lost him forever." Tears stung my eyes, just from confessing my fears out loud. I willed them to stay hidden, behind my lids, so they couldn't be seen.

"I see," the woman said. "That does happen from time to time." With one final toss she threw the last of her bread down. "Do you love him?"

The question stabbed me, and I pondered it. "I…don't know. I've never loved anyone before."

"Well, I declare," she said softly. "That's about the saddest thing I've ever heard." She half-turned toward me, crossing her skinny little legs at the knee. "You'll know if your heart has been lost when you put his needs before yours. When you'll do anything to keep a smile on his face and pain out of his heart." Her smile sombered. "I met my Sam when I was only thirteen years old," she started. "He was fifteen." She winked. "I like older men." She gave a soft laugh at her joke, then became lost in her story. "We went to high school to-gether, and then he went off to war. That was the summer of nineteen forty-two. He'd come home on a short leave." She winked again. "That's when I got pregnant with our first daughter. When he left, I was terrified he'd never make it back home."

I watched this old, frail woman, lost in memories from so long ago. Her eyes no longer focused on the present, but to those days in the past. Her old life. Before she became alone.

"After Pearl Harbor was hit by the Japanese, the fellas were high strung, ready for revenge. My Sam was no different." Her eyes closed then, just for a split second. "Sweet Jesus, that was a good-looking man. Takes my breath away just to think about him." She opened her eyes and stared ahead, remembering. "Dark blond curls—until the Army shaved it off, of course—sparkling blue eyes, and the grandest laugh you'd ever hear. And I declare, he could dance!"

I sat and listened, completely enthralled. Tossing bits of bread on the ground. Noticing how close the ducks came to my feet to gobble up their snack. I wanted to know more about this love affair from so long ago, and I didn't have to ask for it. She continued on.

"My Sam landed on Utah Beach in Normandy, France on D-Day, although at the time I didn't know it. I'd have driven myself madder than a loon, if I had. But he survived, praise Jesus." She turned to me then, her green eyes clear, crisp, and growing darker as the sun faded. "I begged God that if he brought my Sam back to me that I'd spend ever single day of my life making him happy. God heard me, because my Sam came home." Her eyes drifted again, back to that day, and the wrinkles eased around her eyes a little. I could see her youthful beauty behind the lines of time. "I'll never forget that day at the airfield, waiting for him. When he stepped off that plane I thought my heart would burst clean out of my chest!"

Again, tears stung my eyes, and I was shocked at my reaction.

She looked at me. "How does your heart feel when you see your fella?"

I exhaled softly and held her gaze. "Like my heart is going to burst clean out of my chest."

"Well, then," she said, and reached with that bony frail hand and patted my knee. "If it's true love, it will work itself out, my dear. You just remember what I said." She grasped my hand then, and squeezed. "My name is Clara. What's yours?"

I smiled. "Harper."

Clara nodded, patted my hand. "Thank you for letting me talk about my Sam. Can you come back some time? And feed the ducks and talk some more?"

I gave her a genuine smile. "I'd really like that, Clara."

Her green eyes glittered. "So would I."

Later that night, as I laid awake in bed, I thought about Sam and Clara. I wondered why she was so lonely? I decided Sam must've died, but what of her children? Or grandchildren? She was sweet and kind, and I couldn't imagine having a grandmother like her. I'd spend as much time with her as I could, had I been that lucky.

But I wasn't that lucky. I had Corinne Belle. She was not sweet. Not by far.

Clara, though, had given me hope. Maybe with a little time, things could mend between Kane and I, and we would be able to continue our...what was it? Relationship? All I knew was that I did want it to continue.

Despite my hopes, though, Kane remained silent. Day after day, night after night, I waited, but he never called. I felt like I was on auto-pilot at school, meandering around campus with my fake smile and façade. It was wearing thin on me, I could tell. Becoming harder and harder to convince others that I was some happy-go-lucky, wealthy and well-loved Texas society girl who had everything going for her. With Murphy consumed with her budding relationship with Josh, it was easier for me to keep to myself without question. Inside though, I felt antsy. Cornered. Like I had no idea where to go or what to do next.

It was a week and a half before classes let out. Despite a few disgruntled Deltas who wanted revenge on the Kappas, I'd wiped the Dare from my mind, with everything else that was going on. The foreboding trip I had ahead of me to Belle House; Kane's attack and, most of all, his shunning of me. That hurt the worst. But I think I understood it, really. Wouldn't I do the very same thing? I couldn't deny the hurt, though.

I felt as though that, because I'd seen what had been done to him, his scars, it had in some way caused a riff between Kane and I. As if he somehow connected me to the scar. Of course, these were all scenarios in my mind, but I played each and every one out until the ache it left in me was almost unbearable. I missed him. Missed him more than I'd ever missed another human being in my life.

It was as if he were gone.

"Are you okay?" Murphy asked, suddenly by my side. It was Friday—a week after Kane's accident. Had it already been that long? We'd been at the soup kitchen for the past two hours, bringing in donated canned goods. It was the last load for the holiday.

Murphy wore a Silverbacks ball cap on her head, and her lob was pulled into two pigtails that stuck straight out on each side. She peered closely at my face. "You look as if you might have a bit of the collywobbles."

That did bring a small smile to my face. "I'm fine." Of course I wasn't. Luckily, Kane's attack had been kept hush-hush. I hadn't even told Murphy about it. She couldn't do anything about it anyway, so why burden her?

"Well, there it is." She grinned. "That lovely smile I've gotten quite used to." She stretched. "Right! Off I go." She elbowed me. "Unsure if I'm on the piss or on the pull, but either way," she said, winking, "cheers."

"Bye," I answered, and watched her bounce toward Josh's truck. He leaned against it, arms crossed in front of him, and when she saw him she ran and leapt straight into his arms. They kissed, she wrapped her legs around his waist, and I could only shake my head as they fell against the fender of his truck, laughing and kissing some more. Turning back to the last box of canned goods, I loaded it inside the soup kitchen, waved goodbye to the kitchen staff, and turned to head out.

Kane stopped me dead in my tracks.

Words wouldn't come; I could only stare at his battered face, still black and blue but now turning yellow in some places on his cheekbone. Beneath his shirt I could see the bandages there, binding his broken ribs. Inside, I shook; tears burned my eyes.

"We should talk," he said, and his eyes were already talking, already speaking loud things I didn't want to hear.

"All right," I answered, and simply…waited. I didn't know what to do, where to go, what to say—

In the next second, his hand was on my jaw, his lips were against mine, and I drew in the breath he exhaled. "I've missed you," he breathed, and deepened the kiss.

And I let him.

18. Letting Go

"ARE YOU OKAY?" I asked, the taste of spearmint still on my tongue from Kane's kiss.

He nodded as we walked. "Better now." He looked at me, linked his fingers with mine. "Brax and Gracie left for the weekend." He rounded on me, his gaze steady, clear. "Will you stay with me?" He tucked my head under his chin. "Please?"

I lifted my head and offered him my mouth, which he took, tasted slowly, and sighed against me. "I'll meet you there in an hour."

It was the longest hour of my life. I hurried through a shower, a change of clothes, drying my hair and make-up. My eyes roamed my closet; everything was too formal. Murphy had offered free reign of her closet so I ran to her room, found a pair of worn, faded jeans with a hole in the knee, a navy ribbed tank, and a solid red long-sleeved shirt that had snaps for buttons. Grabbing them all I ran back to my room, and by the time I'd slipped each garment on, I was in love.

How had I not worn jeans my entire life?

I looked at my footwear; no go. Nothing went with the extreme casual dress-down I had on. Running back to Murphy's I found her black Uggs—I didn't think she'd kill me—slipped them on and again. Fell. In. Love.

I'd been missing out. On a lot. I suddenly felt free. Free to possibly be me. It was a breathtaking notion.

It took ten minutes to reach Brax's apartment because of the Friday night traffic, and when I did, Kane was outside waiting on me when I pulled up. Leaning casually against his truck, his smile broke the darkness as I killed the engine. When I climbed out of the Lexus, the smile grew.

"Wow," he said under his breath. Almost not for me to hear. Slowly, his eyes moved from my head to my feet, and back up. "Casual looks good on you."

"Feels good, too," I said, then shivered. He pulled me close, grabbed my hand and led me inside. The lights were out; the candle was lit on the square coffee table. Wordlessly, he led me to the sofa, then followed me down when I sat.

His large, warm hand enveloped mine. "I want to tell you something, Harper," he said in that mesmerizing, quiet voice. Tinged with that unique Boston accent, it intrigued me, and I listened closely. I knew what was coming; things he didn't want to explain. Things I didn't want to hear.

Necessary, both.

"I know Brax told you a little the other night, after," he started. "I'm not going to replay it for you. First, I want you to know something." He breathed, his eyes holding mine. "I'd never put you in danger, Harper. I hope you know that." Fury passed over his face. "When I saw that guy head your way I nearly lost my mind. "

My throat went dry at the storm in his eyes. "I know, Kane. I know what Cory found out. "

He nodded, and that profound gaze bore into me. "But there's something Brax doesn't even know," he shook his head, rubbed his jaw with his free hand. "Man." He struggled; I could tell that. I sat silent, though. Waiting.

"My sister. Katy." A sad smile touched his mouth. "She was my only light back then. So sweet. So small. So helpless." His face grew stormy. "Our father was a big man with a big gut, bigger mouth and an endless temper. Especially when he had a six-pack in him. Which was every day." He turned my hand loose, and rubbed the sockets of his eyes, then looked at me. "I usually took all of Katy's beatings. But one got by me." He closed his eyes, breathed, opened them again. "When I got home he'd beaten my little sister unconscious. He was passed out in the recliner in the dump we lived in." He shook his head, and I knew he was reliving a nightmare. I'd done it before myself. He continued. "I found her on the floor in a heap." His voice caught, tight, cracked, and painful, and it made my insides hurt to hear it. "She wouldn't wake up. She just lay there, her little bony knees and ankles crossed and lying in an odd way on the floor." He cleared his throat. "I knew she was alive, though. So I called 9-1-1. Then I beat my father's drunken, pathetic ass until the paramedics pulled me off." He cleared his voice again, and I eased my hand into his, and he sagged against me. "I didn't beat him hard enough, because the bastard came out of it later that week. He's in prison now, though, and he won't get out in my lifetime." His gaze stayed on our hands for a moment, then he raised his head, and the pain I saw there made me almost gasp.

"My little sister never woke up," he confessed. "She was in a state nursing home at first." He sighed. "They were over-booked, understaffed for the most part, and her care was—I hated going to that place. Hated knowing she was in there." His gaze cleared now, and it was fathomless and fiery and full of shadows. "I quit school during my senior year and ran away from yet another foster home when I got a job running numbers and made a few big checks. The opportunities were endless and I was good at it." He looked away now, and I knew he wondered if I judged him. "I spent every dime I had on a run-down little apartment for myself, and the monthly fee for my sister's care in a decent, private facility up the coast. Out of the city. Harbor Breeze. She gets good care there, and is treated with respect. Even though they say she can't see it, her room really does overlook the harbor. I think she can see it. And I think she hears me when I talk to her. And I've been paying for my little sister that way ever since I was eighteen years old."

My insides sank like a weight had been dropped down my mouth.

His little sister was alive but beaten into a vegetative state by her own father. And Kane had been paying for her care ever since. Words wouldn't come; I could barely swallow my own saliva.

Kane's knuckle lifted my chin, and our eyes held. Tears rolled from mine. His were deep, wet, glassy. "And so you see,

Harper, that's why I run numbers. It's why I can't stop. Ever. Not for a second." His mouth lifted, somber, sweet. "My little sister is my heart. And she deserves only the best."

When Kane's voice cracked again, I fell against his chest, slid my arms gently around him but didn't squeeze, and nestled into his lap. He rested his chin on top of my head, silent, cautious. "I've only told you," he admitted. "Just you."

I looked up, into his eyes, those eyes that spoke every emotion. "You're safe with me," I said softly, and I ran my fingers through his tousled hair. "You can trust me."

In his eyes I saw gratitude. Desire. And something else I was unfamiliar with. "I can, yeah?" he asked. His thumb found my bottom lip.

"Yes," I answered, and the sensation of his roughened thumb against the sensitive skin of my lip sent tingles across my spine.

He pulled me to him, his mouth against my ear. "Thank you," he whispered. Then he kissed me there, and my hands sought his face, marveling in the scratchy feel of his unshaven jaw against my fingers. It was all so new. So many emotions. Sensations.

I shifted my weight and leaned into him, and he grunted slightly. I jerked back, my eyes drawn to his ribs. "I'm sorry," I muttered. "I—"

His mouth closed over mine, silencing me for several seconds as he tasted, suckled, and he smiled against my mouth. "I'm fine," he whispered. "Just a little sore." Sliding his hands along my hip, the curve of my backside, he slid them beneath my sweater, my tank, until he found my skin. My breath caught, and he stopped.

"No," I said, and brushed my mouth against his. "I don't want you to stop, Kane." He looked at me, his eyes liquid pools, and they asked me silently if I was sure. "You trust me," I said quietly, "and I trust you. I've never wanted to share this part of me with anyone." His eyes regarded me, made my insides heat. I didn't want to tell him it was forbidden. A sin, in my overbearing grandmother's eyes. Not now. "I want it to be you, Kane McCarthy."

Without closing his eyes, he settled his mouth gently against mine, and he swept his tongue along the seam of my mouth, and I gasped. "Are you sure?"

I kissed him back, mimicking his movement. I drew back. "More sure than I've ever been."

"I didn't bring you here to seduce you," he said quietly.

"But you did," I answered, then gave a timid smile. "I'm pretty sure I am one hundred percent thoroughly seduced."

His smile came easy then, and he rose from the sofa with a slight grunt, pulling me with him. Bending down, he grabbed the mason jar candle with its alluring scent curling from its mouth, laced his fingers with mine, and led me across the studio to a small hallway. In the room where he'd been taken after the attack, he set the candle down on the nightstand, pulled me inside and closed the door.

Why wasn't I freaking out? Why weren't the deluge of terrifying memories, of consequences washing over me? Was it because Kane was right? He and I together were right? That all along what I needed was to find trust in just one single person?

As his room closed in on me, I allowed Kane to replace the terror.

19. Kane

CHRIST, WHAT WAS I doing? Part of me knew I should stop. Just get up and walk out the door. Go outside in the forty-degree weather and cool the fuck off.

Harper's hand reached toward mine, slid her delicate fingers through my big ones, and her large eyes looked like pools of seawater as she stared at me. She just stood there, inching closer, leaning in. The flowery smell of her shampoo drifted up as she tucked her hair behind her ear. "I've never wanted anyone to touch me before," she said in that quiet, breakable voice. "I want you to."

I was gone then; just four words, and I was fuckin' gone. I gathered her face in my hands and inspected every feature, every curve, and then my mouth was on hers, so hungry, so starved like I hadn't eaten in weeks. Her lips were full, soft, pliable, inexperienced yet moved exactly where mine did, traced my path, tasted where I tasted. Her hands rested lightly against my chest, slid down to my stomach, and I was already so far gone, just from that brave touch, that I had to check myself. I pulled back, and she looked at me, and her mouth curved into the most beautiful smile I'd ever seen on her face. This smile wasn't broken. It was real. And it was mine.

"I like the way you kiss me," she admitted. And even in the candlelight of the room, I could see her cheeks redden. Her eyes cast downward, then back up. Shy. Brave. And in her eyes, desire.

I lowered my head again, moved my lips over hers, and moved my hands over her collarbone, down her shirt where I unsnapped it, pushed it off her shoulders and dropped it to the floor. I touched her as easily as I could; she seemed so delicate, small, and she then mimicked me, reaching for the buttons on my shirt until they'd all been undone. Just like me.

She pushed my shirt open, and her eyes widened when she saw the ugly black and blue across my ribs, and her fingers were there, tracing the marks, then the ridges of my abs. She looked up at me, slid her hands around my neck, and pulled my mouth back to hers.

I picked her up in my arms, and it hurt, but I didn't care. She didn't weigh hardly anything, but my ribs were still broken. With her wide eyes on mine, I laid her down on my bed, but her arms didn't leave my neck. Her mouth didn't leave my mouth. We shared the same air, the same matter, same space. We might as well have been one.

We lay beside each other, and her kissing grew as hungry as mine, and when I slid my hand along her hip, her thigh, feeling every curve through the soft jeans that hugged her skin, she moved closer, groaned. My hands moved under the thin tank she wore, her skin soft, untouched, and I hesitated. I leaned back, searching her eyes in the soft light, searching for answers without asking for them. Searching for acceptance. Consent.

She sat up then, pulled the tank over her head, dropped it to the floor. And she reached for my shirt, and I let her pull it off my shoulders. Then she reached for me again, and I went.

Our mouths fit, no matter which way I moved, like locking pieces of a puzzle, and when her fingers moved over my back—skimming that offending memory scarred there, kissed my chin, my jaw, and my throat—it felt healing. It felt fucking perfect. Like I'd waited my whole life to find her, just to trust with the darkest parts of me. She'd seen that darkness, and had accepted. I devoured her. It still wasn't enough.

My hands moved to her jeans, the snaps, and her hip bones, her taut stomach, the rise of her ribs just before her breasts curved made my mouth go dry. I didn't have to ask her anything; she lifted her hips, and I pulled the jeans off and tossed them to the floor. With one snap I released the lacey bra she wore, and she lay there, trusting me, her eyes wide and her hair spilling around her like an angel. I literally lost my breath. I didn't say anything; I reached for her hand, pressed it against my heart, and her eyes filled with liquid wonder when she felt how hard my heart raced and pounded against my chest. I stood, kicked my jeans off, my boxers, and she reached for me once more and I went once more.

With her soft body beneath mine, we melded together, like two pieces of metal that had been brought to liquid then merged to form one solid piece. I didn't mind that she touched my scars. It didn't shame me that she saw. As I tasted her, kissed her neck, that hollow dip in her throat, and those sweet, full lips, my hands found the rest of her just as perfect, just as pliable, just as fitting to mine. She was the most beautiful thing I'd ever seen.

Finding my wallet on the night stand, I flipped it open, reached for the condom there, tore it open, and slid it on. Grasping the delicate edges of her panties, I pulled them over her hips, down her long slender legs, and dropped them onto the floor. I moved over her slowly, hesitantly yet trying to reign in my own out-of-control hunger, kissing her, urging her thighs open with my knee, and I filled her then, capturing her gasp and swallowing it, then lying as still as I could until she grew used to me. To us. I nearly lost my mind, waiting. Then I slid my mouth along her bottom lip, pulled it into mine, and she kissed me back. Her legs went instinctively around my waist, and we moved together then, like one, and I was gone again, lost again. I saw her eyes widen, squeeze shut, and the moan of pleasure escape her beautiful throat. I exploded then, wave after wave nearly taking my breath until I collapsed beside her. We were out of breath, and I pulled her to me, her entire body tucked against mine, and I kissed her damp forehead. We were quiet as our hearts slowed, our bodies quieted, and our breathing eased.

I looked at her then; so soft in the candlelight. Her mouth swollen from kissing, and her eyes damp. "I can't stop staring at you," she said in that soft voice, and her fingers dragged over the ridges of my stomach. "With my eyes or my hands."

If a girl could make a guy's heart melt, she just did. I pushed her hair over her shoulder. "So there you are," I murmured.

She tilted her head. "What do you mean?"

I traced her lips with my thumb. "I've been looking for you my whole life."

Then her face eased into the most beautiful smile I'd ever seen, and she pulled my head to her chest, and I drifted off into the most settling sleep I'd ever had, with Harper's arms around me, her fingertips trailing over my skin, through my hair. Her lips grazing my temple. Healing me.

When I woke, the early hours of daylight, hazy and ethereal, moved through the room. I shifted, still entwined with Harper's legs and arms, and as I looked up, her wide eyes were watching me, still filled with wonder.

"I told you I can't stop staring," she grinned, and then her brows pinched together. "I'm sore."

I gave her a slow smile. "That's normal."

"You're…so big."

I quirked my brow. "That's what all the girls say?"

She whopped me with a pillow. "I'm serious!" Then her eyes looked down. Saw my arousal. "Whoa," she gasped.

I couldn't help but laugh. Her lush body called to me, but I knew she was too sore. I would hurt her. "Let's go make some pancakes."

Her eyes softened. "Okay."

I thought about jumping into a cold shower first, but I passed that idea up and gave her one of my shirts to wear. It nearly hung to her knees. And she looked adorable. She sat on the counter while I made pancakes from a box mix, and then we ate together on the sofa. It felt so…normal. So right with her. As if all the shit and hell I'd endured as a kid had led to this moment. To this girl. To the one who would make everything okay.

And the weekend passed too fast. I couldn't keep my eyes, my hands off of her. I almost felt like a virgin myself. Everything with Harper was different than it had been with anyone, ever before. Unique. Special. Totally Harper. She filled a void I'd always know I had. The only thing is, I never thought it'd be filled. I'd never let anyone in, so close they could see the raw me. It'd been so easy to let Harper in. So fuckin' easy. And now that she was there? I didn't want her to ever leave. I'd only loved two people my whole life: Katy and Brax. Now, for the first time, I felt like there was room for more. It made me consider things. Consider my future. To have Harper in my life meant no more numbers. How could I fuckin' pull that off?

It was Sunday afternoon when Brax and Olivia made it back. We walked outside to greet them.

Olivia, wearing a backpack, climbed off Brax's bike and started unstrapping her helmet. Brax followed. "Bro, how's it goin'?" he asked. "Half-pint?"

I pulled Harper close against me. "Perfect," I answered.

Olivia smiled. "I've been feeling Brax's stomach growl against my hand for miles," she said, and looked at Harper. "We...were going to go for pizza. Want to join us?"

I felt Harper tense beside me; but then I also felt her breath leave her in a long exhale. A breath no one saw; only I felt.

"That...would be great, Olivia," Harper said slowly. Hesitantly. "Thank you."

Olivia flashed a quick smile to me. I couldn't stop the wide, stupid grin from spreading across my face. And Olivia beamed as though she'd just made a great discovery. A final break through. Harper looked up at me and her eyes shined.

209

Harper had agreed to go and, for some reason, I thought that was a major milestone. I couldn't quite figure out why she was so resistant to having a good time, even if it was just going out with friends for dinner. The small amount of food she consumed bothered me. Over the weekend I'd actually hear or feel her stomach growl with hunger. But I'd ask her to eat and she'd say she wasn't hungry. For anything, but me. That had made me smile, but it also concerned me. I knew she trusted me, but there was a room full of Harper that she hadn't allowed me entrance into. Hopefully, one day, she would.

But for now, she'd accepted Olivia's invite, and she'd even agreed to see me in public. Another milestone. I'd broken through at least the outer wall she had carefully constructed around herself, and all was good. I later waited in the common room of the Delta House while she ran upstairs to change.

And that's when I overheard something I wished I'd not have.

"I still think Harper was wrong," the girl said. She and two others stood by the hearth. I stood by the front door. They hadn't seen me and even if they had, they probably didn't know I was waiting on Harper. "The Dare was her idea. She wanted to get back at the Kappas. And that loser brother of Brax Jenkins' was specifically her choice from the get-go. Her test subject." She formed air quotes. "Her big reformation project."

My breath froze in my lungs. Maybe I was hearing them wrong?

"I heard her tell Murphy that he was a lost cause," another said. "That there was no reforming him and that she didn't want to get in trouble with the law. I bet that's why she called off the Dare. She just didn't want to lose."

"Probably," the other said. "Kind of lame if you ask me. She's our president. We were supposed to be getting vengeance for Olivia and Macie."

I'd heard all I needed to hear.

I'd been part of a fucking sorority prank?

I didn't look back. Didn't look at the girls.

I just walked out the door.

20. Broken

WHEN I STEPPED OFF the staircase, I saw Kane's back just as he was leaving out of the front door.

Why was he leaving?

"Hey, Harper," a voice called. It was Anna.

"Hi," I answered, and headed out the door. Kane was half-way to his truck. "Kane!" I called. He didn't stop, and I hurried faster. "Kane, wait!"

He stopped, but kept his back to me. Even when I reached him, he didn't turn around. His broad shoulders sagged, and he was looking down. Brax and Olivia stood by Brax's bike, watching silently from afar. Confusion on both their faces.

Then Kane turned and faced me. And I saw pain in those coffee eyes.

"A dare, Harper? That's what I was a part of? An experiment?"

Fear froze my words. He wasn't shouting. Not with his voice. But his eyes screamed at me. "No—oh, no, Kane. How...did you find out?"

Anger flashed in his eyes. "So it's true?" His voice was calm, but anger simmered just beneath the surface. Anger and hurt. Both I sensed like they were mine.

I nodded. "Yes."

He stared at me, those eyes blaring as he searched my face. "No buts? No excuses?"

"No," I said quietly. "There was a Dare. In the very beginning. But I—"

He shook his head. "I don't want to hear it, Harper." He turned to open his truck door, then turned back to me, leaned close for only my ears to hear. "I. Trusted. You," he said harshly, emphasizing each word as they cut into me. His eyes dug into mine, angrier than I'd ever seen him. I wanted to explain. I wanted to tell him how wrong he was, how wrong I'd been, but I couldn't. I knew it would be useless. Silently he turned, got in his truck, and didn't look at me once as he started the engine and pulled away.

Inside, I trembled. My stomach hurt. My breath wouldn't come.

What had I done?

I stared at his taillights as they disappeared into the darkness, and an ache came over me, a pain that hurt worse than anything had in a long, long time.

Olivia hurried over to me. "Harper, what's wrong with Kane?"

My lips were numb; I trembled where I stood, and an ache so painful it almost caused me to double over, started in my stomach. I couldn't even bring myself to look at her. All I could do is stare into the direction Kane left in. "It's…my fault," I said quietly. Brax had come to stand close to us, but he remained silent. "I came up with a plan to get back at the Kappas for their annual Dare," I said slowly. "For what they did to you, and then Macie Waters this year." I sighed, while Olivia and Brax both silently listened. "I came up with a reformation plan to get back at the Kappas." I looked at her then. "A bad boy makeover." God, how stupid it sounded now. "Three of us chose our subjects." I sighed. "Kane was mine."

"Christ almighty," Brax muttered under his breath. "Gracie, let's go." He turned and headed back to his bike. His gait was fast, determined, and angry.

"He's just protective of his brother," Olivia offered kindly.

I shook my head. "I don't' blame him," I said. "I was an idiot."

Olivia placed her hand on my shoulder and smiled kindly at me. "Just give it some time, Harper," she offered. "These things have a way of working themselves out." Then she turned and crossed the lot to Brax's bike, climbed on the back and pulled her helmet on, and they left. I watched Brax's single tail light as it disappeared. I stood beneath the lamp light in the Delta's yard. The night air surrounded me, and although people were milling about—even the Kappas' rowdy music poured out of their house—I still felt completely and utterly alone.

I stayed there, outside, letting the chilled December air nip at my cheeks, my hands, for some time. How dumb could I be? I should've told Kane a long time ago about the Dare. At the very least, I should have told him about my reservations, and about calling it off. Instead I'd put it behind me. I'd

214

greedily allowed my newfound joy with Kane to consume me in a way that I'd let my guard down. About everything.

How could I have hurt Kane like that? I knew he'd been through pain, like me. Yet I'd just added to it. Was Olivia right? Would this work itself out? For some nauseating reason, I didn't think it would. Kane was the kind of guy who gave someone one chance to earn his trust. When you earned it, you truly earned it.

When you lost it? That was it. The trust was gone.

Just like it would be with me.

Tears came to my eyes and I let them fall freely. I couldn't help it.

I'd just shredded everything Kane and I had gained to bits.

Finally, I ambled back inside to Delta house, and climbed the stairs to my room. Any hunger pangs I might have had earlier were gone. I readied for bed, climbed beneath my covers, and turned on my side.

In my heart I felt as though I'd just seen the last of Kane McCarthy.

Closing my eyes, I cried myself to sleep.

*   *   *

THREE DAYS PASSED BY and not once did I see Kane's truck on campus. He'd packed up his business and if he were still in town, he wasn't at the school anymore. I'd wandered from class to class, meeting to meeting, once again on auto-pilot. I'd tried to call him, but he wouldn't answer. I tried texting, too, but he didn't respond to that, either. It was the longest three days of my life. The newfound freedom I'd acquired with Kane slowly started slipping away, and my old ways and old fears returned. Without my consent. They just...returned. Maybe even worse now. My appetite had fled, and sometimes I wouldn't even finish the one meal I'd chosen for the day. I felt cold inside. Empty. Empty, without Kane. I missed him. And my heart ached knowing that I'd hurt him. His words haunted me; during the day, but mostly at night.

I. Trusted. You.

He'd laid his soul open to me; more than he had anyone, probably. And I'd yanked the rug out from under him. Guilt swamped me, and I had a difficult time keeping up the mask I'd carefully worn for two years at Winston. Three days. I couldn't take it anymore.

Finally, I got the nerve up to go over to Brax's. Inside, my stomach was a massive ball of rabid butterflies, all flapping around at once. The thought of facing Kane now scared me. But I had to do it.

When I pulled up to Brax's apartment, my heart sank. Kane's truck wasn't there, but Brax and Olivia both were. Before I made it to the door to knock, they'd both stepped outside.

"He's gone, sweetheart," Brax said to me. "He's pretty hurt, but I guess you know that."

I nodded, and tears stung my eyes. "I didn't mean to hurt him."

Olivia's hand found mine. "Brax must be forgetting what it's like being in your shoes," she said gently. "Right, Brax?"

Brax sighed, rubbed his head with his hand. "Look, Harper," he said, not too rough. "I know my brother. He doesn't let people in. He lets them in just so far." *Fah.* He shook his head. "But he let you in. You got to him. So it makes the hurt that much worse." He pulled Olivia close, tucking her head beneath his chin. "And yeah—I know what it's like to be in your shoes. It fuckin' sucks."

A tear slipped past my lid. "I never meant for any of this to happen," I said, then looked at first Olivia, then Brax. "Did...he leave Texas?"

"I'm pretty sure he did," Brax said. "Can't say for sure. Kane's his own man. He answers to no one." Brax surprised me then and pulled me into a fierce bear hug. "Give him some time, sweetheart," he advised, then kissed the top of my head. "See what happens."

I nodded. "Thanks." My eyes then found his. "I didn't know him then. I thought he was just some...random bad boy who needed reforming."

A crooked smile tilted Brax's mouth. "Well, that's not too far off the mark now, is it?"

"Only he's anything but random," I said. Then, I looked at Olivia. "I'm sorry."

She hugged me. "It's okay, Harper. I understand why you did it."

"He won't answer my calls," I said, and my voice cracked. "I'm just...so sorry."

Olivia's kind gaze sought mine. "If it's true, and it's meant to be," she said, giving me a soft smile. "It will be. Trust that, if anything."

I looked into Olivia's wise eyes, and grateful for her friendship, I gave a nod. "Thanks, Olivia."

I left after that, my heart clenched in pain. In fear.

Fear that I'd never see Kane again. And that I'd hurt him beyond repair.

*   *   *

THE FOLLOWING EVENING WAS the Dash-n-Date. It was an event I didn't have my heart into. Not at all. But I'd done everything I was supposed to do. Delta House was hosting desserts, and wearing a sleek red velvet dress with long sleeves and silver pumps, and fitted with an organza holiday apron, I stood with my sisters in the kitchen and served cherry almond cheesecake. Christmas music played on the CD, and the Deltas had decorated our small artificial tree and had it lit up in the corner of the common room. Garland hung along every surface, and along the bannister on the stairway. I pasted on a smile as I slid pieces of cheesecake onto sturdy paper plates with a silver serving spoon. Murphy was beside me, spraying the top with whipped cream and adding a cherry. She paused and glanced at me more than once.

"Something's wrong," she said. "I know I've been in my own little Josh world lately, but I see it now. You've slipped."

I glanced at her and smiled weakly. "Slipped?"

"Aye," she said. "Back to the old Harper Belle. You know? The one before Kane."

The last of the date dashers passed through, sorority girls with their fraternity boys on their arms, everyone dressed in cheery holiday garb. After Murphy and I loaded the last of the cheesecake, she set her whipped cream down and tugged me by the arm.

"Let's go," she said.

"Where?" I asked.

"Upstairs." She glanced at her me over her bare shoulder, and the hall light caught the shimmering silver in her off-the-shoulder dress. "Confession time, love."

On Murphy's bed, I told her nearly everything that had happened between Kane and I. Including the beating he'd received by the outside group of men he'd run numbers on. And, his finding out about the Dare. I kept the rest to myself, though.

"Bollocks," she whispered. "Damn, Harper. I'm so sorry." She squeezed my hand. "He'll come 'round. I'll bet my life on it." She offered me a smile. "The way that boy looks at you? A simple misunderstanding about a sorority dare won't keep him away."

I sighed. "I hope you're right." I looked at her then. The one person I'd called a friend, besides Olivia, I supposed. "Thank you, Murphy."

"Anytime, love," she answered.

That night, I lay awake in my lightened room, staring at the ceiling. Thinking of Kane. I tried again to call him, but it went straight to voicemail. I hung up, the hole in my chest growing larger by the day. Finally, I drifted off to sleep.

*   *   *

IT WAS THREE MORE days before Winston let out for the holidays. I'd not heard one word from Kane. No text. No call. Nothing. My heart felt cold, empty. Dull. Part of it was fueled by shame. I knew the Dare had been wrong from the beginning. I hadn't counted on falling for my subject. Falling so fast.

Falling in love with him.

Just as fast, I'd ruined everything. And now Kane was gone.

I'd visited the park, sat on the bench with Clara, and we'd talked. I'd somehow found comfort in her company. She was sweet and wise, and just hearing the stories of her life uplifted me. Until I went to bed, where my fears and thoughts kept me awake. Kept my heart heavy.

I'd just left the library with Murphy, and she glanced over. "No word, eh?"

I shook my head. "No."

She hugged me now, offering consolation as best as she could.

"Oy, love, he'll be back," she said. "Once his bruises are mended, he'll realize he can't live without you. Give him time." She winked. "You'll see."

I nodded and, not wanting to be a total bummer, pasted a smile on. "How are things with Josh going?"

A slow smile broke her face. "Very well, thank you. He's driving to meet my parents the day after Christmas." She wagged her brows. "I can't wait for the encounter with me father. Lord, that's one big, intimidating Welshman." She grinned. "I'll be sure and video the occasion." She hugged me once more. "If things change you call me, okay? You're always welcome to the Polk house!"

"Thanks," I replied. "I might—"

"Harper Belle?"

I turned at the sound of my name to find an older man dressed in a gray suit and long coat standing in the quad facing me. He was tall, with silver hair at his temples. Alert blue eyes stared down at me. Kind. Perceptive. He smiled.

"I'm sure you don't remember me," he offered. "We met a very long time ago." His hand shot out, and I grasped it. "Detective

Frank Shanks. May I have a word with you in private? I may have some news regarding your parents' case."

I stared at him, stunned. My mind whirled, and suddenly the sounds around me dulled. Even his mouth was moving, but I no longer heard his words. A wash of memory fell over me, sucking the breath from my lungs and making my knees go weak. The man who'd pulled me from that kitchen sink was here. The waves crashed over me then, standing there with my hand in Detective Shanks' large one, his eyebrows furrowed as he ducked his head closer to me. My lips grew numb, and I began to gasp for air. Of course I remembered him. Had never forgotten him. Never would.

Oh Jesus, no! Don't let this happen! Don't let them see what's inside of me!

As if on a fast-spinning carousel, I spun, faster and faster, and in the next instant I saw Murphy's face, Detective Shanks' face, and back and forth and spinning by so fast until I slipped, falling, my body jerking uncontrollably. I couldn't breathe. I couldn't see. The monster was out of me, I just knew it. I felt myself choking, coughing. Someone was going to see. I'd be put in an asylum. Tremors began to shake my body, uncontrolled, jerking.

Then, an ominous wall of darkness fell completely over my eyes.

*   *   *

"HEY, THERE YOU ARE."

My eyes slowly fluttered open. Murphy stared down at me. A man—Detective Frank Shanks—stared down at me, too.

Along with what looked like half of Winston U.

221

"Harper, you had a seizure," Detective Shanks offered. "Do you have epilepsy? How do you feel now?"

I tried to sit up, but he kept his large hand on my shoulder. "No, honey," he said. His voice was gruff, sandy, but steady. "You stay right there. I've called an ambulance."

I pushed up against him, my head spinning. "No, call them off," I said. "I don't need an ambulance. I'm fine." I looked at him, and my fears returned. "No…epilepsy."

I sat up now, and he allowed it. I glanced at Murphy, and her face was drawn tight in concern. Behind her, others were drawn in horror.

"You are a difficult girl to locate," Detective Shanks said. "You're all grown up now." His face pulled in worry. "Just rest, Harper. Take it easy until the ambulance arrives. We can talk later, okay?"

Talk later? What had he found out? Had anyone heard his words? My eyes darted around at the eyes peering down at me. "I'm…fine. Really. Can I stand?" I wasn't; my head hurt, and my insides felt sick. Detective Shanks brought back all of those horrors from so long ago. That night. The days I stayed crammed beneath the kitchen cabinet. He helped me stand, and I forced myself to be steady.

"You'll have to come back," I said hastily to Detective Shanks. I turned and wobbled, but forced my legs to carry me. To push me through the crowd. "I…can't talk right now. No ambulance."

He didn't follow me; that surprised me. I pushed my way through the onlookers, and their faces all blurred as I passed by. They stared at me as if I were a monster, just like Corinne Belle had said they would. I had to leave. Had to get away, before someone came to take me to the asylum. My legs were weak but still I hurried, as fast as I could, until Delta House was in sight. Murphy was right behind me.

"Harper, wait," she kept insisting. "Harper!"

I climbed the steps, stumbled to the door, and stood. I'd left my bag. My purse. My key. Tears began to fall, and then Murphy was beside me.

"Here, I've got it," she said softly. "I've got your belongings, too." She swiped the key and we both went inside. I ambled to the steps, and she followed right behind me. "Harper," she said. "Love, you've got to rest." Inside my room, I aimed for my bed. Murphy followed me there, and set my belongings on the floor. When I laid down, I turned on my side, facing away from her.

"That detective gave me his card," she said, and set it on the nightstand. "I'll stay with you. Harper, what's going on?"

It was the first time Murphy had ever questioned me about my personal life. "I can't say, Murphy. No," I mumbled. "Please don't stay."

"I can't just leave you here. After that."

"Yes you can," I answered. "Just go."

"You call me if you need me," she offered quietly. "I'll be around until tomorrow."

I didn't say anything. Then I heard the door close, and finally, I breathed. My eyes drifted shut, and tears fell down my face as I once again cried myself to sleep.

Detective Shanks. How had he found me? And what did he want? After all this time, he'd brought the nightmares back to me. I didn't want them. I wanted them gone. Forever.

I suppose that just wasn't going to happen. Ever.

*   *   *

I SLEPT THROUGH THE night, and by morning, the news had spread about my demons. My psychotic breakdown had finally happened, right in front of the whole school. And just like Olivia, I'd become an overnight YouTube sensation at Winston. Corinne Belle had warned me it would happen if I wasn't careful. No one really knew the extent of my demons, though, and for that I was grateful. Brax and Olivia had come by, Murphy had let them in, and I'd spoken briefly to them both. I'd pasted on a brave face, told them very little, and had sent them on their way. Olivia's face was drawn in concern, but I tried to convince her I was fine. Despite my humiliation of becoming a campus star, I found I wanted to just…disappear. Leave. And hopefully, everyone would forget the incident over the holiday break.

"Won't you change your mind and come with us for Christmas?" Olivia offered. "It'd be good for you to get away."

"Thanks," I said. "But my grandmother is expecting me."

Olivia watched me for a moment, seeing through my façade, but she nodded. "Okay," she answered. "But I'm only a phone call away." She cocked her head. "You shouldn't be driving, Harper."

"I'll be careful," I insisted. "Thanks, Olivia."

I watched her and Brax leave, and not too far behind them, Murphy left. But she first begged me once more to come home with her. I graciously declined. Finally, I was the last one at Delta House. The campus already had that empty feeling that I usually didn't mind. Now? It felt like a shell. An empty husk. Like me. Gathering my belongings, I shouldered my bag, placed it into the trunk of the Lexus, and left Winston.

The drive home consumed me. My heart felt as if it'd been run over. My stomach felt knotty, like it had been punched. Some of my secrets were out at Winston. What was I going to do about that when I returned?

Worse, there was a hole, a void, something missing and I knew it was Kane and that I was the reason he was gone. Would things had been different had I come clean with him right away? The moment I realized I no longer wanted to participate in the Dare? And that he actually meant something to me?

It was a long, long drive to Belle House. I stopped at the little local market and picked up a few things to eat, some bottled water and bananas. Then I drove to the house. Darkness had blanketed the property, but just as I'd left it, every single light blazed from the windows. I parked, gathered my meager groceries and overnight bag, and trudged to the front door. Kicking up the mat, I grabbed the key, opened the door, and went inside.

I hadn't turned on the heat, so a chill hung in the air as I sat my belongings down. I went straight to the hearth, busied myself making the fire, and once it was lit, I opened my blankets up and lay down. I wasn't hungry. I wasn't thirsty. I didn't want to shower. I didn't want to think.

I just stared into the flames, letting the heat wash over me, until my eye lids grew heavy and I fell asleep.

In my dreams, Kane was there, making love to me, touching me, kissing me with his mouth, his eyes, but then that dream had turned into a nightmare, and I was locked in the dark room upstairs, naked of clothes, and that dank smell of the kitchen cabinet clung to my nostrils. I saw my mother's pale hair, streaked with blood, and her glassy eyes wide and staring at me as she lay on the floor in an unnatural way. She wouldn't wake, no matter how hard I shook her. Her eyes wouldn't close. Only stared. Then the voices. I ran. I hid. Crammed into the cabinet. Shanks found me, and I was in his arms again, but then it was at Winston and I screamed as the monster inside of me showed itself to Murphy, to everyone.

I woke in a panic, in a sweat, the cold air striking it and making me shiver. My breath came harsh. My heart pounded against my ribs like a hammer. Somehow, I drifted back to sleep. When I woke the next morning, the fire had gone out, and I was left cold on the outside and on the inside.

I trudged around for two more days. I chopped wood. Got more blisters. I finally did shower. And I read. I walked the property, noticing how run down the place had become, and felt a ping of guilt for letting it do so. Kane, though, always interrupted my thoughts. I even kept my phone on me, just in case. But he didn't call. Or text. And I was too ashamed to call or text him.

Christmas Eve had arrived.

I was once again alone with my ghosts.

21. Demons

I SAT IN FRONT of my fire at Belle House, eating a turkey sandwich I'd made. Christmas Eve. Alone in Belle House again. I'd gotten a grip on myself. Somewhat, anyway.

I couldn't wait for tomorrow to end.

Sleep wouldn't come; I'd napped earlier and I just wasn't tired. The nightmares had made me sleepless and I felt off kilter. I'd brought a book to read, but I didn't feeling like reading Emily Bronte. I didn't feel like reading at all.

I wanted Kane. I wanted to tell him everything. To ease the burden I'd carried for so long. I wanted him so badly, it hurt to even think his name. To bring his face, his eyes, and that mouth that had made me writhe with pleasure, to mind? The gaping hole in my heart grew. I'd never felt more alone than I did on Christmas Eve.

Restless, I began to wander the halls, and I knew what sort of trouble that invited. Memories I had no business remembering. Fear I had no business surfacing.

But the pain? I deserved that, after all. Corinne Belle had said so.

I was sick of it. Sick to hell of it all.

A thought stole over me, and I ran outside in the cold. Grabbed the ax, and made my way to the dark room on the third floor. I recalled that day, my first day arriving at Belle House. Corinne Belle had made me strip in front of her, made me shower off the retched dirty little girl she loathed, and never once allowed me to mourn the loss of my parents. Never once hugged me, or soothed me. Never consoled me. She'd taken my belongings, burned the only picture I had. Left me alone. Locked me in that dark room, naked, for trying to get my stuff back. For trying to hold onto a piece of me. Of my life. She made me suffer consequences. Told me I was dead.

Down that long hall sat the dark door. I marched to it, my breath in my throat, my heart pounding. Tears fell down my cheeks. I screamed once.

I took that ax, and I swung it, embedding the blade into the door. I hacked it, over and over and over until the door was splintered, laying on the floor. Breathless, I sobbed, dragged the ax downstairs to my old room, every memory and nightmare assailing me. Kane. God, how I wished he were with me.

I felt that loneliness again, now. And it was my own fault.

As I pushed open my old room, fears cloaked me. I squeezed my eyes shut against the wash of memories, yet almost felt as though I deserved them. So I stayed. Walked to my bed and sat down.

And cried.

Visions slammed into me now, of that night the police officers had found me, and so vivid were the visions that I gasped. Jumped up. Ran from the room as though demons chased me. They did. They were there. They were always there.

Down the stairs I dropped the ax and flew, skidding across the hall and flinging myself onto my makeshift bed in front of the fire. I pulled the thin blanket up, over my chin, my eyes, and only then did the tears crash, turning from sobs to wailing. I fell asleep crying; I didn't even remember when they stopped. But by the time my eyes opened again, rays of light fell across my face. It was morning. Christmas morning. Cold. Hollow. Alone. I pushed my despair over my past, my lost childhood, and my newfound love in Kane McCarthy. It was time to face an old demon.

Quickly, I readied myself for another visit with Corinne Belle.

At Oakview, Ms. Baker greeted me as always, as though she hadn't seen me just a few weeks ago. I'd dressed in a trim green velvet maxi dress and a pair of expensive black pumps. I'd left my hair down, tucked behind my ears. I'd carried a fruitcake for the staff. It felt like a brick in my hand, but they always seemed to enjoy it.

I went through the usual greetings and braced myself for the icy stare I'd receive when I stepped inside Corinne's room. She didn't open her eyes when I entered; she'd been dressed in a red plaid flannel nightgown that had a white collar. Her hair, snowy white, was pulled into a bun. Her face was relaxed, void of the angry lines usually there. My heart began to beat fast, and I drew a deep breath.

"Merry Christmas, Grandmother Belle."

Those icy blue eyes didn't flash open. Those snowy brows didn't collide into a terrorizing scowl.

I moved closer. Slipped my hand to hers as it rested on top of her quilt. It was as icy as her stare. Cold. Stiff.

My heart lurched. "Grandmother?"

Corinne Belle didn't flinch. She didn't move. And she didn't breathe.

I stood there, staring down at her, waiting for those awful mean eyes to flutter open, focus on me, and blaze. They didn't. My body began to shake. My breath quickened, and so did my heart. How could this be? How?

"Merry Christmas! So, how are we doing this morning?" Ms. Baker announced as she walked in.

My eyes didn't leave Corinne Belle's body. "She's…" my voice quivered. Cracked.

"Oh my dear child!" Ms. Baker gasped. "Ms. Belle!" She hurried over to my grandmother's side, patting her hand, her cheek. She raised her worried gaze to mine. "I just bathed her an hour and a half ago," she said, tearful. "Ms. Harper, I'm so sorry."

Tears didn't fall from my eyes.

Not for Corinne Belle.

No one knew the things I knew.

And it'd stay that way.

Forever.

"Ms. Belle! Darling, are you okay?" Ms. Baker crooned.

I saw the monster in the bed. Her eyes were closed. And they weren't opening. My hands gripped the side of the frame, so tightly my knuckles were white. I eased my breathing as much as could.

I looked at Ms. Baker. "I'm perfectly fine. For the first time in my life."

The monster was dead.

And I was alone.

The staff rushed in then, Ms. Baker cooing and pushing Corinne Belle's hair back and disconnecting her feeding tubes. I sat back and watched, quietly. Confusion kept me there. What was I to do?

"Ms. Belle, don't you worry about a thing," Ms. Baker said, squatting beside me in the chair I sat in. "Your grandmother was a gracious woman, I can tell. She has all of her final arrangements in order." She patted my hand. "You won't have to do a thing."

The words were almost comical to me. I didn't blame Ms. Baker for not knowing. Although how she couldn't see the pure hatred shooting from those icy blue eyes like lightning bolts was beyond me. Still, I stared at Corinne Belle, even as the staff fussed over her, making her stiff head comfortable on the pillow, the quilt tucked just so around her skinny frail neck. They had no idea about the monster they were tucking in one last time.

"Is there someone I should call for you, dear?" Ms. Baker asked.

I didn't look at her. Only at my dead grandmother. "There's no one," I answered. "No one except me."

*   *   *

CHRISTMAS NIGHT, I LAID by the fire in Belle House. I wondered what would happen now. What I'd do next. I didn't know who I was. Who I was supposed to be. Was I free now? Or would I always be trapped inside this prison Corinne had set for me. Would I ever be normal? I wanted to call Murphy. I'd shut her out completely, but now I wanted to let her know things. My past. Why Detective Shanks was at Winston. It'd feel good to release those demons without fear of repercussions from Corinne. Would it be that easy? Just…release?

And that's when an idea struck me.

I had something to do first. Then I'd call Murphy.

I sat up, found my phone, and called information.

"City and state please," the operator called out.

"Boston, Mass," I offered. "I'm unsure of the city, actually. The listing is Harbor Breeze Care Facility."

"That's in Revere, hold for your number."

So I did.

*   *   *

AFTER I'D MADE THE call, my thoughts rampaged. For the first time in my life, I'd known who I was with Kane. Even if for a little while, I'd known. It was the first time I'd felt real my whole life. Now, he was gone. I was truly alone. And I didn't know what to do. I wanted him back. So very badly.

Finally, sleep overcame me. Corinne's face appeared before me as I closed my eyes, almost like a ghost from a Charles Dickens novel. Her eyes flashed fury, dripped with icy blue frost, and her brows plowed together as she drew close to me, staring, damning my soul. Threatening to lock me away in an asylum. I think she wanted to haunt me, truly. I forced my eyes to stay shut. Forced her vision to leave. Forced sleep.

I drifted then, in and out of nightmares and the past and under beds and in cubbyholes and in dank dirty kitchen cabinets. Visions of that night flashed before me like an old movie projector, faces pale, angry, screaming. And the blood.

"No!" I screamed with my eyes shut. My lips were numb, my heart raced wildly against my ribs and, despite the cold in the hall, I poured sweat across my brow. Tears flowed from my eyes, and I sobbed. "No! Please! Don't lock me in an asylum! I'm not bad! I…I am not psychotic! Please, grandmother!"

"Harper, Harper," a voice crooned. Familiar, soft, husky. "Open your eyes."

I noticed the hand that covered my shoulder. Felt the body heat that crouched beside me. When my eyes fluttered open, my breath lodged painfully in my lungs, and I couldn't breathe. I gasped, gasped again, and tried to get up. Run. I needed air. I couldn't breathe.

Kane was there, somehow, and he held me fast, pulled me against his chest. Was he a vision? Was I hallucinating? With his big hand pressing against the side of my head, he held me steady. He felt real. Had to be real. "Feel the rise and fall of my chest," he said gently. "Feel my air moving in. Out. Feel my heart, Harper. Be like me."

I listened. Focused.

"Breathe, baby," he whispered. "Breathe like me."

Confusion warped my thoughts; made the inside of my head all buzzy and hazy. But I breathed. In. Out. Again. Until my lips weren't so numb. Until my heart didn't pound so hard. Kane's piney scent wrapped around me, and I leaned away. Reality struck.

"How are you here?" I whispered.

His eyes searched mine. "I found you."

He had. Old fears struck me. I couldn't help it. "No one…knows."

His hand reached out, grazed my cheek, my jaw. "Tell me, Harper. Tell me about the dream you just had."

"I'm so sorry, Kane," I said first, then fell against his chest. I slipped my arms around his waist. He was here. Really here, and I didn't want to let him go. "I wanted to tell you about the Dare, end it right away, and I just...didn't." I looked at him. "I never meant to hurt you."

His eyes softened. "I know that. And I'm sorry for not giving you the chance to tell me. I'm sorry for running off."

I drank him in. His dark tousled hair. Alabaster skin, although there were a few fading bruises still remaining. And those profound, expressive eyes that spoke to me. "I still can't stop staring at you," I breathed.

He pulled me to him. "Then don't ever stop," he said against my temple.

Kane held me that way for some time. Tears fell; I hadn't known they'd started back up. I wanted to squeeze him so tightly to me, but I didn't dare because of his ribs.

"You're not going to hurt me, Harper," he whispered against my ear.

So I squeezed.

"This place," he urged. "What's going on, honey?" He lifted my chin, forcing me to look at him. "What'd they do to you?"

With a resigned sigh that seemed to set free any inhibitions or reservations I had about telling another soul of my past, I told Kane everything I remembered.

Even the things I'd kept locked away from myself.

22. Kane

I LISTENED. IT WASN'T easy. Wasn't easy at all. Her story lasted until morning.

Seemed like life tried to fuck us both over.

To hear Harper recall the painful memories of her childhood past was like watching a small child being punished for spilling a drink on white carpet. No matter what memory she recalled, she felt it was her fault. Her parents were both hooked on crack. Harper's fault. Penniless and living in squalor. Harper's fault. Had not only watched her parents be murdered by a disgruntled drug lord's lackey but then stayed locked in the run-down apartment for days, with her dead parents inside, until the cops found her. Harper's fault. Why? She'd let the lackey in. Had opened the door. At age eight, she'd shouldered the blame.

And her grandmother had allowed it. Had taken her in. Forced her to ignore her past, forget her parents. And then had tormented her. Threatened to lock her away in an institution. Convinced her spies watched her continuously, even at school, ready to report back any wrong-doings. Any sin. Jesus Christ, what sort of monster did that to a kid? When Harper had fallen asleep, I'd held her for a while, then decided to wander around. Upstairs, I found the dark room on the third floor. The one Corinne Belle had made Harper strip down and stay locked in. For consequences. Harper had taken an ax to it and ripped it to shreds. Good.

Harper was never beaten physically. She'd been beaten down all the same. Forced to pretend her past hadn't happened. Forced to be something she wasn't. All in the name of keeping the Belle family out of the black. Corinne Belle had terrified Harper, even after she'd grown up and moved off to college. Even after she'd had a stroke, unable to harm Harper. She still had managed it. Probably known it, too. She was no better than the loser bastard of a father I had. That crazy old woman had convinced Harper that she had something evil living inside of her. That to have relations with a guy was sinful. That she'd allowed me to even touch her once was a miracle. It'd take a long, long time to get past some of the stuff she told me.

I wanted to be the one she could lean on. To trust.

To love.

"Your back," she said softy. "Why?"

Dark memories washed over me, but I'd beaten those demons years ago. When I'd almost killed my own father. "It was just my sadistic father's way of controlling me," I said. "Called me stupid. Every day. He knew I'd take it to keep Katy from getting beat." I laughed harshly. "Hurt like hell, every single letter, but it was worth it. Katy was so frail. I always knew she'd never survive one of his thrashings if he got ahold of her." I looked at Harper, and her eyes had softened, and her hand found mine. "I was wrong about that," I said. Katy's small twisted body flashed before me. The way it was then, that night so long ago. And again only a handful of days ago. "She's still in there, my sister," I continued. "I don't care what any doctor says, or any of the nurses. She knows I'm there." I nodded, gripping Harper's hand. "I'll always be there."

"She knows you love her," Harper said, and laid her head against my chest. "She knows it."

We were both silent for a few moments, but then she looked at me. "Do you think I'll ever be normal, Kane? Or do you think the nightmares will always be here?"

"We'll learn to be normal together," I offered.

She didn't say anything else but her small arms tightened around me, and she sighed against my skin. An exhale of relief, maybe? Only time would tell. I knew it'd be a long road ahead. For us both. But mostly for her.

Harper drifted off to sleep again, and when she woke, she woke crying. Terrified. Screaming about being locked in an asylum. I smoothed her hair, held her, and when she was finished, her sobs still bubbling up and catching her breath, she told me the next thing that blew me away.

"I found Corinne Belle dead in her bed yesterday."

I looked at her. I didn't know what to say, so I held her hand.

Harper gave an acerbic laugh. "Even in death, she had to have one final jab at me."

"What was that?" I asked.

Harper's seagreen eyes searched mine. "She took Christmas away from me a long time ago, Kane. Yesterday?" she folded her hands in her lap. "She made sure of it."

A thought came to mind.

"No she didn't," I said gently. When Harper's brows bunched in question, I gave her a soft smile. "We're taking it back. Today."

She cocked her head. "What?"

I stood, extended my hand. "Come with me."

With a hesitant smile, she grasped my hand and I pulled, her feather-light body easily rising. That was something else I'd have to work on.

Somehow, Corinne Belle had forced Harper into believing she was so worthless, that she needed to treat herself sparingly— including her intake with food. Just the thought of that old bat infuriated me. I was glad she was dead. And I'm glad Harper found her. It'd provide closure one day. And I aimed to help her get it.

At the door, I grabbed Harper's black wool coat, helped her into it, found the ax she'd dropped on the floor and grabbed that, too, and outside, the cold December air bit at my face. The new leather jacket Brax had given me for Christmas kept it from sinking into my skin. I pulled Harper to my side and strode toward the woodpile. I glanced around.

"What are you looking for?" she asked.

I kissed her temple. "You'll see."

I saw them then—and headed straight for the wood line. It was a decent walk, with the early morning day after Christmas cold wind biting at us both. She snuggled against me, and I knew I loved her. Loved feeling her body next to mine. The smell of her hair. The softness of her skin. And the look of adoration in those seagreen eyes. We were alike, she and I. We shared demons. We shared fears.

We'd share the healing, too.

At the wood line, we stepped in, and although mostly pines, we found some that looked like a Christmas tree. Small, it looked more like a Charlie Brown tree. It didn't matter.

It'd be our first. The first of many.

"Stand back, woman," I teased, and set Harper back. I eyed the tree and whacked it with the ax until it cracked. I pushed it over, and looked at her.

"You're crazy," she said sweetly.

"You like crazy," I corrected.

"I do if it's you," she warned.

I grabbed the tree by the stump and we dragged it back to Belle House.

With no tree stand, no lights, I propped the tree, now leaking sap, against the stone wall near the hearth. It wasn't big—maybe four feet tall.

Next year, we'd do Christmas right.

This year? It was more of making a point. Of letting go of the past.

Of kicking the past's ass.

Grabbing her narrow shoulders, I urged Harper to sit by the tree. "Be still. Keep your eyes closed," I warned. "Don't open them until I say to."

She closed those beautiful eyes. "Okay, okay."

I ran out to my truck, opened the door, and grabbed the box Olivia had helped me wrap. I took two leaps and was back up onto the porch and I flew inside. I dropped down beside Harper, and all at once I couldn't take my eyes off her.

"Can I look now?" she asked.

I continued to stare, marveling at every single feature. "Not yet."

A soft grin claimed her lips, and then I did, brushing my mouth over hers. She exhaled, and I swallowed it.

Then I put the box in her lap.

"Open your eyes," I said.

And she did.

She looked at it. Fingered the big red bow. She did that for several moments—so long, I almost ripped the bow off for her. Then she lifted her face, and my heart seized in my chest. Those wide eyes were wet with tears.

"It's so beautiful," she said, and her voice cracked.

I reminded myself to breathe. "Open it, silly."

I knew then that, despite the word carved in my back by a radical drunk of a father who never, ever deserved children, I was far, far from stupid. Nope. Not a stupid boy at all.

I watched Harper then, slowly tug the bow loose, ease open the taped ends of the box. I saw her hands shaking, and for a moment it saddened me to think she'd been given so much in life, yet so very little. The simple things that would've made her happy. Like a red bow on a box.

So little as to not have experienced a personal gift from a loved one.

That was about to change, starting now.

She looked inside the box. She blinked. She looked at me. And then threw her arms around my neck, the box trapped between us.

"A new camera!" she said excitedly. "Kane!" She covered my face, my mouth, my forehead with kisses, then my throat, and then settled on my mouth with a long, slow, erotic sort of kiss that made me wonder how she'd only just started kissing in the first place. When she finished, she looked at me, and her eyes shined with something you don't see in many people anymore. I know people. And I don't see it. Ever.

Gratitude. Pure. Raw. Gratitude.

And something else I dared to hope for.

Love.

"I love it," she said, and she grazed my stubbled jaw with her smooth fingers. She kissed me again, and then looked at me, close, our faces a breath apart. "I...I love you, Kane McCarthy." The words came out on a feathery breath. Soft. So very soft.

My heart seized again. It was a feeling new to me. It was...overwhelming. I kissed her back, slow, deliberate, and sighed against her mouth. "I'm so in love with you, Harper Belle."

Her eyes widened. "You are?"

I couldn't help but laugh. I was. It seemed incredible, but I knew it as sure as I'd draw my next breath. "Yes, I am. And I have one more thing for you. Close your eyes again."

She did, and I reached into my pocket and grasped the small round object I'd found at an antique store a few days before. I grasped Harper's hand, placed it there. "Okay. Open your eyes."

Harper's lashes fluttered, she looked first at me, then her hand. A small gasp escaped her throat, and her small, delicate finger stroked the brushed brass cover of the old compass. She didn't say anything. Just lightly stroked it.

When her eyes lifted they were moist with tears and again, filled with raw gratitude. "Kane," she said, and her voice cracked. "I will cherish this forever."

"For you to always find your way," I said, holding her gaze. "Your way back to me."

She threw her arms around me again, pressing that full, beautiful mouth to my throat. "I'm the happiest I've ever been in my entire life."

I held her to me, pressed my hand to the back of her head. "So am I."

Then, she popped up and her brows knitted together. "I didn't get you anything."

I looked at her then. Searched her eyes with mine. So close, I felt like we could almost read each other's thoughts. Just in case, I told her. "You did. And I'm forever grateful for it, Harper."

She didn't even try not to claim it. "How'd you know it was me?"

I smiled. "Because no one except you knows I have a sister in indigent care at Harbor Breeze in Revere, Mass. That's why." She'd called Christmas night. She'd paid Katy's bill for the next ten years. My heart had burst then, and I'd known right away it'd been Harper. I could never repay her. But I'd die trying. Starting with quitting the gambling life. Getting my GED. Maybe signing up for some classes. I'd tell her that later, though. For now, I just wanted to be with her. In this moment.

In the now.

"Oh," she said. Then she slipped her arms around my waist again. "Tell me again."

I pressed my mouth to her ear, kissed the soft lobe, the soft outer shell. "I'm in love with you, Harper Belle," I whispered.

And she sighed, a content sound that average people don't make.

And then I was lost. Again.

Forever.

EXCERPT FROM
STUPID GIRL

THE MOMENT I SPIED the *Welcome to Killian* sign at the outskirts of town, my stomach dropped and my hands gripped the steering wheel hard. The small Texas college town sat half-way between Lubbock and Amarillo. Two hundred and forty-eight miles from home. Three hours and forty-four minutes by car, going the speed limit.

I hoped to God it'd be enough.

Peering through my shades, I noticed Killian's Sonic parking lot was filled to the gills with rowdy boys, souped up trucks and hot rods. As I passed by, I eyed several girls sitting on the backs of opened tailgates, laughing and flipping their hair. Reminded me of my hometown of Jasper. What was it about a Sonic burger joint? Always seemed to be the popular hang-out spot. Part of me wanted to pull in, tell the hair-flippers to get a grip and leave. But the bigger part of me kept my foot on the accelerator. Stay low, keep quiet, and no one will even know I exist. Just the way I wanted it.

Slowing down, I hit my blinker and pulled into the massive

brick entrance of Winston U. Flanked by huge magnolia trees and planted mounds of petunias and other annuals, a little of my earlier somberness over leaving home eased out of me. It was replaced by an excitement I was sort of surprised by. Things would be different here. I just felt it. No more stares, no more whispers. No more muffled giggles. No more rumors. No one knew me here. I'd just melt in to the population and be a big nobody. Invisible, like a ghost. Perfect.

I started down the main drive leading to admissions, and scanned the grounds ahead of me. Large colorful banners stretched across buildings that said WELCOME FRESHMEN, along with several home-made Greek signs for Rush Week. People were everywhere, on the lawns, the sidewalks, the parking lots. Maybe I should've taken up Mom's offer to come with me today. My brothers had offered to come, too. Even Grandpa Jilly. I'd turned them all down, insisting I could—no, *needed*—to do this alone. What was I thinking? *Stupid, stupid girl.* Too late now, I was in it up to my gills. No turning back. Drawing a deep breath, I pushed my self-doubt aside. *I can do this.*

While not super huge, Winston was mostly well known for their successful baseball and football teams. The Silverbacks. But I'm not exactly a jockette or even into sports, so that's not what drew me. Winston also had an extraordinary astronomy program, with a mega-observatory to boot. They called it the Mulligan, and when it was first installed in 1910 it had been the largest scope in the country. I'd been lucky enough to gain employment in the Science complex through the financial aid department. It was geek-girl heaven, and I'd be right smack in the middle of it.

Literally. I loved the stars, constellations, galaxies, and all that went with it. Staring through my scope at the seemingly infinity heavens had helped me get through the last painful year of high school. To a certain degree, it'd healed me, right along with my family. We Beaumont's all stuck together—except for my dad, who'd pulled a disappearing act long, long ago. Other than my family, astronomy was my life. All I'd ever wanted to do was study the stars, ever since I was a little kid and Jilly had given me my first telescope for my sixth birthday. Finally, it was happening. I just prayed the past would leave me alone. That the nightmares would stay gone, that the relentless fear which had for a while replaced my fearlessness would recede somewhere deep, deep inside of me. And would stay there. Forever.

As I kept my eyes on the street signs, my hand fumbled around on the bench seat of my truck until I found the campus map. Holding it up eye level, I navigated my way through several streets until I found my dorm. Oliver Hall held three stories, double occupancy dorm rooms, each with a private bath, and a common room. I'd been assigned to the second floor, dorm room 21. The parking was split into two sections, with Oliver Hall in the center. I pulled into the not-too-packed left side lot, found a spot closest to the front, and parked.

I pushed my hat back off my forehead and for a moment I sat, just looking out at the red brick building, manicured with boxwood hedges lining the walkway up to the dorm. A huge cottonwood tree, probably a couple hundred years old at least, stood tall and off to the side, casting an arc of shade over the hall. People milled about—mostly girls, since it was a girls' dorm. Laughing. Hollering. Going in and out of the door, everyone loaded down with bags and boxes and belongings from home. Mid-August, it was hot and humid as Hades. And I was here. Alone.

This was my new life.

Somewhat intimidating.

I gave Mom a quick call to let her know I'd arrived and promised to call later. Then, after a big, calming breath, I opened the door and climbed out. The heady scent of freshly cut grass hit my nose, and it actually helped me feel a little less anxious. *These people don't know me. They don't know what happened to me.* A little more apprehension eased out of me. Shoving the truck keys into my bag, I made sure I had my dorm keys, and pushed my cell into my back pocket. I slipped my shades off and tossed them onto the dash, shouldered my backpack, and shut the door. Reaching over the side rails of my truck bed, I grabbed a box filled with astronomy books and desk supplies, and started across the lawn. Not super light, but manageable, and I'd rather get the heavier boxes in first. Looked like I'd be making a few trips to get all my stuff inside anyway. My boots dug into the grass as I made my way to the entrance.

"Heads up!"

Just as I turned, a sudden, powerful force slammed into me, taking me down, and I hit the ground with enough vigor to make the breath *whoosh* out of my lungs. The box flew out of my arms, and I was a little stunned at first, lying in the grass. It wasn't an unfamiliar feeling; I'd been thrown from so many horses over the years, I'd lost count. And this is what being thrown felt like. Maybe worse. My hat had shifted and now shaded my eyes. I concentrated on breathing.

Then, suddenly, my hat was pushed off my face, and *he* was

over me. Arms braced on either side of my head. Looking down. Frozen in place, I couldn't do anything else except stare back at him, and I watched his smile fade as his gaze fixed on mine. He looked about as surprised as I felt.

His face took me off guard. It was … shocking. Not handsome—almost frightening. Rough. The lightest, most startling blue eyes I'd ever seen stared down at me. One of them had a really recent black and blue shiner marring the otherwise fair skin. A whitish half-moon scar started at the corner of the other eye and curved around his cheek bone. Another white scar jagged down from his jaw, just below his ear, halfway down his throat; it was met by a black tattooed inscription that disappeared down his shirt. Super dark hair—almost black—swung over his forehead, and equally dark brows furrowed. We both stared for a few seconds.

Then, his head lowered, and full, firm lips covered mine.

And he kissed me.

COMING SOON
STUPID LOVE

BOOK THREE IN THE STUPID IN LOVE SERIES

Can't get enough of the exploits at Winston University? Stay tuned for book three in the series – STUPID LOVE – to find out what happens next! Sign up for Cindy Miles's newsletter to receive the scoop on the book's upcoming release.

ABOUT THE AUTHOR

Cindy Miles grew up on the Vernon River in coastal Georgia. A best-selling author and a full-time writer, she lives and continues to be inspired by the Gothic Revival and Georgian architecture, the moss-draped squares, ancient cobbles and surrounding coastal marshes of Savannah.

Visit her online at www.cindy-miles.com, on Facebook, Twitter, and Goodreads.

CPSIA information can be obtained at www.ICGtesting.com
Printed in the USA
BVOW02s2249300315

394012BV00002B/53/P

9 781942 356141